W9-BLB-586

# Hang Tough

## A BLACKTOP COWBOYS® NOVEL

# LORELEI JAMES

BERKLEY SENSATION
New York

BERKLEY SENSATION
Published by Berkley
An imprint of Penguin Random House LLC
375 Hudson Street, New York, New York 10014

Library of Congress Cataloging-in-Publication Data

Names: James, Lorelei, author.
Title: Hang tough / Lorelei James.
Description: Berkley Sensation trade paperback edition. |
New York : Berkley Sensation, 2016. | Series: Blacktop cowboys novel ; 8
Identifiers: LCCN 2016027330 (print) | LCCN 2016034167 (ebook) |
ISBN 9780451473790 (softcover) | ISBN 9780698186415 (ebook)
Subjects: LCSH: Ranch life—Wyoming—Fiction. |
BISAC: FICTION / Romance / Western. | FICTION / Romance /
Contemporary. | FICTION / Contemporary Women. |
GSAFD: Erotic fiction.
Classification: LCC PS3610.A4475 H36 2016 (print) |
LCC PS3610.A4475 (ebook) | DDC 813/.6—dc23
LC record available at https://lccn.loc.gov/2016027330

First Edition: November 2016

Printed in the United States of America
3   5   7   9   10   8   6   4   2

Cover art by Aleta Rafton
Cover design by Colleen Reinhart

$\mathcal{G}$arnet Evans was mashing hulled strawberries in an industrial sieve when her phone rang. Thank heaven for caller ID; when she saw the number—and the time—she knew not to ignore it. She used her teeth to remove her right rubber glove and punched the talk button. "So who's got a snootful tonight, Sherry?"

"Not who you'd expect, Garnet." A pause. "Tobin."

That snared Garnet's attention real fast. "*My* Tobin? My word. That boy is always on the straight and narrow."

Sherry snorted. "He's hardly a boy."

"Don't I know it. What's going on with him?"

"I've never seen him like this. He's just so . . . sad. It's breaking my heart."

Garnet slumped against the wall and closed her eyes. For the past six months she'd had a heavy heart too, watching the changes in Tobin, and not liking them one bit.

"Now he's here at the Buckeye trying to drown his sorrows."

"Oh lordy, that's not good."

"Not good at all. And because I know you and Tobin are close, Garnet, I'm gonna break a confidence." Sherry paused. "Normally you can't pry this stuff out of me, but it's important you know where his head is before you come and pick him up."

"Hit me with it."

"Tobin plans to give notice at the Split Rock Ranch and Resort tomorrow. He's made up his mind. He's ready to move on, out of Muddy Gap for sure, maybe even Wyoming altogether."

"How far has he slipped down the bottle tonight?"

"He's not stumbling or picking fights. He's just melancholy and has had too much to drink to drive."

"Get his keys."

"Already got 'em."

"Can you keep him parked on that barstool another thirty minutes? I've gotta call in reinforcements. Lord knows that boy will need to have his truck to go to work tomorrow so we can't leave it at the bar."

"No more than thirty minutes," Sherry warned.

"Don't you worry. I'll be there with bells on before that thirty-minute mark."

Sherry laughed. "Knowing you, Miz G, I'm taking the bells comment literally."

# Chapter One

*One week later...*

*T*obin Hale's cell phone rang for the hundredth time, tempting him to chuck it in the garbage disposal.

So far he'd ignored Tilda's call, Bernice's call, Vivien's call, and Miz Maybelle's call. When Pearl's name flashed on the screen, he knew better than to ignore it.

"Hey, Pearl-es-cent, what's the 411?"

"So your phone isn't broken, you're just screening our calls?" she demanded.

"Yes, ma'am. Shit has hit the fan over here and I ain't in the mood to talk to nobody."

"Well the same thing has happened over here at Garnet's house."

Tobin sipped his beer. "She's mad that I gave Renner notice last week, isn't she?" Now that he thought about it, it was sorta weird Garnet hadn't called to give him what for.

"Of course she's upset. But there's loads more going on than that."

There was a shifting noise on the other end of the phone. "Her son is making good on his threat to lock her away where she can't get into trouble," Pearl whispered. "Don't you remember?"

"Pearl, she was blubbering so damn hard I could barely understand anything she said." Total chaos had erupted inside the lodge when all of the Mud Lilies ladies had shown up.

And he had had his own shit to deal with.

How fucking . . . coincidental that Hugh, the ranch foreman, had decided to lay it all out on the line for their boss, Renner Jackson—on the exact same day Tobin had given his notice. But Hugh had thought ahead and offered to buy the rodeo stock contracting business outright. Great for Hugh, it'd be great for Renner in the long run, but in the short term, that meant Tobin got stuck with doing all the day-to-day work. Again. He'd tried not to be bitter, but dammit. Nothing ever seemed to go his way.

*Not true. You found out today you have a job interview in Albuquerque in three weeks.*

Finally. Tobin felt as if he'd been in a holding pattern. No one knew that he'd updated his resume and started sending out job applications— two months ago. He considered it a sign he was on the right track the day after he'd given notice to Renner when he'd had an e-mail from one of the places he'd applied, requesting more information on his positions as "reproductive project manager at the Split Rock Ranch" and "genetic research development coordinator for Jackson Stock Contracting." Yeah, maybe he'd stretched his job titles a tad, but it wasn't like he didn't have the education and the hands-on experience to it back up. And it had scored him an in-person interview.

"Tobin? Are you listening?" Pearl demanded.

Feeling guilty for tuning her out, he said, "Sorry. You lost me there for a moment. Could you please repeat that?"

"Her son finally has enough 'just cause'—in his mind anyway—after the last couple of Garnet incidents to question her mental stability and her ability to take care of herself. He's sending a moving van to pack up her house and he's put a deposit down at one of those assisted living places"—she sniffled and wailed—"in Cheyenne!"

That garnered his full attention. "What? He can't do that."

"Yes, he can. He's a big-time New York City lawyer. He can do whatever he wants. And ever since Garnet found out, she's been completely nonsensical, which just plays perfectly into his evil and greedy hands."

"Where are all of you right now?"

"Me and Garnet are at her house. She's been making strawberry preserves like she's putting up food for a Russian winter. For an army. Why she'd think them tough military guys would even want fancy fruit spread on their toast rations doesn't make a lick of sense to me, but she keeps insisting that no man is too manly—"

"Pearl. Focus," Tobin said sharply.

"Oh. Sorry, Tobin. I don't have a contingency plan for this."

Things were messed up if organized drill sergeant Pearl was scatterbrained.

"Stay put." Tobin's boots hit the floor. "I'm on my way over."

❧

Garnet's place was only fifteen minutes from the Split Rock Ranch and Resort. Sometimes when Tobin worked in the back forty of the ranch, it was closer to drive to Garnet's for lunch than head back to the office.

A tree-lined driveway led to the two-story house. The style wasn't Victorian, but a few years before he'd come to work at the Split Rock, Garnet had redone the exterior of the house in that "gingerbread style," which she'd taken literally. The house resembled something out of Hansel and Gretel's nightmares—each corner had a pastel theme with what looked like icing dripping down. But the décor fit Garnet's unique and quirky personality.

She had kept the big yard natural grasses, rather than a manicured lawn. At one time there'd been cattle on the nearly one hundred acres, but not since she'd owned it.

He parked next to Pearl's Range Rover, taking the steps two at a time. He knocked briefly on the screen door before he stepped inside.

Immediately the sweet scent of strawberries hit him. "Garnet?" he called out.

No response.

But Pearl poked her head over the swinging "saloon" doors that separated the kitchen from the dining room. "In here."

Tobin pushed through the doors and stopped in his tracks. Chaos wasn't unusual around Garnet. But this? This was insanity.

Garnet had two pails of strawberries on the floor. Across the room on the counter were pint jars of preserves. Stacked three high. In rows of ten.

Four rows of ten.

"Garnet?"

She whirled around. "Tobin! No time to talk, sonny. As you can see I'm busy, busy." She pointed to the opposite counter. "But help yourself to some champagne. It's the good stuff."

"Why don't you take a load off for a few minutes and have a glass with me." Tobin glanced over at Pearl. "You too."

Garnet squinted at Tobin and sighed. "Try harder to convince me, boy. You didn't even whip out them dimples. Go on, give me that charming smile."

Tobin laughed. "You are such a bossy Bessie."

"Only in my own kitchen. Everywhere else I'm as docile as a baby lamb."

Pearl snorted.

"We're breaking out my mother-in-law's hoity-toity crystal for this." Garnet sported a lemon yellow rhinestone-bedazzled do-rag. Her apron, pants and arms were coated in strawberry juice and pulp. She had sugar around her nose and across her upper lip as if she'd been sniffing cocaine.

"I'll get the glasses," Pearl said. "Tobin, you snag a bottle of the cold champagne from the fridge. We're not drinking the warm crap."

In a stage whisper after Pearl left the kitchen, Garnet said, "*She's* the bossy Bessie."

"I heard that."

The next moment Garnet was right in his face. "I'm really mad at you, Tobin Hale. I can't believe you didn't tell me you were giving Renner notice and leaving your job."

"But I did mention it last month. Don't you remember me saying I'd been considering it?"

"Oh pooh. I'm old. I can't remember everything. Anyway, I hope you've applied to places in Cheyenne. I guess that's where I'm moving. At least we'll still see each other sometimes."

He frowned. "Since when are you moving to Cheyenne?"

Garnet flopped down on a kitchen chair. "It's not a move out of choice."

"You always have a choice."

"Not according to my son. He's says I'm incapable of living on my own. He's hired professionals to pack my stuff up. I don't know when he plans to sell the house. But it won't matter because I'll be gone. Playing tiddlywinks in the assisted living place until I'm actually gone for good." She ducked her head to hide her face.

Where did Garnet's son get off meddling in his mother's life and making her cry? As far as he knew, neither the man nor anyone in his family had ever set foot in this house. "Miz G, can you listen to me for a moment?"

She nodded and dried her cheeks with the only clean corner of her apron.

"No one can drive you out without your consent. And if a moving van shows up, you call the sheriff and have him arrest anyone who puts a toe on your front porch. You hear me?"

"Easier said than done. I'm just a little old lady living out in the country by herself. The moving van guys could knock me out and get all my stuff loaded while I'm lying in the gravel drooling. It'd be their word against mine. They could claim I fell and hit my head and I don't remember what was said. Shoot, they could even say I *invited* them in. If I argued that I didn't, well, that'd give my son more reason to have me declared mentally unfit to care for myself." Garnet put her sticky hands on Tobin's arm. "I don't wanna leave here and move to a place where I don't know anyone. Am I really so bothersome just being in this house living my life?"

"Of course not."

"I tried to explain the special circumstances about how I landed in jail and how the gun was more of a prop, but my son refused to listen. He said he'd call me after he sends the movers."

"He's not coming here to personally handle this?"

"Nope. Too busy 'lawyering' in the big city." She snorted. "I wonder if he's throwing other old people out of their homes in the big city this week. I wish I could fight back. But even Pearl doesn't think warning off the moving guys with a loaded shotgun is the way to do it."

"I agree with Pearl. No guns." He squinted at her. "Promise me no guns, Garnet."

She waved her hands in the air. "Fine, fine, fine. No guns. I wish Tilda's dog hadn't died. I coulda sicced him on 'em. He was one hairy scary."

Tobin scrubbed his hand over his face.

Before he spoke, Garnet said, "How long does it take them performance-enhancing drugs to kick in? I could be pretty intimidating if I had 'roid rage." She jumped to her feet and struck a Hulk-like pose, complete with gritted teeth and crazy eyes. "How's this?"

He kept his features schooled. "I don't know that taking steroids is a good option either."

She flopped back down into the chair, dejected. "Dadgummit. I need someone bigger, stronger and scarier than me living here to tell them moving guys to take a hike when they show up." Garnet blinked at him. "Would you consider moving in to help me fight off a coup?"

*Don't do it. Do* not *get involved.*

"It'd be temporary," she added hastily, "since I know you're moving on. You wouldn't have to worry I'm trying to trick you into staying here with me forever because I'll miss you so durn much."

Such a sweet soul. "We both know the forever thing wouldn't work out because you play your music too loud for my taste, rappin' granny."

Garnet's smile was there and gone.

"You're not worried what everyone will say? Even though it's short-term, rumors might get nasty."

"Would it ruin your reputation as a stud if you're babysitting an old fart like me?"

Tobin laughed. "I don't have a reputation to ruin, Miz G."

"Me neither." She snapped her fingers. "Hey! We could tell everyone you're my bodyguard!"

"You wouldn't prefer having your Mud Lilies pals holed up here with you? You ladies have most folks in the county running scared anyway."

She shot a look over Tobin's shoulder. "Between us? I think there's a mole in the Mud Lilies."

"Why?"

"Because how else would my son have known about all of this stuff?" she whispered. "I didn't tell him nothin'. So someone close to me *had* to have tattled to him. It's not like they let any of the stuff we do make the papers."

She had a good point. "You think you know who it is? Or why they're doin' it?"

"Not yet. But I've laid a few traps." She leaned forward. "So are you in?"

The earnestness on her face sucker-punched him. As far as he could tell—and he knew Garnet pretty well—she was just fine living on her own. In fact, it was when she was out and about that she stirred up trouble. "Three weeks is all I can give you, Miz G. Then I'm gone."

"Where are you going?"

"There's a job in New Mexico."

Her eyes narrowed. "You've really been holding out on me, sonny."

He didn't tell her it wasn't a done deal. Nor did he mention that even if he drove all the way down there and didn't get the job, he wasn't coming back to Muddy Gap.

"Where'd you go to get those champagne glasses, Pearl? Timbuktu?" Garnet yelled.

"Quit yelling!" Pearl stormed into the kitchen. "I got the glasses. Bernice texted me back about your hair mask."

"Lordy, lordy, the things I do to keep up my youthful appearance." She sighed and whipped off the do-rag. "I ain't sure whether it's even worth it."

Beneath the do-rag, Garnet wore a plastic cap, covering what appeared to be mashed strawberries smeared all over her head.

*Don't ask.*

"Tobin, get the champagne. And be quick about it because Garnet's gotta rinse the goop outta her hair. The juice is acidic. Let's hope the strawberries haven't eaten into her brain or given her a bald spot."

"That's a cheery thought, Pearl. Especially when we're celebrating good news for a change."

Pearl's birdlike eyes sharpened. "What good news?"

"Tobin agreed to stay here as my bodyguard to keep the moving van people from packing me away."

"Just for three weeks," Tobin reminded her.

"That makes strategic sense. Having this place a transitional space. You'll cut personal ties with livin' at the Split Rock so it'll just be about your working hours." Pearl waited until Garnet turned away before saying in a conspiratorial tone, "If you need to come up with a battle plan, remember, I'm familiar with both sparkler bombs and trip wires."

He raised a brow because, frankly, what else could he say to that?

"My head itches," Garnet complained. "Let's drink."

Tobin peeled the foil back and popped the cork, managing to pour the champagne without spilling.

Garnet raised her glass for a toast. "To friends who come through no matter what."

They touched glasses and he knocked back a big gulp.

Holy crap. Tobin gave his glass a double take. That didn't taste like any champagne he'd ever had.

Garnet bumped him with her bony hip. "Told ya that was the good stuff. I'm only using a little bit in each batch of preserves, because I'm drinking the rest."

"What is this?"

"Cristal."

"Cristal?" he repeated. "The stuff that costs hundreds of bucks a bottle? The kind that rappers are always going on and on about?"

She shrugged. "Now you know there's a reason why they're writing songs about it."

Pearl said, "True dat."

## Chapter Two

❧

"*O*f course, you'll have to drive to Wyoming."

Jade Evans stared at her father, convinced this was an auditory hallucination. She'd indulged in a superlong shower this morning . . . Maybe she had water trapped in her ear. Tilting her head to the side, she attempted to drain it, only to hear her dad say, "For Pete's sake, Jade, are you even listening to me?"

"Sorry. I must've misunderstood. I thought I heard you say you wanted me to drive to Wyoming."

"That *is* what I said." He sighed. "I want you to stay with your grandmother Garnet to gauge her state of mind and her ability to live on her own."

"You're serious."

"As the *New York Times* Sunday crossword puzzle."

"What about my life here? You just expect me to drop everything? Why can't Mom do it?"

Jade watched as her father calmly wiped his mouth with his napkin and laid the white cloth on the table. "Jade. Honey. Your mother is already dealing with your grandmother Celeste, so she can't possibly travel across the country and figure out these decisions for my mother."

"That's exactly right, Dad. She's *your* mother. You should handle this."

"You are her only grandchild."

"So?"

"So, she adores you. She dotes on you. She listens to you."

"Which means she won't suspect me of being there to spy on her and tattle to *you*."

"Precisely."

"Then it's really not fair. GG is the sweetest, most loving and generous person I've ever known. Showing up in Wyoming because—"

"I'm worried about the two-bit hustler in Wranglers who moved in to 'protect' her and likely intends to swindle her out of everything. That is a fair reason to spy on her, don't you agree?"

That tidbit floored her and she fought to keep her temper in check. "Hang on. When did all of this happen? And why is this the first I've heard of it?" Granted, she did work a lot and wasn't around much, but this seemed to be another case of her parents' *Don't tell Jade, she can't handle things like this* attitude.

Things like her mother's breast cancer scare.

Things like her father's business partner making questionable financial decisions and nearly sending the firm into bankruptcy.

Jade hadn't known about either of those major life traumas until months after they happened. As an only child, she had a close relationship with both her mom and dad—even when they weren't living under the same roof. It hurt that they hadn't trusted her enough to tell her the truth or to let her be there for them like they'd always been there for her.

"I first heard about it two days ago," her father said. "One of her more level-headed friends is justifiably concerned about this situation and contacted me privately."

Jade imagined GG coughing "snitch" into her hand and bit back a smile. "That doesn't explain why GG needs protection."

"She *thinks* she needs protection," he corrected. "That's why this slick operator moved in. According to my source, this guy doesn't plan to be in Wyoming much longer. That leads me back to the concern that he's got a timeline all set for ripping her off."

"It sounds like she needs protection from him."

"She does. And yet, she's telling him and everyone else she needs protection from *me*."

Confused, she said, "Wait. Back up. Why would GG say that?" Oh no. Was he afraid GG had developed dementia?

His frustrated gaze met hers. "Last year after the Taser incident, I warned her if she kept getting into trouble I'd have to enforce some changes in her life."

"Dad. You didn't. You know how she reacts to that kind of stuff."

"I was mad, all right? It was a toss-away comment. But evidently your grandmother is convinced that this was the last straw and I'll have her packed up and whisked away to an assisted living facility, never to be seen or heard from again."

"That's not true, is it? You wouldn't just do that without her consent, right?"

"No—only if she needed medical help and didn't have the capacity to make decisions for herself. Or if I believed she might be a danger to herself or others. So with this latest situation . . ." He rubbed the spot between his eyebrows. "I didn't want to share this with you, sweetheart. But GG was arrested last month. She spent the night in jail on a drunk and disorderly charge."

Jade's mouth fell open. Rather than rail on him for yet *another* thing he'd kept from her, she imagined her sweet GG wearing prison orange and playing cribbage for cigarettes. "She's eighty-two years old and they threw her in the drunk tank like a common barfly?"

"Apparently."

"Please tell me you're suing them!"

"No. This next incident should've landed her in jail, but it didn't."

"There's *more?*"

"Yes. She decided to break up an argument between friends and discharged a firearm inside a local resort. Thankfully no one was hurt and the resort owners didn't press charges. Evidently your grandmother owns several guns and she's parading them around town like Calamity Jane in the Wild West."

Jade put her hand over her dad's, trying to wrap her head around this new information. GG had always characterized herself as eccentric, which made her so much fun to be around, but she'd never exhibited erratic behavior.

"Then to top it all off . . . she's on a spending spree. She bought one hundred bottles of Cristal to the tune of twenty thousand dollars—for cooking, she claims. Her friend also let it slip that she purchased a thirty-thousand-dollar horse and she dropped a hundred grand on a bull—I'm still waiting for documentation on those purchases. Who spends that kind of money on livestock?" He answered his own question. "A generous, gullible woman who is under the spell of a fast-talking cowboy, that's who."

A slow burn started in her chest. Jade didn't know who this low-rent lothario thought he was, but she would not allow him to swindle her bighearted grandmother.

"Now do you see why I need you there in person?" her dad pressed. "The only way to gauge if—or how— her mental state has changed is to live in the same house with her."

"And protect her from her 'protector,'" Jade murmured. "Mom is on board with me going to Wyoming?"

"She thinks it will be beneficial for you to spend some time reevaluating things in your life . . . especially after your break—"

"I had the flu, Dad. A really bad case of the flu. That's all it was."

He said nothing. He just looked worried, frustrated and a little sad.

Jade knew her parents were concerned about her. Six months ago her roommate had kicked Jade out so her boyfriend could move in, forcing Jade to move back home. It was humbling to be twenty-four years old and living with her parents. In the two years since she'd graduated from college, she hadn't found a job in her field. So she'd had two choices: suck it up and work outside her field to support herself or return to school for a master's degree. That option hadn't made sense to her. Pay for even more education in an area of study where you currently couldn't find employment? No, thank you. She'd rather work, even if her jobs kept her exhausted to the point she had no time to think.

*Maybe that's why you fill every waking hour with productivity; then you don't have to figure out what comes next.*

"How long would I have to be there?" she asked him.

"At least a month," her dad said.

"A month? I can't take that much time off."

"Jade. Sweetheart. While your mother and I are both proud of your work ethic—you've been slaving yourself with three part-time jobs."

Her chin came up. She knew it looked stubborn and didn't care. "I told you when I moved back in that it wouldn't be permanent. I'm saving as much money as I can."

"And we told you we'd be more than happy to help you out," her father said gently.

They'd had this discussion several times. Jade appreciated her parents' generosity, but proving she could support herself was a point of pride. "Thank you. But as I've said before, you and Mom paid for my education and that's more than enough. I'm grateful I'm not struggling with student loans too."

"We're not . . . discounting the work you do. But it'd be a good break for you, even for just a few weeks, not to work sixteen hours a day."

She almost couldn't fathom that. Not getting up at three thirty in the morning to take the subway to Midtown so she could clock in by four a.m. Then leaving the restaurant by nine thirty and walking to the office building where she answered phones from ten a.m. to six p.m. Monday through Wednesday. On Thursdays and Fridays she worked only until four p.m., allowing her to get to the quintet gig at the upscale restaurant that offered live classical music until the kitchen closed at eleven. Saturdays usually weren't as hectic unless the quartet she played in had booked a daytime wedding and an evening cocktail party. The only day she took off was Sunday—unless their quartet scored a gig, which seemed to happen more frequently lately. Starving artists didn't have the luxury of saying no.

"I know this is a lot to take in," her dad said. "But do you have any questions?"

"What would I do all day in Wyoming?" she asked him.

"Besides keeping an eye on your grandmother and figuring out the cowboy protector's angle?" He shrugged. "I don't know. You could play it by ear."

Jade laughed. "Hilarious. A musician's reference that I can't comprehend because you know I'm a planner and a list maker."

"I'm sure once you get in that drafty old house piled with years' worth of stuff that GG will have plenty to keep you occupied," her father said dryly.

"When would I have to leave?"

"Tomorrow."

She closed her eyes. Giving notice at her receptionist's job wasn't a big deal since she worked for a temp agency. The restaurant had two other prep cooks, so that wouldn't burn an employment bridge. Both the quintet and quartets had backup players for emergency fill-ins. So once she made the calls, she could load up her car and just . . . go.

But could she do it? She'd never been impulsive, so this was asking a lot.

*This isn't impulsive; this is a last-minute family emergency.*

"I'll do it. Under one condition."

He raised an eyebrow.

"That you won't make any decisions about GG's future until I give you my opinion."

"Done."

Jade stood and kissed the top of her dad's balding head. "I'll start packing."

⤳

Since Jade hadn't ever done a cross-country road trip, at first she'd buzzed with excitement about experiencing a rite of passage. But as the miles wore on, she realized it wasn't fun to do alone. Plus, she wasn't a great driver, so she'd white-knuckled it the first day to the point that her hands and forearms actually hurt after a day of driving.

The next day she'd made a conscious effort to try to relax. Her subconscious reminded her this trip was as much about the journey as the destination . . . until her father's voice chimed in with this parting advice. "Don't dawdle. Don't take risks with the speed limit or your safety, but you need to reach Wyoming in a timely manner before GG does something we can't undo."

So she hadn't stopped to see any of the sights that interested her. She spent fourteen hours a day behind the wheel, rested for ten hours and then got up to do it all over again. So it wasn't unlike her normal working days. Time passed in a blur of hitting shuffle on her iPod, stopping for food, gas and bathroom breaks. She'd snapped out of her daze when the GPS instructed her that her destination was two miles ahead.

She'd made it. And for the first time since she'd left home, she allowed herself to be excited. If nothing else, she'd get to spend time with her grandma in her world. And looking around at the topography? Wyoming was a world unto itself.

For hundreds of miles there'd been nothing but flat land. Little in the way of trees, just sickly-looking bushes. She'd been tempted to pull the car over after a tumbleweed—an actual tumbleweed!—had blown across the road. But before she pulled out her phone to snap a picture, the wind bounced it over a fence and into a group of cows.

After cresting a hill, Jade noticed a long line of trees that didn't fit in this rugged setting. The rest of the area was craggy, with rock outcroppings here and there. She slowed on the gravel road and turned onto a driveway—also gravel—that bisected the tree line.

When the house came into view, she couldn't contain her laugh. GG's place was a mishmash of styles, a cross between a Grimms' fairy-tale cabin and something out of a Dr. Seuss book. The front door, curved on the top and painted a glossy purple, made it seem like you could walk through an eggplant.

But her amusement was short-lived when that door opened and a big guy, wearing the kind of cowboy clothes she'd seen on TV, stepped out to block access to the house. With his arms crossed, his legs braced, his face hidden beneath his hat, his body language was perfectly clear: *You will have to go through me to get inside.*

That got Jade's back up. Who did this macho yokel think he was? She was Garnet's granddaughter. She had every right to be here. Him? Not so much.

Before Jade decided the best way to circumvent Mr. Large and In Charge, GG appeared beside him. She paused, grinned, clapped her hands and barreled down the steps.

Jade scrambled out of the car and met GG halfway.

GG had always been stronger than she looked, but still, GG shocked her when she picked Jade up and spun her around in a circle. Then she set her down and hugged her hard.

"You are as beautiful as ever." GG trapped Jade's face in her hands. "But I'm a little ticked off that your dad sent you to do his dirty work."

Jade knew her best defense was an attempt at ignorance. "GG—"

"Don't deny it, K, cutie pie? It'll save us both a lot of round and round if we lay our cards on the table from the start."

"I am happy to be here and very happy to see you."

"I'm happy to see that you didn't pull up in a dadgum U-Haul." Her eyes narrowed. "Or are you the lead car and there's a parade of moving vans behind you?"

So she *was* paranoid. "No, GG. It's just me."

GG looped her arm through Jade's and started toward the steps. "You're here in time for lunch."

When they reached the porch, Jade noticed the cowboy sentinel now blocked access to the stairs.

"Tobin, you can lower them hackles. Come over here and meet my granddaughter."

His boot heels struck the wooden planks in measured steps that seemed to echo the beat of Jade's heart. She didn't look up until the man cast a shadow over her.

And her heart stopped completely. Oh man. He was steal-your-breath-and-common-sense handsome. Tall and broad and just . . . big all over. The stubble on his jaw wasn't affected like the city guys she knew who didn't shave in an effort to appear more manly. This guy probably scared his razor away. He probably hadn't shaved because he had important manly stuff to do and didn't waste time with trivial stuff like running a blade over that beautifully chiseled face.

Her gaze wandered up to his eyes, which were an arresting blue-green. Had to be contacts. No one's eyes were that color without enhancement. Regardless. Those eyes were as cool as his standoffish demeanor. His lips were flattened into a thin line too.

She bristled when his gaze slowly took in every nuance of her face as if attempting to put the pieces together. That scrutiny prompted her to step forward until they were boot tips to flip-flops, their bodies almost touching. Mr. Rugged Sexy-Eyed Cowboy needed to know that he didn't intimidate her.

"I'm GG's only granddaughter, Jade Evans. I can see by your confusion that I wasn't what you expected, so let me clear it up for you. Yes, I was adopted as a baby, but that doesn't mean—"

"Whoa, there, tiger. I wasn't questioning your parentage. And since I haven't seen pictures of you or your parents—*ever*—anywhere in this house, let alone seen any of you bother to step foot in Wyoming, I had no preconceived ideas about you."

Not the answer she'd been expecting. But he had managed to get in a dig about her family anyway.

"Now, now, no fighting. No need to get indigestion before we eat lunch, is there?"

Jade watched a sweet smile bloom across the man's face as he looked at GG.

"If you're truly making liverwurst sandwiches, Miz G, I'll guarantee indigestion."

"Oh, you." GG flapped her hand at him. "I know you hate it, so of course that's not on the menu for today."

The way he pandered to GG ticked Jade off. "Excuse me, but I didn't catch *your* name."

That aquamarine-colored gaze winged back to her. "Tobin Hale."

"Tobin Hale," she repeated. "Is that one name? Like Billy Bob?"

He raised an eyebrow. "You're making a lot of assumptions about me, for us just meeting, Jade."

She smiled at him. "Assumptions about you, Tobin Hale, are *exactly* why I'm in Wyoming." She faced her grandma. "Since this is the first time I've been here, can you show me around after lunch?"

"I'd love that. Let's go inside. This bickering between you two is eating into Tobin's lunch hour. He needs to get back to work."

Tobin pushed open the screen door and held it for them. "No need to rush now, Miz G. I believe I'll take the rest of the afternoon off so I can help you show Jade around."

*More like show me over the edge of a cliff*, she thought.

The interior of the house was as whimsical as Jade had imagined. The kitchen with its bloodred walls, crisp white cabinetry, dark gray countertops and wide-planked floor had a warm, welcoming country kitchen vibe. On the antique sideboard Jade noticed stacks of jelly jars. "GG, are those your strawberry champagne preserves?"

"You remembered! I put up a big batch."

"I finished the last jar you gave me just this week."

"This is the primo stuff. Better ingredients and all that. I'll hook you up with a case."

Jade felt Tobin studying her so she met his gaze head-on.

"I'll even load it in your car before I send you on your merry way," Tobin said helpfully.

*Back where you belong,* went unsaid.

"Tobin, dear, would you get out the plates?"

"Sure, Miz G."

"Jade, be a doll and grab the milk out of the fridge."

"GG, I haven't had milk with lunch for years."

"The milk is for Tobin." GG squeezed his biceps. "How do you think he got so big and strong?"

"I assumed from lifting cows or whatever."

Tobin laughed. "Well, darlin', I'll take that *assumption* as a compliment that you think I'm capable of lifting a twelve-hundred-pound cow by myself."

GG snickered. "You're gonna get quite the education, girlie, on life in the West. I guarantee it's nothing you learned at Columbia."

Blushing, Jade grabbed the milk out of the fridge and set it on the table.

Tobin carried two plates, one loaded with sandwiches, the other with fruit, and parked himself between Jade and her grandmother.

Not a subtle move at all.

GG set a glass in front of each plate and passed out *Hello Kitty* napkins. "No liverwurst on the sandwiches, just turkey, ham, roast beef and salami." She patted Tobin's muscled forearm. "I eat more meat when you're around."

"The food is just an extra bonus for living here with you," Tobin said.

So . . . was this where she just jumped in and asked *why* Tobin was living here? Or did she let the conversation develop naturally? Jade had zero stealth skills. She'd never needed any. Thinking back to all the episodes of *Veronica Mars* she'd watched where the sleuth tricked suspects into spilling their guts without much effort . . . well, she was drawing a blank on that technique.

"Are you havin' a sandwich? Or are you some kind of vegetarian?" Tobin asked.

Jade blinked, noticing he held the plate of sandwiches in front of her. "Now who's making assumptions? No, I'm not vegetarian. Not that there's anything wrong with it."

"Agreed. It ain't my business how folks choose to live their lives." His eyes gleamed. "In fact, I find it disturbing when people who haven't got the first clue about a person's life presume to horn in and take over."

And it looked like the gloves just came off.

Good.

Before Jade responded, GG pushed back from the table. "Shoot. I left my pills in my room. Gotta remember to take them with lunch." She quickly vanished through the swinging doors.

Tobin leaned close enough she could see the golden hair mixed in with the darker scruff on his face. "You might as well get in your car and hightail it back to New York City and tell your daddy that he won't succeed in throwing Garnet out of her house. I won't let that happen."

"Why are *you* here, Tobin? Exactly what kind of . . . relationship do you have with my grandmother?"

"You watch yourself," he warned. "I have nothin' but the utmost respect for Miz G, and that is why I will not let her family—a family that's *never* been here to visit even *one* time in the years I've known Garnet—think they have the right to enforce any kind of decision on her. Your father does not know what's best for her and neither do you."

"And you do?" Jade asked him with a sneer that matched his.

"Damn straight. I'm here to ensure that a moving van doesn't pull up and start dismantling Garnet's life piece by piece as she stands by helplessly and watches them haul it away." He shook his head. "Not happening to her on my watch."

Jade started to correct his assumption about the sudden appearance of moving vans as paranoid speculation on GG's part, but she decided to let his mistaken judgment ride and see where it led. "She's out here in the middle of nowhere—"

"That is a lame argument. She's been fine living on her own here for years."

"Because she's heavily armed?" she retorted. "Lately she's been exhibiting the type of behavior that forces us to question her ability to make sound decisions." She took a breath. "You think it's *fine* for her to shoot off guns in a public venue? It's *fine* for her to get arrested and spend the night in jail? It's *fine* to spend twenty thousand dollars on champagne? Or on—"

"It's her damn money," he said irritably. "If she wants to drop that kinda cash on bubbly, it's not your father's concern or yours."

"But it is my concern how much she's paying you for 'protection services.' I highly doubt you're doing it out of the kindness of your heart."

"You don't know a thing about me. But here's a hint. I'm stubborn as fuck. And you just showing up here out of the blue proves my point about there bein' way more at play than Garnet making a couple of bad decisions when she's defending her best pals." Tobin pointed to the door. "That woman is selfless and nobody is taking advantage of her for that. Especially not her family who think they can lay down the law for her from thirty-five hundred miles away."

"Happily, I'm not that far away anymore. I'll be living here for as long as it takes to get a feel for what she needs."

Tobin eased back. "You know what Garnet needs? Honesty. Don't play off your sudden appearance like you got a wild hair up your ass to leave your fancy city lifestyle so you could experience the modern-day West. You'll hurt her if you allow her to believe you give a shit about her life in Wyoming."

Jade felt her cheeks heat. "I would never hurt her."

"You don't think not knowing anything about her life or her community doesn't hurt her? As you so annoyingly pointed out first fucking thing, you are her only grandchild. So how come I've never seen a picture of you?"

The blush spread from her face to heat her neck and her chest. "I don't know."

GG sailed back into the kitchen. "Aw. You two didn't have to wait for me to eat. You should've just dug right in."

*He got plenty of digs in, all right.*

Jade watched as Tobin turned and smiled at GG. "I'll sort through those tools in the shed and see if I can't find that missing bit. You enjoy lunch with your granddaughter. I'm sure you two have a lot to catch up on."

"Aren't you gonna eat? I know you're starved, young man. You told me so yourself."

He grabbed a sandwich off the table. "It'll be a working lunch, same as always." He locked his gaze to Jade's. "But don't you worry. I'm not going anywhere."

# Chapter Three

≈✦≈

*T*obin didn't even taste a single bite of his sandwich after he stormed out of Garnet's kitchen.

He crossed the yard and headed straight for the machine shed. He threw his shoulder into the wooden door because it always stuck—not because he was pissed off.

But he *was* pissed off.

After slamming the door behind him, he didn't bother with the light. He didn't need anything out here; he just figured it was a place where neither Garnet nor her granddaughter would follow him.

Her annoying, pain-in-the-ass, argumentative granddaughter.

Her goddamned beautiful granddaughter.

Holy hell the woman was the most stunningly exotic beauty he'd ever laid eyes on. The round face with those almond-shaped smoky-topaz eyes. The warm caramel hue of her skin, her full mouth that almost distracted from the tip of her stubborn chin. And that hair. Glossy black that fell in a straight line below her shoulder blades. She was small—he topped her by at least a foot, but she had some delectable curves.

By god the woman had some balls showing up here and accusing him of having ulterior motives. Maybe he did; he refused to let an adult woman be railroaded into life changes that would put her in an early grave. Yanking her away from her home and her friends . . . everything that made Garnet vibrant would wither away with no one around to appreciate it. He'd never doubted that's why she donned such outrageous getups. It got a reaction. It got people outside her normal circle talking to her. Or rather, Garnet talking to them.

He'd taken her to the farm and ranch supply store in Rawlins about six months after they'd become friends. He'd gone to get his supplies, which took ten minutes, and in that time he'd lost track of Garnet. When he found her, by the warmers where the baby chicks were penned, he watched her scoop up a baby chick and bring it over to an elderly woman sitting on a bench by herself.

The woman's hands were gnarled and she could only stroke the chick's downy head with a misshapen finger, but she wore a big grin the entire time Garnet cupped the chick in her hands. When the woman started to talk, Garnet listened. A harried woman around Tobin's dad's age came over and chewed the woman out for wandering off. Garnet held the chick out to the woman and told her the world would be a better place if everyone had more patience with children and old people. Kids because their excitement came from how they saw potential in everything and old people because they had to give up the things that were important to them, and that had defined them.

It'd really struck home that this sweet, kooky woman had such a big heart. She'd gone out of her way to forge a connection with someone who looked as if they needed it. That was the first of many times he'd witnessed Garnet's generosity.

He'd bet that Jade had benefited from that generosity. But how well did Jade know her grandmother beyond that?

*You're just hopeful she's not the bad guy because she's hot. And a little mouthy.*

Heaven help him, but that kind of woman was catnip to him.

Tobin had been prepared to square off against a moving company.

Nothing had prepared him for the mixed emotions she evoked with one haughty look.

But there was no doubt in his mind he'd still be squaring off against her.

🙠

After killing a couple of hours outside, he jogged up the steps and saw Jade lounging on the love seat next to the porch swing. Beside her was a laptop, a tablet, a cell phone and an e-book reader.

"Before you grill me on GG's whereabouts, I promise I didn't put sleeping powder in her tea. She conked out on her own in the sitting room."

"Look, I never said I thought you intended to harm her. I said I didn't want you to *hurt* her. And before you go all 'I'm an English major' on me or something, I'm aware of the similarities in the meanings of those two words. But that means you're also aware of the differences in their meanings."

She smiled. Not a sarcastic smile, but a genuine *you amuse me* smile and damn if that didn't just cause a funny tickle in his gut.

"Pull up a chair, Tobin, and let's see if we can have a civilized conversation this time. Because looking at you..." Her gaze wandered across his shoulders and lingered as it moved down his arms. "I know I would lose badly in an arm-wrestling contest against you."

Tobin laughed, but holy hell. That almost seemed like a compliment.

*So that's her game. She'll use her beauty, her body and her charm to distract you and make you think she's not the devil.*

"Why would we be arm wrestling?"

"For GG's affections of course. I've never had to share them."

"Feelin' a mite competitive and jealous?"

Jade blinked those stunning topaz eyes and gave him a weak smile. "As a matter of fact... yes. And I do realize that sounds petulant."

"Well, darlin', that's the best part of Miz G. She's got affection in spades." Tobin sat across from her. "I feel the need to point out . . . a little slip of a thing like you? I don't see arm wrestling bein' one of your skills."

"It's not. But that's my clichéd way of saying I'll go to the mat to do what's best for her."

"Then when you're done you'll pack that mat up and send it to Cheyenne along with the rest of her stuff?"

She glanced at her watch, then back at him. "Wow. We didn't even make it to the two-minute mark that time without taking potshots at each other."

At least she'd said *we* and wasn't placing the blame for sniping solely on him. "Let's try again. Did you get the grand tour of the house?"

"No. I unpacked my car and dumped everything in my room. That took a while. GG was sleeping by the time I finished."

Tobin frowned. "I would've helped you haul your stuff upstairs."

That surprised her. "I'm used to doing everything myself. And it wasn't bad. The last place I lived was on the sixth floor. The elevator didn't work ninety percent of the time. I think that room is bigger than that entire apartment was."

"Miz G put you in the daffodil room?"

She nodded. "I did have some serious envy that you'd already claimed the rose room."

"Why?"

"The bed is bigger."

"That's the king-sized bed I brought with me. A guy my size doesn't fit well in a double."

A moment of awkward silence passed.

Then Jade said, "It looks like we'll be sharing the upstairs bathroom, so I feel the need to warn you about leaving the toilet seat up."

"As long as we're goin' with clichés, I'll warn you not to use my razor."

Jade's thoughtful gaze roved over his face. "Doesn't look like you have much use for a razor anyway."

He scratched his cheek. "Just not today. I wasn't aware we'd be expecting guests. Did she know you were coming?"

"Yes. She didn't tell you I was on my way here?"

"Nope. How long are you staying?"

"Depends."

"On?" he prompted.

"This and that."

He eyed her electronics. "You don't have a job to go back to?"

"Not a full-time career-type job."

"Got a boyfriend pining away for you?" he asked, suspecting a woman with her type of delicate beauty wouldn't be single.

"Not one of those either." She paused. "How about you?"

"No boyfriend for me. Or girlfriend for that matter."

Jade laughed. "I was going to say the same thing."

"What are your plans while you're here?"

"What's with the twenty questions? Are you afraid I'll be boxing up the crystal and the silver personally so I know that you don't abscond with it?"

He grinned, appreciating that her quick wit hadn't masked her antagonism. It'd be interesting to see how hard he'd have to poke her buttons before that sharp tongue took over. "I'd be asking Miz G before you move stuff around here. She's particular about her things. It probably looks like chaos. But trust me; she knows *exactly* where everything is in this house. But if you don't believe me? Knock yourself out. See how lovey-dovey she is with you after she catches you messin' in her china cabinet or her kitchen."

Jade sipped her tea. "Speaking of the kitchen. She made you lunch today, but do you cook for her?"

"Nope. I buy the groceries."

"So you do the dishes and clean up after she cooks for you?"

He shrugged. "I hang out with her in the kitchen while she's cooking and cleaning up. She asks me to chop veggies, I'll do it. She asks me to scrub a fry pan, I'll do it. It's not like I've got a defined list of chores."

She made a face but didn't respond.

Tobin rested his forearms on his knees and leaned forward. "What's put that wrinkle in your brow, darlin'?"

"Don't *darlin'* me," she warned. "I'm not so easily swayed by sweet-talking cowboys."

"Been around a lot of *gen-u-wine* cowboys in New York City, have you?"

"Sadly, no, but that's beside the point. I've only been here a few hours and I've already seen you use those sweet-talking ways on GG. So what has she promised you in exchange for your protection?"

Tobin knew his eyes had turned frosty, but he kept his tone even. "She did mention something about giving me forty acres and a mule." When he realized Jade didn't get the reference, he backtracked. "Why are you so damn suspicious of me?"

"Seriously? You're a good-looking, unmarried cowboy who has moved into my grandmother's house and taken on the role of her protector. You can't see why my dad would have a problem with that?"

"Then your dad oughta nut up and confront me about it in person."

The screen door banged open. Garnet strolled onto the porch, yawning. "Guess I needed that nap. That's where toddlers and old-timers are alike; we don't want to nap, but if we don't we're cranky-pants the rest of the day." She squinted and her gaze flitted between him and Jade. "What's going on? Looks like you two were having words."

"We were talking," Jade said.

Tobin snorted. "Call it what it is, darlin'; we were arguing. Jade was trying to act all cute and charming, but I didn't buy any of it."

"Jade? Charming?" Garnet slapped her leg with amusement. "Oh, sonny. That's a good one. Jade is as cute as a bug in a rug, but she's so shy she failed charm school twice, didn't you, sweetie?"

"GG!"

"You failed twice? Now that I'd believe," Tobin drawled.

Miz G poked his arm. "Your charm doesn't work as well as you think, or else you'd already have hooked yourself a girlfriend or a wife, wouldn't you?"

Jesus.

He'd forgotten about Garnet's equal-opportunity blunt streak.

"That's probably because he argues about everything," Jade said.

"The hell I do. I argue when it's warranted."

"I don't like arguing in any way, shape or form," Garnet said.

"Then we'll stop," Tobin said. "It'll be easier for some of us than others."

"Yes, it'll be very easy for *him* to stop," Jade said sweetly, "since he wasn't winning anyway."

"Hard to get my point across when I'm bein' accused of everything from freeloading, to having undue influence, to expecting payment for my services."

"I never said any of that," she said hotly.

"But you sure were thinking it, weren't you, darlin'?"

"Oh, so you're a mind reader now too?" Jade leaned forward. "Tell me what I'm thinking right now."

Tobin clucked his tongue. "Miz G doesn't like to hear that kind of foul language, Jade. As her *only* granddaughter, you should already know that."

"Omigod. You are the most infuriating man I've ever met."

"And I'm considered a nice guy around these parts."

"Not exactly a badge of honor when the population around these parts is like . . . ten," she retorted, "and half of them are animals."

"If there aren't enough people around to suit your needs, why don't you trot your little self on home to New York City?"

"Because I like it here. Present company excluded. So suck it up, cowboy. I'm not going anywhere."

"Right." He smirked. "Bet you don't last half a day, *cupcake*, when I tell you the nearest Starbucks is in Laramie . . . eighty miles away."

"Enough!"

They looked at Garnet and then each other. How had they forgotten she was here?

Garnet said. "Zip it, both of you, and listen up. I'd hoped I was wrong but I can see that it's worse than I imagined." She pointed at Jade. "I don't care what you said to Tobin in the kitchen earlier that had him scurrying off, but it was more than just a little tiff to get that man to forgo lunch." She focused on Tobin. "And I've no doubt you were equally at fault by goading her into it."

"Me?" Tobin said innocently.

Jade whispered, "Why don't you just *nut up* and admit it?"

Miz G said nothing to *her* about her snarky comment. How was that fair?

*Jesus. How old are you? Nine?*

"I won't listen to this kind of grade-school bickering. I'm too damn old. I'll state the obvious. You two are oil and water. You have nothing in common. You'll be at each other's throats at every opportunity, so I simply won't allow them kind of opportunities." She paused, her steely-eyed stare moving back and forth between them. "Do you understand what I'm saying? You two will steer clear of each other at all times for the duration of your stay with me—however long that'll be."

"How are we supposed to 'steer clear' of each other, GG?" Jade demanded.

"Yeah. We're sharing a house, a bathroom and . . . time with you, Miz G."

Jade muttered, "Suck-up."

"I'll divide up the mealtimes with a schedule so you *both* get equal

time with me. I'm giving you ten minutes to figure the rest of it out.
Then I don't want to see you two anywhere *near* each other after that,
understood?" She shook her finger at Jade, then at him. "Don't test me
on this. You both know how stubborn I can be." Miz G paused again.
Her eyes filled with tears. "I won't watch two people I care about deeply,
ripping each other down either in front of me or behind my back in my
own home. Got it?"

"Yes, ma'am."

Jade said, "Of course, GG. Whatever you want."

As soon as Garnet was out of earshot, Tobin leaned in. "This was
your doin'? Whining to *GG* how mean I was to you at lunch and seein'
how fast she'd freeze me out?"

"News flash, cowboy. I didn't bring up *your* name at all. Maybe she
finally sees what you're up to and is taking precautionary measures."

"That right there? Is why us steering clear of each other won't be a
problem."

Jade stood and said, "Ditto." She gave him a wide berth and hustled
down the steps, her hands in her pockets as she wandered up the driveway.

Tobin watched her until she disappeared over the hill, wondering
why the hell he didn't just get in his truck and leave. He didn't need this
crap.

## Chapter Four

～ぺ～

*T*obin hauled himself out of bed earlier than usual the next morning. But he still hadn't gotten up before Garnet.

He thought about their conversation as he completed his usual daily chores, feeding the herd, checking the outlying areas for cows that might've strayed. He did a quick run-through of the Split Rock grounds, but he didn't see anything the groundskeeper had to worry about.

Out of habit he checked the stock in the pasture across the road. Hugh, the former foreman, and Ike, the former cattle broker, now leased that section to house their rodeo stock that once had belonged to Renner. Now that Jackson Stock Contracting was a separate entity from Jackson Cattle Company—both of which were separate businesses from the Split Rock Ranch and Resort—the daily care of those animals was no longer Tobin's responsibility.

Hard to believe six years had passed since Tobin had finished grad school. He'd started at the Split Rock as a hunting guide and within a year he was second in command of the livestock operation. The money wasn't bad, and he did have his own place. The longer he worked there, the more responsibilities were passed off to him, but none of those responsibilities utilized his degrees. Tired of being a glorified ranch hand, tired of watching all his friends—except him—find a life partner, Tobin knew he needed a drastic change.

He'd expected things to be awkward between him and his boss, but the truth was Renner understood loneliness and the need for a change better than anyone else. He'd uprooted his own life in Kansas to build the Split Rock and expand his cattle company. In doing so, he'd met Tierney, the woman who'd become his wife, his business partner and the mother of his children.

Two hours later, Tobin's thoughts were pulled in a dozen different directions when he wandered into the office section of the barn.

Renner was pouring a cup of coffee in the break room. "Hey. Please tell me you didn't stick around because you have bad news."

"Nah. Everything checked out fine this morning. But number 224 ran off again and I tracked her to the bottom of the ravine. Third time this month."

"Damn jumpy heifers are the bane of my existence," Renner said dryly. "What else is goin' on?"

"Let's go into your office. It takes that ancient computer of yours fifteen minutes to start up, so you can get that goin' while I bend your ear."

"Hilarious." Renner started down the long hallway.

Tobin grabbed a soda out of the fridge and followed. In the office, he dropped into the chair opposite Renner's desk and sighed heavily.

Renner said, "So?"

"I know I've filled you in on the Garnet situation but it just got a whole lot more interesting."

"Moving vans haven't shown up already, have they?" Renner said sharply.

"No. Garnet's granddaughter Jade showed up yesterday instead."

"Jade?" Renner frowned. "I don't recall ever hearing that name."

"Exactly."

"What do you know about her?"

"She's beautiful," popped out of his mouth first thing. "Got an attitude too, that's for sure. She was in my face from the get-go, which was a challenge for her since she's like five foot nothin'. She accused me of manipulating her grandma. I questioned why Garnet's family took an interest in her only when they wanted to imprison her."

"Yikes."

"Yeah. Not a productive conversation. Long story short, Jade has moved in and is bein' vague about how long she intends to stick around. I can't just abandon Garnet, especially after . . ." Tobin scratched his jaw. "You know how Miz G always wears them funky clothes? The more outlandish the better? This morning she was wearing khakis. Khakis! And a plain, long-sleeved tan shirt. She even put on those preppy loafers. Not in vivid orange or bright pink but in basic brown. No jaunty scarf tied around her neck or worn as a headband. No jewelry. No rhinestones or sparkles anywhere. She looked like a Sears appliance saleswoman." Tobin swigged his soda. "So I asked her, 'Is it laundry day, Miz G, and that's all you have left to wear?'"

"How'd that go over?"

"Dammit, Ren, she got teary-eyed. She said the time had come for her to toe the line and act her age." He tamped down his anger. "Then she asked if I'd drop off the eight garbage bags of clothes she'd removed from her closet and bring them to the Salvation Army donation center. I told her I would, but only if she was sure."

"Was she?"

"Up until her gold lamé disco pants fell out of the bag I was carrying to my truck. When she picked them up and hugged them, I had to turn away. I hoped when I turned around I'd see that she'd run those garish pants up the flagpole as a sign of rebellion. But she just handed them over and said, 'You dropped these, sonny.'"

"Christ." Renner's gaze flicked to his monitor and then back to Tobin. "All those bags are in your truck now?"

He nodded.

"Take 'em to Harper at the clothing store and explain what's goin' on. There's plenty of storage in the back room. She'll keep an eye on them for a while in case Garnet changes her mind."

"Thanks. So in light of this . . . I'll be sticking around longer than I planned."

"How much longer?"

Tobin blew out a breath. "I'm hopin' just a week."

Renner sipped his coffee. "What about Albuquerque?"

"I told them I had a family emergency." He'd hated calling to postpone, but he'd tossed and turned half the damn night and hadn't seen an alternative.

"While I believe what you're doin' for Garnet is admirable, don't let it interfere with your plans any more than it already has."

"Any applicants for my job?"

"Not a single one."

"That sucks."

"Tell me about it. Anyone worth their salt knows bein' a ranch foreman is a lot of work. Anyone with a map can see we're highly isolated here. Those two things together . . ." He shook his head. "Anyway, my personnel issues ain't your problem."

Tobin stayed silent. It'd been so ingrained in him to be a team player that for the hundredth time he had to bite his tongue to stop himself from telling his boss he'd stay until a replacement had been found.

"Before I forget . . . the guest from Schenectady wants the full rodeo experience. Since you'll be working cattle with Teddy tomorrow, I asked Kyle and Hank to come by."

"Good."

"Was there anything else?"

"Nope. Thanks, boss. I appreciate it."

Tobin returned to Garnet's house to find Jade teetering on the kitchen counter, pulling down Garnet's cookbooks from the shelf that stretched above the sink.

He paused outside the swinging doors, watching her in a desirous daze. She'd donned a tiny pair of jean shorts that did fantastic things for her ass. Plus he got the bonus of seeing her beautifully toned legs, which shouldn't look that long since the woman wasn't bigger than a minute.

Despite being mesmerized by the glossy fall of her hair swaying enticingly across the middle of her back, he realized when she reached for the cookbooks on the back of the shelf that she hadn't compensated for the weight of the books already piled in her left arm. She bobbled the books, and her body listed to the side.

Rather than trying to catch her, he opted to stabilize her; his hands landed on her ass just as she started to fall backward.

Jade screamed and lurched forward, scrambling for a handhold on the shelf. The shelf separated from the wall, sending the rest of the books crashing around them like bombs.

Bombs that landed on Tobin's head. "Ow. Ow. Fuck."

Jade whirled around and glared at him. "What is *wrong* with you? You see a woman standing on the counter and decide to cop a feel?"

Tobin stared at her, dumbfounded. "The only reason I grabbed your ass was to keep you from falling on it!"

"I had it under control."

"Like hell you did." Now he was pissed. "So excuse the fuck out of me for trying to keep you from getting hurt. None of the cookbooks beaned *you* in the noggin, did they?"

She blinked those golden-brown eyes at him. "No."

"Lucky you. Three bounced off my head. I'm still seeing stars."

Then she smirked. "More's the pity none of them hit you hard enough to knock you out."

Un.Be.Lieve.Able.

"But since you're here and your contribution to GG's household is using your muscles, can you reattach the shelf so it won't crash down again?"

His first response—*If you think you're so smart, why don't you fix it?*—remained trapped in his throat. He couldn't leave it half-assed and let it crash down and hurt someone. "Fine. I'll get the ladder, which is a pretty handy tool for climbing up to retrieve things out of your reach. Have you heard of one?"

"Ooh, cowboy charm has a bite. Yes, I've heard of a ladder. I actually searched for one. But since GG isn't here—"

"Where is she?"

"Lunch at the Lions Club with her Mud Lilies friends. I guess they planned to teach some cougars a lesson about . . . poaching?" Confusion clouded her eyes. "Do you have any idea what that means?"

"It means the Mud Lilies are stirring up shit in Rawlins." He stacked the books on the table. "What were you doin' with all the cookbooks anyway?"

"Moving them." She gestured to a two-tiered shelving unit filled with knickknacks. "GG has better access to them there."

That actually made sense. But . . . "Did Miz G ask you to do this?"

"No. I was bored so I thought I'd surprise her." Jade jumped down. "I'll get out of your way."

And she'd stayed out of his way.

Until Miz G came home and Jade threw him under the bus.

Tobin just happened to be putting away his tools in the mudroom when Garnet strolled into the kitchen. She gasped. "What's this? Why are all of my cookbooks down here?"

"You don't . . . like them there?" Jade asked warily.

*Yeah, sweetheart, you probably should've cleared this "surprise" with her first,* Tobin thought smugly.

"I'm not one for change, Jade," Garnet said mulishly. "I like things the way I like them."

"But it's not entirely my fault! I was up on the counter, getting some cookbooks, when Tobin barreled into the kitchen, scaring the life out of me. I lost my balance, fell forward and grabbed on to the shelf. All of the cookbooks crashed down—"

"On top of you? Oh, sweetheart, that's awful! Were you hurt? Are you okay?"

Tobin rubbed the bump behind his right temple, annoyed she hadn't clarified that *he'd* borne the brunt of the falling books.

"I'm fine. But your shelf? Not so much. Tobin tried to fix it, but he claims the shelf wasn't meant to hold heavy cookbooks. That's why I swapped out your knickknacks."

*Oh, you little liar.*

But she hadn't really . . . lied. She'd merely twisted things around to save her own cute butt.

*Tactical error, darlin'. One that's gonna cost you.* Because now? It was on.

Tobin opened and closed the back door as if he'd just waltzed in. "Hey, Miz G. How was your lunch?"

"Boring. No Jell-O fights. No hair pulling. Pearl didn't even get to whack anyone with her cane." Her eyes turned shrewd. "Next time you think about messing around with any of my stuff without asking first? Don't."

Jade looked guilty as hell.

"Understood."

She patted his arm, as if all was forgiven. "Now be a dear and grab the bags of top soil out of my trunk."

"You didn't have to buy dirt. I would've dug up soil out of the garden for you."

"I appreciate that. But my potted petunias are looking puny and my buddy Tony the Stoner said my soil might be worn out and I need to repot them."

Jade choked on her glass of water.

Miz G whacked her hard on the back. "Lordy, I'd hate to imagine how badly you'd fare after a prairie fire shot if you choke on water, Jade."

Tobin hid his smirk, waiting to see how she'd respond to that.

"I choked after hearing you mention Tony the Stoner! How on earth do you know someone like that? Did these Mud Lilies friends of yours introduce you to him?" she demanded. "Because I think they're a bad influence on you."

She'd done it now.

But Miz G just blinked. "What in heaven's name are you talkin' about? The Mud Lilies have nothin' to do with this. I've known Tony for years. I've been buying pot—"

"Omigod, GG! I do *not* want to hear this. You know I have to tell my dad about the stuff you're doing that might be wrong or illegal!"

"Take it down a notch, Jade, and listen up," Tobin interjected. Then he addressed Garnet. "Where does Tony work and what does he do there?"

"He works at the building center in Rawlins. He usually runs the masonry department. In the summer months he's in charge of the home and garden section." Miz G looked baffled. "Sonny, have you been drinking? You know all of this. Tony the Stoner did the stonework up at the Split Rock."

"And you call him Tony the Stoner . . . because he installs stone."

"What else would I call him?" She huffed out a breath. "Although, now that you mention it, when he changed departments to the garden center he did ask me to stop calling him Tony the Pot Pusher."

Tobin busted out laughing because Jade looked totally poleaxed.

*Welcome to daily life with Garnet Evans.*

Miz G flapped her hand at him. "I don't see why that's so funny."

"I'll let Jade explain it to you while I unload some more dirt."

Tobin had dropped two bags around the side of the house, when he saw Jade lumbering toward him with a bag of soil clutched to her chest.

"Dammit, Jade, let me do that." He snatched the bag out of her arms and tossed it on the pile. "I do the heavy lifting around here."

"I wanted to help."

"I don't need it." He leaned against the side of the shed. "But I will take an apology for you blaming the broken shelf and cookbook re-arranging on me."

She shoved her hands in her pockets. "I'm sorry. I panicked, okay? My brain got stuck on the fact I'd screwed up and I'd disappointed GG on my second day here."

*Disappointed* was an interesting word choice. "So it was better to have her mad at me?"

"I said I was sorry. I didn't know GG would be so adverse to one small change."

"Wrong answer, darlin'." Tobin pointed at her. "I warned you—several times—that she hates change of any kind. Ain't my fault you chose not to believe me."

He saw that moment when the lightbulb clicked for her.

"This is your way of proving that if she freaked out about her cook-book collection being relocated, she'll be near hysteria if she's moved out of her house."

"Bingo." Tobin stared at her hard. "But maybe if you keep rearrang-ing her personal belongings when she's not at home, that'll ease her into seeing them boxed up? That *is* your plan?"

"I don't have a plan."

"That's right. You're here following Daddy's plan, aren't you, tiger?"

"You calling me *tiger* isn't some shot at my Chinese heritage, is it?"

His gaze locked onto hers. "Not a shot at your ethnicity. I call you tiger because your eyes remind me of a tiger's eyes. Especially when you're pissed off and backed into a corner."

"Oh." She blushed and that seemed to annoy her. "At least mine are real."

*Do not check out her chest.* "What's real?"

"My eye color. Obviously you wear contacts."

"What?"

"You wear contacts because no one has eyes that color."

His nostrils flared. "Poke your damn finger in my eye if you need proof, darlin', but this eye color? All mine. And what the hell does it matter anyway?"

"I was trying to pay you a compliment." She jammed her hands in the back pockets of her shorts. "The color of your eyes . . . it's . . . extraordinary."

Tobin didn't buy it. Why would she be nice now?

*Because she wants something.*

"Stick with insults. You're much better at them." He walked away.

*Chapter Five*

⤜⤚

The following day at GG's house, Jade had reorganized her closet, rearranged her room and had gone for a run—all before noon. She had that itchy feeling between her shoulder blades that she should be doing *something*.

But after yesterday's cookbook fiasco, she wouldn't actually move or change anything.

So after lunch, she'd familiarized herself with the kitchen, she'd checked out the barn and the machine shed—that place needed to be organized in the worst way. Then she'd cleaned out the inside of her car and scrubbed the windows in the garage door.

And she still had a couple of hours to kill until GG returned from her meetings.

Restless, with itchy feet and idle hands . . . what was she supposed to do with herself?

Tobin wasn't even around to argue with.

GG had informed Tobin that he had to stay away until late afternoon. Not that Jade had heard any of this firsthand—she had, however, received a terse note from Tobin that he'd oh-so-thoughtfully stuck to the bathroom mirror:

*I can't be here until later, but there will be hell to pay if I see so much as a single packing box anywhere in this house. Don't test me on this, darlin'. You will lose. T~*

Jade had fumed for a while at his audacity. Then she created and discarded witty comebacks designed to get under his skin. And what fine, fine skin it was. Even when he annoyed the crap out of her, it'd been hard not to notice how the muscle in his cheek flexed in that broodingly sexy way few men pulled off. Or how the intense way he argued heated his magnetic eyes into a deeper shade of blue.

*Stop. So the big, rugged cowboy is hot. And commanding. And imposing. And insistent. He's clever; he figured out how to push your buttons and that's why you should do as GG says and steer clear of him.*

For now . . . she needed something familiar to calm herself, and the best way to accomplish that was through music.

Jade set up her music stand on the front porch. Playing outside for her own enjoyment was a rare treat. The wind blew harder than she expected, requiring clothespins to keep her sheet music from blowing away. But she'd played this piece so many times she had it memorized.

Perched on the edge of the chaise, she held her bow above the strings and inhaled a deep breath before she launched into "Summer" from Vivaldi's *The Four Seasons* and everything became right with her world again.

❧

GG returned home around six o'clock, completely frazzled. "Sometimes I want to strangle Maybelle and her insistence on our community involvement. We don't even have a school here in Muddy Gap, say nothin' of any of us havin' grandkids or great-grandkids that attend school in Rawlins."

"What's going on?"

"A 'meet the teacher' carnival thingy tomorrow night. We sure didn't have one of them when I was a kid. We considered ourselves lucky we had extra chalk to draw on the pavement with at recess."

Jade folded her arms over her chest and watched GG pace as she went off on a tear.

"There's a cakewalk at this carnival. Last month or sometime, I don't remember, I said I'd donate, thinking because it's a cakewalk . . . it oughta be a cake, right?" She shook her head. "Wrong. Because no little ankle-biter should ever feel left out, every cakewalk participant gets his or her own cupcake—in addition to the chance of winning a gol-durn cake!"

"What does that mean?"

GG flopped onto the couch. "That means instead of relaxing and havin' a glass or two of bubbly with my beautiful granddaughter, I have to bake and decorate five dozen cupcakes tonight. Sixty stinkin' cupcakes for rugrats who'll be so hopped up from a mini-donut sugar rush or zoned out on fumes from the face-painting booth that they won't appreciate my hard work."

Jade perched on the edge of the recliner. "Why don't you just buy the cupcakes and save yourself the hassle?" A woman who dropped twenty k on champagne shouldn't balk at spending fifty bucks on baked goods.

GG patted her leg. "Oh, honey, I forget you're not from around here. You don't get it."

"Yes, I think I do. This is a competition where you have to go all Martha Stewart and craft your cupcakes from scratch, then decorate them with golden coins, silver swirls and crystal flakes, or else you're afraid you'll be a laughingstock at the town hall?"

"Whoa. Take it down a notch, tiger."

Jade spun to see Tobin lurking in the doorway. "Back off, buttinsky. You were *not* invited into this conversation. We're persona non grata to each other, remember?"

GG ignored Jade's outburst and peered over her shoulder at Tobin sauntering in. "Did you get the stuff?"

"What was left. Ended up with two boxes of lemon cake mix, so you've only got four flavors instead of five."

Jade muttered, "No one ever listens to me."

"Speak up, Jade. Miz G can't hear you mumble," Tobin said in that sexy drawl.

"Why didn't you just buy the premade cupcakes when you were already at the store?"

"Sweetheart, there is one grocery store in town and I doubt they keep more than a hundred cupcakes on hand at each location." GG sighed. "Even if I'd wanted to buy them? Others have also been saddled with cupcake and cake duty. Everyone goes to this carnival. They're projecting a thousand attendees."

"Supply and demand and limited resources. You have to bake your own."

"Isn't that what she told you from the start?" Tobin inserted smarmily.

"All of us Mud Lilies are doin' our duty." GG glanced at Tobin again. "Didja get sprinkles and red licorice?"

"Yes ma'am. And gumdrops. And icing. And some fruit-shaped hard candies. No golden coins or silver swirls or crystal flakes, Miss New York City."

"Do not start, you two. I mean it," GG warned. "I'm extra poopy-doopy today and I'm blaming it on wearing khakis. Boo for bland. I miss my rainbow spandex, feathers, glitter and neon Converse. Dressing upstanding makes me want to upchuck."

Tobin grinned. "Amen, sister."

Jade had no idea what they were talking about, but wow. Tobin had one really big dimple when he grinned like that. She stared at his mouth, hoping to see that divot again, and noticed he had nice lips when they weren't forming a scowl.

Tobin made a noise and her gaze zoomed to his.

She didn't see smugness or a cocky smirk, just genuine surprise that she'd been transfixed by his mouth.

GG clapped her hands and Jade jumped.

"We have a busy night on the cupcake express. So let's discuss—not argue—who is doin' what. I need one of you as a baker's helper and the other as a decorator."

"I'll help you bake them," Jade jumped in before Tobin could.

"What the hell? *I* bought the stuff, I should get to choose first," Tobin complained.

"That's why you should decorate them. You went to all the trouble to choose the special finishing touches. I'd hate to deprive you of your chance to create magical fruit rainbows and gumdrop mountain master-pieces."

Tobin gifted her with that dimpled smile. "Ah, sugar, is that your way of hinting you want me to build a rainbow friendship bridge between us?"

"How about you survive frosting and decorating sixty cupcakes before you add more work into your night?"

GG slowly rose to her feet. "I'll get out the mixer and the pans."

After GG was gone, Tobin walked over and parked himself in front of Jade. "In the spirit of cooperation, I will let you swap jobs with me."

"Not a chance. I'm sure a macho cowboy like you who doesn't cook or bake at *all*, isn't the least bit concerned that his decorating skills might be subpar and would embarrass Miz G in front of her pals."

He shrugged. "I'm not worried. I just wanted to give *you* a chance to shine for your grandmother."

"Oh really?"

"Yep. But it's your loss. I'm gonna decorate the hell out of those cup-cakes. They will be a sight to behold."

"I can't wait to see your creations. Maybe I should take notes." She cocked her head. "Luckily I happen to have a piece of paper right here."

She dug the note he'd left her out of the front pocket of her jeans, slowly unfolded it and slapped it on his chest. "Do not delude yourself that you have any right to tell me what or what not to do."

"Tiger's got claws," he murmured.

"What did you hope to accomplish with that note?"

"Look, I wrote it last night when I was pissed off at you, all right?" His gaze briefly dipped to her mouth before connecting with her eyes again. "After I left for work I was hoping it fell down and you didn't see it because, believe it or not, I don't want to fight with you."

She said, "'*There will be hell to pay*' and '*don't test me on this*' were code for 'let's kiss and make up'?" Her face flamed. Why in the world had she said that?

And why did Tobin's eyes gleam as if he considered that a great idea?

"Jade? Are you coming to help me or what?" GG yelled from the kitchen.

Saved by the yelling granny. "Be right there." She crumpled the note in her fist and tossed it at him.

Tobin caught it before it bounced off his chin. He grinned. "You added hearts and flowers to this, didn't you?"

"More like daggers and skulls." She sidestepped him and hustled into the kitchen.

❧

Of course Tobin didn't stay out of the kitchen.

Within ten minutes of GG heading to her "boudoir" for a long bubble bath, he wandered in. He invaded Jade's space so completely she caught a whiff of the soap he used.

"Smells great in here. Are there any extra samples you need me to try?"

"Should've gotten here sooner for that."

"Damn. So are any of them ready for me?"

"No. They have to be cooled completely before you can frost them. I just took the last batch out of the oven fifteen minutes ago."

"How much longer until I can start?"

Jade stopped wiping down the counter and peered over her shoulder at him. "An hour probably."

"Are you gonna help me?"

She laughed. "Nice try."

"Why not?"

She faced him. "A, I didn't see you in here the past two and a half hours helping *us*. B, you seem to have forgotten the 'we're not to occupy the same place and are supposed to actively ignore each other' rule. C, well, there is no C presently, but I'll probably come up with one the longer you stand there breaking rule number one."

Tobin grinned. "You *are* Little Miss Rule Follower, aren't you?"

"Yes. This is where you tell me that you aren't big on following the rules."

"Actually, I'm totally a by-the-book guy." He rubbed the back of his neck. "Does that surprise you?"

She found herself saying, "Yes," almost automatically. "So as long as you're here, Mr. By the Book, check out the schedule on the fridge."

Tobin pushed away from the counter. "A schedule for what?"

"When GG plans to eat with you and me, but she isn't dining with us at the same time at all, nor is she letting us dine together."

"This is just plain damn ridiculous."

"Maybe if you hadn't been so argumentative and antagonistic since the moment I arrived, things would be different."

"I'm taking the high road and ignoring that comment, which is also proof that I can follow the rules. But I'll forgive you for your rules breach if you stay and help me frost these damn cupcakes."

She smiled. "You wish."

"Not fair to deny me a taste."

Her focus went straight to his mouth and she managed, "What?"

"You must've had a taste, because you have batter on your face." Tobin's hand slid beneath her hair and he pressed his fingers against her neck, letting the rough pad of his thumb glide across her jawbone.

Jade didn't move; she couldn't breathe as he gently rubbed on the spot. The heat from his body hit hers as if she'd opened the oven door.

"I got it off," he said, his deep voice gruffer than normal.

"Ah. Thank you."

He dropped his hand and stepped back. Then he jammed his hand through his hair. "So, uh, yeah. I'll . . . ah . . . be back in an hour."

Then he was gone, leaving Jade to wonder what had just happened.

❧

Tobin was fucked.

Seriously fucked.

And not because he'd almost fucking *kissed* Jade in the kitchen two hours ago.

Goddammit. He'd immediately gotten hard when he'd touched her smooth skin and her hair had brushed his knuckles like the finest silk. When she'd parted her lips and a sexy sigh had escaped, just a quick hitch in her breath that sounded like an invitation . . . he'd forced himself—and his cock—to stand down.

He oughta get a cupcake for not devouring her.

*Focus, man.*

Keeping in mind Jade's comment about not embarrassing Miz G with, oh, just plain old sprinkles on the cupcakes, he'd actually attempted to be creative. Using the banana-shaped candy and two of the orange-shaped hard candies, he'd tried to make a bird with a curved beak.

So his first tray of cupcakes looked like an erect dick and balls.

Fucking awesome.

He hadn't fared much better on tray two. He'd nestled two gumdrops side by side, placing a dot of icing on the center of each gumdrop to make them look like a pair of eyes.

Except . . . they looked like a pair of tits.

That's when he grabbed a beer out of the fridge. Miz G would blow a gasket when she saw the X-rated decorations that he'd constructed.

He powered through with tray three when he found a cookie mold and pressed the shape into the frosting, which allowed him to outline with icing. Then he filled it in with colored sugar and sprinkles so they resembled flowers.

Tray four—and beer two—he fashioned the pi symbol out of the hard candies on each one. Hey, educators always claimed kids never had enough math.

He was on a motherfucking *roll* for the last tray. Slicing the licorice whips in random lengths and poking them into the cupcakes so it resembled a porcupine or something out of a Dr. Seuss book. Add in some rainbow sprinkles . . . and ta-fucking-da. Done.

Jade pushed through the swinging doors. "Oh. You're still decorating?"

The woman had the worst poker face ever; he didn't believe for a second she wasn't checking up on him. "I just finished."

"Mind if I have a look?"

"Knock yourself out."

She smiled at the flower tray. Laughed at the pi tray and said, "Pi on cake. Clever, cowboy."

Tobin shrugged, but he was pleased.

She laughed again at the porcupine tray. "These are awesome. Kids will go crazy for them."

And then . . . she reached the other two trays. She shifted her stance a couple of times before her gaze sought his. "So what happened here?"

"What do you mean?"

"You *know* what I mean."

He manufactured a confused frown. "They look fine to me."

"Really? Because they are completely inappropriate."

"How so?"

"You cannot send cupcakes decorated like breasts and a dick and balls to a school carnival, Tobin."

"They're not that bad." Belligerently, he folded his arms on his chest. "Maybe you just have a dirty mind."

Jade stared at him. "There is a phallic-shaped piece of fruit sticking up between two oranges—not a huge leap to see an erect cock and balls. And your gumdrops have nipples."

"Huh. Well, the adults will get a charge out of them."

"No, they will charge GG with indecency."

"Shit. You're right."

She inhaled a deep breath. "What were you trying to make?"

"With which one?"

"The gumdrop nipples. What's the small dot halfway down? Because it looks like a belly button, which really makes those look like boobs."

Tobin rubbed the skin between his eyebrows. "It was just a mark to know where to put the licorice smile."

"Adding that in might fix it."

"Except I used all the licorice."

"Awesome." She leaned over the other tray. "I can't wait to hear your explanation on this one."

"An attempt to re-create Gonzo from *The Muppet Show.*"

"While you get points for creativity, I think Gonzo's eyes are blue."

"Yeah. And that would've been so much better. Blue balls *and* a banana dick nose."

Jade laughed.

God. She was even prettier when she laughed.

She'd look even better with swollen lips after he kissed the daylights out of her.

"Good luck figuring out a way to fix them," she said.

He shook his head to clear it. "They're done. I'm not a creative guy on my best days. Today was grueling, moving livestock with one less helper than usual, and I'm fried. I get to get up at five thirty and do it all again."

Jade slipped her hands in the back pockets of her jeans. "Was any of the livestock you moved yours?"

Strange question. "I don't own cattle. I'm just a hired hand."

She studied him. "Somehow . . . I don't believe that."

That hadn't sounded antagonistic, just curious.

When Jade realized she'd been staring at him, she backed up. "Anyway, see you tomorrow."

"Did you get what you came for?" he asked when she'd almost reached the door.

"Pardon?"

"You're in the kitchen. You haven't grabbed a snack or a drink. So I have to ask, Little Miss Rule Follower, why you came in here when you knew us inhabiting the same space is against the rules?"

Jade blinked innocently—but couldn't quite pull it off. "I thought you would've finished long ago."

"Wrong. You knew I'd be struggling with this, didn't you?"

"I suspected you'd exaggerated your skills. So . . . maybe I came down here to peek at your cupcakes so I could secretly snicker at them and feel superior."

He hadn't expected that much honesty from her. "And the verdict?

"Split decision. Those three pans? Very clever and unique. No snickering. However the boobs and dick ones? I'm totally feeling—"

"Superior?" he supplied.

"More like bad for you. Because dude. Those seriously suck." Her eyes lit up. "Can I snap a picture of them and post them online as a Pinterest fail?"

"I have no idea what that even is, so I'm gonna say no."

"I'd let you do a Pinterest fail on me if the situations were reversed."

All Tobin heard from that was *do me.*

*Yeah, baby, I'd do you in a fucking heartbeat.*

*Wrapping that silky black hair around my hands as I ate at that sassy mouth. Feeling your legs clamped around my hips as I powered my cock into you slowly, making you wait to get off because you like it fast and hard.*

Whoa. What the hell was wrong with him? He shouldn't be fantasizing about fucking Jade; he oughta be fantasizing about her fucking *leaving.* He didn't even like her.

*Actually you don't even know her.*

"Tobin?"

He offered her a hangdog smile. "Sorry. It's late and I zoned out there for a moment."

"I said thanks for helping out with the cupcake emergency tonight."

Her hair had fallen in front of her face, giving him a glimpse of the shyness Miz G had spoken of. "You're welcome. And don't worry, tiger, I won't tell Miz G about how blatantly you broke the rules tonight since I know how worried you are about disappointing her."

"The 'rule' is pretty absurd. But if you know my grandmother as well as you claim to, you also understand the more times we tell her how ridiculous or unenforceable her rule is, the more stubborn she'll get about it. If she thinks we're going behind her back and purposely breaking it? She will be a hard-core pain about it. We'll never hear the end of it."

Tobin laughed. "That's true. So what are you suggesting?"

"Nothing. This conversation never happened." She flashed him a grin and left the kitchen.

❧

Tobin thought everyone was sleeping early the next morning when he walked out the front door, heading to work.

He'd only reached the top porch step when he heard, "Tobin Hale. I need a word with you. Right now."

He faced Miz G and bit back a groan. She hadn't bothered to take out her curlers or change out of her flannel pajamas and fuzzy flippers. "I'm running late. Can't it wait?"

"No. Kitchen. Now. And don't dawdle, sonny."

Shit. She'd already seen the titty and dick cupcakes. He hadn't figured out a way to fix them last night, so he'd just left them and gone to bed.

Sure enough, Miz G stood by the counter, her arms crossed over her bony chest, the bunny head on her slipper flopping side to side as she tapped her foot impatiently. She'd peeled back the aluminum foil halfway on each pan. "Care to explain these?"

Tobin had decided to claim he was drunk—sad when that lie was better than the truth. So when he saw the pans she was pointing to, he did a double take. The dick cupcakes looked like pinwheels with the banana-shaped candies pressed into the frosting. And the titty cupcakes were flowers—flattened pieces of gumdrops shaped to resemble sugared rose petals, arranged around a hole in the center of the cupcake that was filled with strawberry-champagne preserves.

Jade. That little sneak. She'd come back down here last night and saved his bacon.

Totally unexpected.

Totally sweet.

He laughed with relief and delight because once again, Jade had shocked the hell out of him—in a good way.

Then Miz G's bony finger was drilling him in the chest. "I don't find this funny in the least. Dadgummit, boy, why didn't you tell me you had a flair for cake decorating?"

*Flair?* Oh hell no. He had to nip this in the bud ASAP. "It was a fluke."

"Horse puckey. Tell me the truth."

It wouldn't be fair to drag Jade into this so he said, "I used to make cupcakes with my grandma."

A beat of silence passed.

"And after she passed on . . . you couldn't do it without thinking of her. Gol-durn it boy, I thought you were getting teary-eyed looking at the frosting last night, but I figured it might've been from fear that you'd gotten in over your head." Her chin wobbled. "I'm sorry. It'll be our secret."

He hadn't lied, but she'd gone a little farther with the half-truth than he'd expected. "I'd appreciate it."

She patted his cheek. "Have a good day at work, dear."

## Chapter Six

After tossing and turning in bed for an hour, Jade got up and slipped her clothes on.

She opened her bedroom door slowly, unsure if it creaked. Not that she thought it'd wake GG, tucked away in her bedroom on the main floor.

The hallway light had been turned off. Two plug-in night-lights sent a bluish glow across the wood floor. She closed the door behind her, noticing Tobin's door was shut.

As she passed the sitting room, she debated on playing a few hands of solitaire to wind down. She'd had that itchy need-to-do-something feeling from the moment she'd woken up. It hadn't helped that GG left her to her own devices again, all day, so she'd cleaned the house, scrubbing bathrooms, vacuuming everything, dusting and mopping floors. After lunch she'd talked to her parents and that had been a fruitless endeavor, attempting to explain her continued restlessness. Their advice? To relax.

Relax. Right. She'd never mastered that particular skill. And people telling her to chill out when she *knew* she couldn't only increased her feeling of inadequacy. What was wrong with her that she couldn't even take a nap in the afternoon? Instead she'd practiced her violin for two hours. Then she'd watered the flowers, cleaned off the porch and by that time GG had returned home. Even a heavy meal and several glasses of champagne didn't flip the switch to shut off her brain when she crawled between the sheets.

So here she was . . . wandering around at midnight.

Jade stopped in front of the liquor cabinet. Whiskey might lull her to sleep, but she didn't see herself swiping the bottle of Jameson and sneaking it back to her room. There was something pathetic and dangerous about drinking alone in this kind of mood; it could easily become a habit.

*Get some fresh air. Clear your head.*

On her way outside, she snagged an afghan off the back of the couch.

The front door wasn't locked—a fun thing to bring up with her grandmother tomorrow since she'd promised they'd spend the afternoon together.

Jade quietly closed the screen door after she stepped onto the porch.

The night air did smell sweeter here. She leaned against the porch pillar and tried to check out the stars, but the overhang blocked the sky. To get the full view, she'd have to stand at the bottom of the steps, and that seemed like too much effort.

Great. Now she was restless and lazy.

"Couldn't sleep?" A voice came from the corner of the porch.

Jade whirled around.

Tobin sat on the chaise, kicked back and holding a beer.

She pressed her hand to her heart. "You scared me. Good thing I'm not a screamer."

His immediate flash of teeth in the darkness told her the dirty direction of his thoughts.

Or maybe *she* was projecting. Tobin's grin was far more wicked than innocent. "What are you doing out here?"

"Waiting for my fence to pick up this pillowcase full of silver frames, candlesticks and silverware I've secretly stashed under my chair," he said without his usual humor.

"Now that you mentioned it . . . I thought it looked like a few forks were missing earlier."

"I wouldn't know since I wasn't allowed to dine with y'all."

She called him on his crappy attitude. "Bad day on the range, cowboy?"

"Shitty day all around, thanks for askin'." He paused. "Sorry. I'm still in a lousy mood."

"That makes two of us. My day wasn't rainbows and butterflies either."

"Speaking of . . . thanks for fixing my cupcakes, cupcake. That was the last bright spot in my week."

Jade smiled. "You're welcome. GG said they were a big hit. So what made your day lousy?"

"Besides getting kicked, stomped on, yelled at, equipment breaking down and running out of supplies?"

"Yes, besides that."

"There is nothin' besides that."

"You win. Your day was worse than mine."

Tobin grunted. "Why're you out here?"

She tugged the afghan around her shoulders. "It's too quiet. I couldn't sleep. I'm used to constant noise."

"Now that would drive me bat-shit crazy."

"You get used to it. Or in my case, I grew up with it."

"Did Miz G visit you often in the big city?"

"Never as often as I wanted, but at least four times a year."

"So you didn't spend time hanging out with her here during summer vacation?"

"She'd come to us. Then we'd go to the Jersey Shore or the Catskills or some other place."

"I find that odd. Wouldn't you think your dad would want to come back home once in a while?"

Jade frowned at him. "My dad didn't grow up in this part of Wyoming."

His beer bottle stopped in front of his mouth. "Really? I thought Garnet was local."

"Maybe in her childhood, but not during the years she was married to my grandfather and raising my dad. They lived outside of Jackson Hole—I never visited there either. GG sold the house my dad grew up in after my grandpa died. Then she bought this place."

"Huh. That's news to me."

So he didn't know everything about her grandma. "My dad said this wasn't his home. His home didn't exist anymore and he had no reason to ever waste time here."

Tobin sipped his beer. "Well, except for the tiny fact his mother lives here."

Given his mood, she'd ignore his digs. "What about you? Are you local?"

"Depends on how you define local. My family's ranch is near Saratoga. South of here about an hour and a half."

"How often do you go home?"

"Almost never." He pointed his bottle at her. "Wipe that smirk off your face. It's not the same thing. I've never been close to my family."

"I'd hate that," she said softly. "I'm close to both of my parents."

"I was always closer to my mom than my dad." He swigged his beer. "That makes me wonder . . . are your dad and Miz G close?"

"Like do they talk on the phone every day? I don't believe so."

"They send each other jokes via e-mail because they have similar tastes in humor?"

"I'm not sure. Why?"

"Tryin' to get a handle on the Evans family dynamic. Does Miz G tell him about all the things she does with the Mud Lilies? Does he brag to her about the cases he wins?"

Jade suspected she wouldn't like whatever he was building up to. "Why are you grilling me on this out of the blue?"

He snorted. "It's not out of the blue. We've been goin' round and round with this since the second you stepped out of your car."

"*I* didn't bring it up tonight; you did. But since you're in a lousy mood—by your own admission—by all means, please take it out on me and let's just keep arguing the same points over and over."

Evidently Tobin missed the sarcasm because he lit into her anyway. "You're here, acting on your dad's behalf because he thinks he knows what's best for his mother. And I'd argue the point that he doesn't know her at all."

"But you do?" she retorted.

"I've got a helluva lot better perspective on Garnet than her own son does—I guarantee that."

"This superior perspective happened before you moved in with her? Or after?" He'd pushed her; now she'd push back. "Tell me, Tobin. Will you continue this fantastically close friendship with her after you bail out of Muddy Gap?"

His look of surprise indicated he hadn't known that she knew about his future plans.

"Will you talk to her on the phone every day? Will you be her e-mail buddy? Or once you've gotten whatever it is you want from her, then it's *buh-bye*? Out of sight, out of mind?"

"You're still assuming I want something from her. That I'm a taker and that's all I care about—making sure Miz G can do something for me. Not everyone is like that." He shook his head. "Christ. Why am I even bothering tryin' to reason with you?"

"You started this, so don't act like *I'm* being unreasonable by asking you the same questions that you're demanding answers for from me."

Tobin considered her. Then he pushed to his feet.

She expected him to storm off.

Instead, he moved to lean against the porch pillar opposite her. "I'm sorry. I'm bein' a dick."

"Yeah, maybe you are a little bit."

He brooded at the darkness.

She let him. But she kept sneaking looks at him.

Finally, he said, "You've asked me why I'm here. I'm tired of the bullshit between us, Jade, so I'll level with you."

Her stomach knotted but she forced herself to take the four steps separating them so she could look into his eyes.

"But I don't expect you to believe me."

"What makes you say that?"

"It'll sound staged. A little too coincidental."

"Try me."

Eventually Tobin gathered his thoughts enough to speak. "My grandma Hale lived close by when I was growing up. My brothers never gave her much thought—behavior they learned from our dad. Bein' a ranch kid meant after-school chores. Since my brothers had it under control at our place, I went to Grandma's twice a week to help her out."

"How old were you?"

"Eight? Ten maybe? Somewhere in that age range. I split logs and filled her wood boxes. Shoveled snow. Dragged in any supplies she needed." He smiled. "She always fed me. Man, that woman could cook. Course, I never let my brothers know."

She laughed softly. "Didn't want to share?"

"Nope. She taught me how to play cribbage. She let me poke around in my granddad's tackle boxes. She told me stories of her growing-up years as a kid and then as a newlywed. She gave me advice on everything from buying the right fishing bait to showing me how to sew on a button."

A funny tickle started in Jade's belly. "I take it this story doesn't have a happy ending?"

Tobin blinked and shook himself out of the memory. "No. When I was thirteen, Dad decided she couldn't take care of herself anymore and sent her to an old-folks' home."

That tickle in her belly twisted into a knot.

"When I found out, I asked my dad how he thought *he* knew so much about Grandma's ability to live on her own when he never spent any time around her."

Now it made sense why Tobin had asked her about GG's relationship with her son.

"Dad said he didn't answer to a snot-nosed kid who could be bribed to look past the truth with a couple dozen cookies." Tobin scratched his cheek with the beer bottle. "Maybe he had a point. But when I asked why Grandma didn't just live with us, Dad said he wouldn't put that burden on Mom."

Jade had wondered the same thing, even knowing her mom struggled with her own elderly mother's care. "What did your grandma do? Did she fight it?"

Tobin shot her an odd look. "How could she? First of all, stuff like that wasn't done by ladies her age. Hiring a lawyer would've taken a bite out of her meager savings. When I told her I'd go to court and ask to be declared an adult so I could take care of her . . . that was the first time I'd ever seen her cry." He knocked back another drink of beer.

"Did that change anything?"

"Nope. The next time I saw her she lived in Sunny Acres Rest Home. She had one room, which served as her bedroom and her sitting room. At the ranch, she'd used a walker to get around her house. Within four months of living there, she'd become wheelchair-bound."

His icy tone had her pulling the afghan more securely around herself.

"I assumed she was easier to take care of if the workers could just plop her in a wheelchair and push her wherever *they* wanted her to go. Even within the first month, she wasn't the same chatty woman who'd ask about my day at school, which would lead her into a story about her childhood. She'd pat my leg and say, 'That's nice, dear,' and return to watching TV. It got so I couldn't visit her anymore. It never occurred to me, until years later, that maybe I was the only one who visited her besides my mom. After I stopped . . ." He drained his beer. "She only lasted a year in that place before she died."

"I'm . . . sorry."

Tobin looked at Jade. "Is that really what you want for your grandma? To die alone? With only her TV for company? Because the thought of that rips my fucking guts out." He set his bottle on the railing and bounded down the steps.

The weight of this decision about her grandma's future sat in the pit of her stomach like a stone.

After a few minutes, Jade followed him.

He stood next to the water pump, his hands propped on his hips, staring into the dark night.

"We're not on opposite sides, Tobin. We both want what's best for GG. Your experience with your grandmother is heartbreaking, but it's also skewed from the perspective of a young boy."

"Great. You gonna psychoanalyze me now?"

"No. But you can't deny that maybe you didn't have the whole story. You have no way of knowing whether your grandma was diagnosed with anything serious. And before you argue with me, that exact scenario happened to a friend of mine. Her grandpa was fine for all appearances, then her family moved him into a nursing home. She also believed it was laziness on the part of the nursing home workers that within two weeks he was wheelchair-bound. Within three months he was completely bedridden. Within five months he was dead. Would things have been different if her mom had admitted that her grandpa was diagnosed with a fast-moving bone cancer that necessitated an immediate move into a nursing facility?"

"Not the same thing, Jade."

"But you don't know. Maybe your grandmother asked that her health diagnosis wasn't shared with you. That even happened to me with my own mother just recently. When I found out, I was so angry with her and my dad for keeping the truth from me. They thought they were protecting me. Maybe your dad and mom thought they were protecting you."

Tobin didn't say anything for the longest time. Then he looked at her. "I'll concede that argument. You can bet your ass I'll ask my dad about that the next time I see him."

Although their conversation appeared to be at an end, Jade had no desire to go back into the house. She meandered to the end of the driveway. Closing her eyes, she tipped her head back and welcomed the cool breeze blowing across her face.

Shuffling footsteps stopped beside her. The clean cotton and earthy scent she'd started to associate with Tobin drifted over her.

"Tryin' to escape my charming company?" Tobin said.

"Always. But it doesn't seem to work, does it?"

"Not for either of us." He sighed. "Look. Believe it or not, I'm not usually a grumpy, self-centered jerk. You said your day sucked ass too. What happened?"

"Nothing."

"You won't confide in me even a little?" he cajoled her. "After I tried like hell to get you to believe that I'm just a good old boy who's always had a soft spot in my heart for grandmotherly types and widows?"

Jade laughed. "You weren't telling me a tall tale to gain my trust."

"You're sure?"

"Yes. A true con artist would've cried at the end of the story to gain additional sympathy. You just got more pissed off. That's an honest reaction."

"That anger wasn't directed at you, Jade."

"I know."

Tobin bumped her with his shoulder. "Come on, darlin'. Your turn to let fly. What happened today?"

"I already told you. Nothing."

"Bullshit."

"No, I'm serious. *Nothing* happened today and that's why I ended up in a mood."

"Ah. I see." He paused. "You're missing the pace of your life in the big city?"

Jade turned her head toward Tobin, but he wasn't looking at her. He stared straight ahead, granting her a perfect view of his chiseled face in profile. Moonlight looked amazing on him. So maybe the fact she didn't have to gaze into those assessing eyes encouraged her to speak honestly. "I don't know if that's it. Yes, I'm used to going a hundred miles an hour, seven days a week, but not because I love it. I do it out of necessity."

"Can you explain?"

She felt him looking at her quizzically, but she didn't meet his gaze. "I work three part-time jobs to maintain my . . . what did you call it my first day here? My *fancy, big-city lifestyle?*"

He groaned. "I'm an asshole sometimes."

"I don't have a lifestyle because I don't have much of a life. I'm too busy working to take advantage of all the city has to offer. My friends have moved on—either out of the area or they've scored jobs that have given them a lot more disposable income than I have. The few friends I've kept in contact with . . . their invites to hang out have tapered off because I always say no. I can't even remember the last time I went on a date." She let the afghan slip down her shoulders. This personal confession caused her to overheat from her forehead to her chest. "It's not a 'poor me' tale to gain your sympathy. I truly don't know what to do with myself when I'm not on the clock fourteen to sixteen hours a day."

"Jesus, Jade. Now I feel like a fuckin' slacker."

"That wasn't my intent, Tobin."

"So what have you done the last couple days?"

Jade rattled off as much as she could remember. She'd probably forgotten a few things.

He whistled. "Did you do any of that at Miz G's request?"

"No. She takes off early in the morning and doesn't come back until right before you stroll in after work."

Tobin opened his mouth. Then closed it. When he started to speak, she braced herself, assuming she wouldn't like his observation. "You've been here what . . . five days?"

"Something like that. Why?"

"Have you left Miz G's place at all?"

"No."

"You need to get out," Tobin said gently. "Maybe you're just suffering from cabin fever. I know there are a million options of things to do in the big city, and the offerings in Wyoming probably look lame in comparison—"

"Don't say that," she said, meeting his gaze. "How would I know what my options are here if I haven't checked them out? Being in Wyoming isn't the issue, Tobin. *I'm* the issue. I'd feel this way if I was in New York and had four days to fill. The last time I had free time? Was when I had the flu and couldn't get out of bed for a week."

*Are you still calling it the flu? You know what it really was. You know that's part of the reason you're here.*

"Darlin', no offense, but you know bein' sick doesn't count as free time."

"Which, again, proves that I am lame, not the location." As soon as she admitted that to this hot hunk of man, mortification sunk in. If yanking the afghan over her head and sprinting toward the house wouldn't have made her look even more pathetic, she'd be halfway down the driveway by now. Instead, she stepped back. "Sorry. It's late, I'm babbling. I'll see you later." She turned and started to walk away.

But Tobin was bigger and quicker. He grabbed a hold of the afghan and spun her around. "Whoa. Why are you running off?"

"I'm tired."

His eyes roamed over her, from her eyes to her mouth to the pulse jumping in her throat and then back up. His lips quirked. "You can't lie for shit; you know that, right?"

Jade didn't bother to deny it. "I hate that it's so obvious."

"I like it."

"Why?"

He leaned closer. "Because I'm a terrible liar too."

She laughed softly.

"And I'm great for comic relief."

Her smile stayed in place as she watched emotions play across his handsome face.

"Seriously, sweetheart . . ." Tobin stroked the underside of her jaw with the back of his knuckles. "Thanks for talking to me. And without overstepping my bounds or jeopardizing this truce between us, you need to remind Miz G that at least part of the reason you're here is to spend time with her. But even if she blows you off for her friends? Take a break. Get out of the house. It'd be good for you, Miss Workaholic, to get in your car and drive around aimlessly."

"You're right."

"Just make sure your GPS works. City slicker like you . . ." He smirked. "I'd hate for you to get lost. I'm sure all gravel roads must look the same."

"Thank you for the reminder."

Tobin lowered his hand from her cheek. "My pleasure."

"Thank you for listening. I never talk about this stuff."

He grasped the edges of the afghan and pulled it up to cover her shoulders. Then he smiled again. "Same goes."

This sweetness . . . threw her off. No, Tobin threw her off. He wasn't turning out to be the kind of man she—and her dad—thought he was.

"You ready to go back in?"

She nodded.

They walked back to the house side by side, in silence. Once they were in the entryway, Tobin said, "You go on upstairs. I'll lock up down here."

"Thanks."

Jade had made it halfway up the dark staircase when she heard him say, "Sweet dreams, sweetheart."

*Chapter Seven*

❧

$\mathcal{J}$ade didn't see Tobin at all the next day, and GG pulled her disappearing act again.

So the following morning Jade left GG a note—in case she arrived home before Jade returned—letting her know she'd gone out. Being vague suited her purposes; she had no idea where she was going.

After reaching the main road, she turned right. The blacktop dipped low and rose up like a long black ribbon. The cool morning temps tempted her to roll down the window. She passed fields dotted with cattle. The black hides stood out among the red dirt, cream-hued rocks and gray-green sagebrush.

She hung a right at the WELCOME TO MUDDY GAP sign. Once inside the city limits—calling it a "city" was a stretch—she cruised up and down every street. Were residents peering from behind curtains, wondering why a car with NY state license plates was puttering around their neighborhood?

Main Street had more businesses than she expected. The various denominations of Christianity were represented. There was one bar. One small grocery store. One hair salon. One insurance agency. No medical facility. No school.

Back at the crossroads, she checked the clock. Now what? That detour had only killed twenty minutes. She started back the way she came, when she noticed a sign for the Split Rock Ranch and Resort.

On a whim she followed the signs until she came upon a huge rock with a split down the middle. Her GPS cut out but she could see a large angled roofline, so she had to be close.

She hung a left, bumping along a gravel road. Just when she thought she'd reached the resort, the road curved and she found herself on a steep incline with no place to whip a U-turn.

Jade's hands tightened on the steering wheel. At the end of the road was an enormous barn. As she put her car in park to try to figure out where she was, she looked around nervously, thinking it'd be her luck if gun-toting rednecks showed up to chase her off private property.

That's when she noticed the field across from the barn, teeming with cows going every which way. Three guys on horseback were in the fenced-in area among the chaos.

At first glance all the men looked the same, wearing light-colored long-sleeved shirts, cream-colored cowboy hats, jeans and boots. Then the guy closest to her reined his horse to the left abruptly, giving her a view of his broad back and shoulders.

She knew that was Tobin.

Holy crap, did he make a stunning visual all cowboyed up.

And that didn't take into account how fluidly he moved. Shifting his entire body weight nearly off his horse to block a cow's escape. Spinning back around and calling out to the guy on the other side, then dodging and weaving through the herd.

After Tobin reached the other side, he conferred with his pen partner. Their heads were up as they kept a constant visual on the animals, but their faces were shadowed beneath their hats. Tobin had one gloved hand holding the reins. His other hand rested on his thigh. So he was ready at a moment's notice to snatch up the coiled rope hanging off the side of the saddle?

That's what she wanted to see, Tobin tearing across the field on his horse at full speed, twirling a rope above his head, all power and grace. His back muscles straining, his legs gripping the horse's belly, those ropy forearms flexing, his biceps rippling, his concentration absolute as he closed in on his prize.

Whew yeah. Tobin Hale on horseback? The epitome of sexy. A prime example of rugged beauty. A powerhouse of raw masculinity. A glorious vision of virility.

The man made her thighs quiver and her mouth water. Or, more accurately, he made the insides of her thighs wet and her mouth ache to know the feel of his lips on hers.

And she might actually burst into spontaneous orgasm if she saw him wearing a pair of those fringed leather pant-things and heard the *ching ching ching* of his spurs as he ambled toward her with that intense look in his eyes and that wicked smile.

Jade watched him working the cattle for about thirty minutes until the corral was mostly empty. When she saw him dismount, providing her with a very nice view of his buns, she knew it was time to go before he caught her gawking at him.

After Tobin handed the horse's reins to a smaller guy, he crossed the road and headed straight toward her.

*No, he's heading to the barn. He doesn't know you're here creeping on him ... fantasizing about climbing on and riding him.*

And yet, Tobin did mosey over, dust kicking up with his every boot fall. His head tipped down, his hat putting his face in shadow so she couldn't see his eyes.

But Jade wasn't looking at his eyes; she was still drinking in every-thing about him. The closer he got, the more she noticed the marks of his hard work: fine dust covering his hat, brown and green smears on his shirt, hay stuck to the clumps of mud on the frayed hem of his jeans. She'd never seen a man embody a stereotype and yet, transcend it.

So that's probably why she'd frozen completely when Tobin crouched beside her car and signaled for her to roll down her window.

*Please don't let me be totally tongue-tied.*

But she was so flustered she hit the wrong window control buttons. Twice.

She finally got the right one. As soon as the window opened, the barnyard scent floated past Tobin on a hot breeze, along with the clean cotton scent that lingered in the bathroom after he showered.

Those aquamarine eyes connected with hers and she sort of melted.

"You lost?" he asked in that deep, shiver-evoking voice.

Jade had to clear her throat before answering. "Yes, actually, I am."

"I figured. No one ever parks on this side of the barn."

"Am I breaking some kind of rule? Because I didn't mean to park here; I was looking for a place to turn around. Then I saw you in the middle of all those cows and I got sucked in to watching you do your cowboy thing."

Tobin smiled. A wide, happy smile that she hadn't seen before. "'Cowboy thing.' Rancher thing is more like it."

"I'm not well versed in the differences."

"Well versed." He laughed softly. "No, bein' from New York City I don't suppose you are. But, tiger, I aim to change that." He pointed to where several pickups were parked in a line. "Park down there and I'll give you a tour."

"Really? Because I don't want to be a bother and interrupt you."

"It's a quiet morning. Just me, Ted and Renner. And I don't gotta worry about introducing you to either of them, bein's one is married and the other is jailbait."

Weird comment. "Okay. I'm moving." She chugged over the deep ruts in the road, but it still jostled her around. As soon as she parked and killed the engine, Tobin opened the driver's-side door, offering to help her out. "Thanks."

He didn't let go of her hand. "I'm happy to see you out and about."

"I thought I'd take your advice and see the countryside."

"And you like what you see?"

When she locked her gaze to his and said, "Very much," they both were aware she wasn't referring to the scenery.

Tobin squeezed her hand. "Glad to hear that. We'll start in the small barn."

"You won't have me milk a cow or something?"

"Nope. We're not a dairy, so no milking machines."

She followed him to the door. Before they walked inside, Jade stepped in front of him. "I'll probably have a million questions, so please be patient with me."

"I'm a patient man." Tobin's gaze zeroed in on her mouth. "Until I'm not."

*Do not bite your lip.*

Then those hypnotic eyes were on hers again, as if he knew exactly what she'd been thinking. He said, "This way," and rested his hand on her lower back to guide her inside.

The barn had a musty smell. "What's in here?"

"This time of year? Livestock we're doctoring. It's out of season for births. Although if we do end up with a cow or two that calve in the fall instead of the spring, we'll keep her in here until she delivers."

She blinked at him. "Calve? Rancher speak for giving birth?"

"See, darlin', you're catching on."

They walked to the end of the center section, which on either side had been divided into stalls.

"Is Miz G out with her Mud Lilies pals again?"

"Yes. I drove through Muddy Gap. Then I saw the signs for this place and here I am."

Tobin shifted closer. "Would you like to tour the whole resort? Or just the ranch portion?"

Jade hip-checked him. "I want the whole enchilada."

"Cool. Walk? Or ride up to the lodge?"

"Ride," she said slowly. "As in ride a horse?"

"Ride in a golf cart."

"There's a golf course here?"

"Nope. That'd be a waste of grazing space and natural resources. We use golf carts to get around the resort. They don't make as much noise as the four-wheelers. And here at the Split Rock, we're all about providing guests with the relaxing atmosphere we promise."

Jade raised an eyebrow. "Is writing ad copy for the resort brochures one of your special talents too?"

He laughed. "Sounded a little rote, didn't it?"

"But sincere."

He put his mouth next to her ear as he ushered her outside. "We're headed up a slippery slope, sweetheart. You get scared or jumpy, you hold on tight to me."

The rumble of his voice and the heat of his breath on her skin distracted her from dwelling on a deeper meaning to his words. Tobin kept his hand on her as they walked to the golf cart. Every time his touch shifted to a different spot on her back, that swooping sensation in her belly overtook her.

After they were situated, Tobin whipped the cart around and headed up the road she'd driven down.

"So this road . . . isn't a road, is it?"

"It's mainly for cart traffic, but once in a while we use the shortcut to drag supplies back and forth between the lodge and the stuff stored in the barn office."

Once they reached the top, Jade was able to see where she'd missed the turn to the lodge. But how had she missed the big red sign warning NO ADMITTANCE or the arrows pointing the opposite direction? She groaned.

Tobin shot her a sharp look. "What?"

"I'm a terrible driver."

"Why do you say that?"

"I just got my driver's license two years ago."

"There's not much need for you to drive in New York City, is there?"

"No. And New York drivers are so aggressive. I ended up taking my driver's test out of the city after I failed it." She paused. "Because I rear-ended a cab."

Tobin cringed. "Damn."

"At least we knew the air bags worked."

"That's looking on the bright side."

"I prefer to focus on the good rather than the bad." She sent him a sideways glance. "I'm sure our conversation the other night would make you question that statement."

"Wrong. That was the first honest conversation between us, so I'm done making assumptions about you." Tobin drove around the edge of the parking lot, stopping in front of the main entrance, so she could see the entire layout.

"This is a gorgeous place."

"It is now. It was a worthless piece of land because the topography is different from the surrounding area. But once bulldozers tiered the slope, it became usable. The lodge is open year-round except for two weeks at Christmas. I oughta be able to tell you the occupancy rate, since Renner and Janie, the Split Rock's GM, talk about it all the damn time, but I tend to tune them out."

"If a conversation doesn't revolve around cows, it's not interesting to you?" she teased.

He grinned. "Something like that. But Janie, who is married to a rancher, returns the favor when Renner and I talk about cattle."

How could anyone ever tune out Tobin's sexy voice? Not too deep or too raspy, as if he smoked a pack of Camels every day, but smooth like warm honey.

"You want to walk down to the pool?"

"Not really. I'd rather see the scenery." When Jade saw the steep incline, she said, "Can we make it down? Or should I get ready to pedal like *The Flintstones*?"

"Funny. But rolling this cart would be a shitty way to end the tour."

"The tour is over already?"

He looked at her. "You sound disappointed."

"I am."

"Then we'll go the long way around." His slightly devious smile made her blush.

"So you don't come in the main entrance when you come to work?"

He shook his head. "My day begins and ends at the barn. There are three sections I check first thing. Cows and bulls are kept in different pastures. We have trail horses that are separate, but Ted usually does that check now."

Tobin mentioning horses sent her thoughts back to how she'd lusted after him, seeing him in his element. Had he known he'd affected her that way? Is that why he'd been acting friendlier?

*Friendlier? Mr. Sexy Voice had his hand on your butt as he whispered in your ear. From the moment you showed up here, you know you skipped straight from adversaries to . . .*

"Am I boring you?" Tobin asked, startling her out of her thoughts.

"No! Why would you ask that?"

"Just paranoid, I guess. Some people say I talk too much."

"I could listen to you talk all night."

His heated gaze rolled over her with such intensity her palms—and other places—started to sweat. "You know I'm gonna make you prove that sooner rather than later."

Holy moly. When Tobin turned it on, he turned it *on*. She had to look away. That's when she noticed they were headed for a tree. She yelled, "Look out!"

He reset their course, but she swore they'd gotten close enough the golf cart would have scratches from the bark. "Relax, sweetheart, I've got it under control."

She muttered, "I'm glad someone does."

Tobin kept his focus on the road until he parked next to a white metal fence. "Hop out and I'll show you the rodeo grounds."

They walked slowly, side by side up a walkway made out of crushed rock. He stopped and rested his forearms on the top of the fence.

"Not that I know anything about rodeo, but isn't it unusual that this place has rodeo grounds?"

"The Split Rock caters to those looking for a 'real' western experience. We provide guests with an opportunity to ride a bull or a bronc."

Jade frowned. "Why would anyone choose to do those things?"

"Some guys want to try it and there's criteria to meet besides bein' macho. The local guys who help us out used to rodeo. I can't think of another place like this that has a bullfighter and a bull rider at their disposal."

The pride in his voice was unmistakable. "Are you a former rodeo cowboy?"

"Nope. Too risky for my blood."

"I'm not a huge risk taker either."

"I'm not surprised. It's your type A personality."

Jade shook her head. "I'd be more successful if I was type A. I'm more type . . . C plus."

He laughed. "You? With three part-time jobs? Doubtful. How many degrees do you have?"

"Uh, one."

"One bachelor's of science and one bachelor's of art kind of thing?"

"No. One bachelor's of arts, but I did double concentrations, not that it counts as two majors. Heck, it barely counts as *one* degree."

He studied her. "What's your degree in?"

"History with concentrations in medieval and Renaissance studies and music."

Tobin blinked at her.

Jade poked him in the chest. "Yes, Mr. Hale, it *is* exactly what you're thinking. That is not an employable degree, as I've discovered."

"Your parents were fine letting you pick that major? Of all the—"

"Useful, employable majors I could've chosen? Why yes, they thought it was admirable I turned my love of obscure history into . . . well, it should've been a career. Hence the need for three part-time jobs." Jade wondered why her parents hadn't pulled her up short and demanded she pick a normal major. "What about you?" Right after she'd said it, she wanted to take it back. Chances were that Tobin hadn't gone to college; he'd probably gone straight to work.

He dropped his hands and adjusted his cowboy hat.

Of course the question put him on edge. Before she could tell him to forget it, he sighed.

"I graduated from the University of Wyoming. I have a bachelor's of science in animal sciences with a minor in reproductive biology. I have a master's degree in animal sciences."

Stunned, Jade kept her jaw from hitting the dirt.

That seemed to amuse Tobin. "Shocked, Miz Columbia?"

"Actually, I'm embarrassed for assuming . . ."

Tobin shrugged. "No worries. We agreed to no more assumptions. Besides, most people see the cowboy first and never a scholar."

"Is that what you consider yourself first?"

His gaze shuttered. "To be honest, Jade, I don't know anymore."

The allusion of defeat in his tone, the lack of guile in his eyes and his body language . . . confused her. She waited for him to say something else, but he remained mum. "Tobin? You okay?"

He shook himself out of the moment of melancholy, smirked and gave her a light punch in the arm. "Peachy keen, jelly bean."

"Dude. Did you punch me in the arm like we were in third grade?"

He blushed a deep red. Opened his mouth. Closed it. Rubbed the back of his neck and released a soft laugh that resembled a groan. "Yeah."

Omigod. He was adorable.

Then Tobin was in her face, cocky grin in place, oozing the offbeat charm that had her heart racing and her hope rising. "And if you're really lucky, tiger, next time I'll yank on your pigtails to show that I like you."

*Oh, cowboy, you can pull my hair anytime.*

His eyes darkened as if she said that out loud. Then he murmured, "Damn, woman. You are—"

"Hey, Tobin. I wondered where you'd disappeared to."

Tobin muttered, "Never fucking fails." Then he stepped to the side and dropped his hand to her lower back, nudging her forward. "I've been giving Jade a tour. Jade, this is Renner Jackson, the mastermind behind the Split Rock Ranch and Resort, owner of Jackson Cattle Company and . . . my boss."

His boss? Crap.

Renner offered his hand. "Nice to meet you, Jade. You're Garnet's granddaughter?"

"Yes." Tobin's boss was really good-looking. And like every time she met an attractive male, she reverted to her shy state.

"Tobin mentioned it's your first trip out west?"

"Uh-huh. Everything is so big." *Brilliant, Jade.* She glanced up at Tobin. Some of her tension eased when he smiled at her. "Speaking of GG . . . I'd better get back."

"What are the two of you doin' today?"

"She hasn't said."

"Well, you already cleaned the house the other day." His eyes narrowed. "You never told me what you accomplished yesterday."

"Maybe I heeded your advice and took the day off."

"Liar." He reached out to tug on her hair. "You did laundry, didn't you?"

Jade put her hand on his chest and playfully pushed him. "I didn't do yours."

"I'll leave it in the hallway for you tonight. I'd hate for you to run out of stuff to do."

"So, I'll see you back at the office," Renner said to Tobin.

Her face flamed. She'd forgotten Tobin's boss was right behind her. She shoved her hands in the back pockets of her jeans and backed up. "I won't keep you. Thanks for the tour."

"I'll walk you to your car and point you in the right direction so you don't get lost."

She started to tell him it wasn't necessary, but something in his demeanor had changed and she wanted another minute alone with him. They wouldn't get that at GG's house.

"Drive safe and tell Garnet hello," Renner said.

"I will."

Once again, as they crossed the parking lot, Tobin had his hand on her. More possessive than friendly. She liked it. She really liked it when he curled his hands around her biceps and pressed a kiss to her forehead. A simple kiss that should've felt chaste, but the glide of his lips near her hairline and his ragged breathing kicked it up a notch.

She trembled.

He murmured, "We'll talk later, tiger," and retreated into the barn.

Jade didn't realize he hadn't given her directions until she was halfway home.

## Chapter Eight

*Tobin*'s head was filled with images from the past hour with Jade when he strolled into Renner's office. "What's up?"

Renner sighed. "You sure you want to play it this way?"

He spun the chair in front of Renner's desk around and straddled it. "Play what?"

"The fact that a week ago you were convinced that Garnet's grand-daughter was the Antichrist. And today, she just happens to show up at the Split Rock and you gave her the grand tour?"

"She took a drive and ended up here. What was I supposed to do?"

"Maybe not look so damn happy to see her for one thing." Renner tapped a pen on the desk and gave him a considering look. "Not that I blame you because Jade is a very attractive woman."

That was an understatement.

"And if you tell me you really hadn't noticed, then there's way more goin' on between you two than what I saw."

Tobin removed his hat and ran his hand over his hair. "Oh, I've noticed how beautiful Jade is, trust me. But I'm not lyin' when I say we seem to annoy the hell out of each other. Lately . . . there's the added complication that we're drawn to each other."

"You sure it's not some kind of ploy on her part to get you to come around to her way of thinkin'?"

"Because no woman could actually be attracted to me, right?" Tobin said sharply. "She'd have to want something from me to even give me the goddamned time of day?"

Renner held up his hands. "Whoa. You took that completely wrong, Tobin."

"Did I? Don't you think I know what people around here call me? Boy Scout. Do-gooder. Mr. Straight and Narrow. And they're the ones I consider friends." He curbed the bitterness in his tone, but not his tongue. "Yeah, maybe I was overly enthusiastic and just plain damn happy to be working when I took this job. Part of the reason I agreed to bein' a glorified ranch hand was I saw it as a stepping-stone to utilizing my degree in genetics." He glanced up at Renner. "You told me that creating a better breeding program was your long-term plan."

"I'm aware of that. Things change."

"That first year the Split Rock opened . . . chaotic all around, tryin' to decide exactly what type of place this was gonna be. A working cattle ranch with a rodeo stock contracting company on the side? Or just another dude ranch? I was pretty pumped at the prospect of having a voice in that decision, especially since my dad and my brothers made no bones about the fact my help wasn't welcome in their ranching operation.

"First year passed. Then the second. I retained hope some of the things we'd discussed would get implemented. In my off hours I hung out with a decent bunch of guys. Men I respected. But even when I was just a few years younger, I kept that reputation as the fresh-faced kid. Ike and Max were the only ones who didn't treat me like one." Tobin held up his hand when Renner started to speak. "It is what it is. Fletch and I both knew that summer Tanna lived here that you were spread too thin and your idea for a separate genetics and reproduction facility was more a dream than an actual plan. In addition to my ranching skills bein' prized over my college degree, I had to watch my buddies pair up. What sucked for me, is that every new woman who entered the small world that is Muddy Gap, Wyoming . . . saw me the same as everyone else. A kid. A friend. No matter what I did, nothing changed that."

Tobin sighed and rubbed the stubble on this cheek. "It got mighty lonely. Maybe it makes me a pussy for admitting that, but I'd spent enough time by myself, not only working during the day, but now the guys I'd hung out with had wives and girlfriends to go home to. And every fucking night I went home to that shitty trailer and crawled in bed alone. I'd started to feel pretty damn miserable about everything in my life. But again, no one seemed to notice. Except Hugh and Ike, but it wasn't like we talked about it beyond jokingly calling dibs on every new attractive woman who crossed our radar. When Harlow came back? I knew Hugh's history with her and that he wanted another shot at her. That's when I finally realized I would always be that bachelor 'kid' if I didn't make a plan and stick with it to start over someplace else."

Renner didn't say anything and Tobin kept his gaze aimed at his hands. This was more truth than he'd ever admitted to his boss. More personal than he'd ever intended to get. But Christ, it fucking stung to be perceived as the kid that he hadn't been for a long damn time.

After a bit, Renner sighed. "First off, I'm not makin' this about me when I say I know exactly how you feel. I dealt with that loneliness for years. It sucks. It's maybe one of the worst feelin's in the world that you're not . . . seen as you'd like to be. Then you wonder if you're just kiddin' yourself that you'll ever find that woman who gets you and gives you a place where you belong.

"Look. I'm not big on spilling my guts, either in a work situation or personally, so I appreciate you talkin' to me about this. I'll admit, with all that's happened in my life the past six years I seem to have blinders on when it comes to people outside of Tierney and the kids."

"You know I didn't tell you this to make you feel like a shitty boss, right?"

"Maybe I oughta feel like one." He picked up the pen again. "So much stuff just slipped out of my control, or I thought, 'I'll deal with that later,' and later never came. It was a huge blow, not to my ego or to my pride, to hear Hugh mention he hadn't hired on with me to be a ranch foreman. I knew that. But I got so wrapped up in what *I* wanted, I failed to remember in a business, it's more about what's best for the collective than what's best for the individual."

Tobin smirked. "Sounds like something Tierney would point out."

Renner smirked back. "I have no problem admitting my wife is a helluva lot smarter than me. I've always maintained that I was the one more in tune with people. That we balanced each other out because I have the people skills that she lacks. Even that hasn't turned out to be true. So that was a long damn answer to my question about what is goin' on between you and Jade."

"There's something. If she gives me even half a sign that she's moving in that direction? I'll take it."

"Don't bite my head off when I ask this, okay? But it's not just because she's convenient?"

He shook his head. "Besides the fact she's hot as hell, and smart, she's funny. She's uptight, yet she's shy. We both keep finding reasons to break the rules and talk to each other."

"What rules are you talking about?"

"Garnet's rules. Jade and I wound up in a couple of yelling matches the first day she showed up. Miz G said she wouldn't have that kind of behavior under her roof so she forbade us from 'engaging' with each other."

Renner threw back his head and laughed.

"I don't find it funny that she might be pitting me and Jade against each other for her own amusement."

"Well, whatever Miz G is doin' it ain't workin'. It's obvious Jade is into you."

"How'd you pick up on that? She said like five words to you."

"I spied on you, of course."

Tobin rolled his eyes.

"I assume the Mud Lilies have met her?"

"No, they haven't. I think that Garnet is hoarding her grand-daughter, for lack of a better term."

"Seems odd, though."

"Odd is the very definition of them old gals."

"True. So back to business. I've always understood doubling your salary wouldn't be an incentive for you to stick around." Renner locked his gaze to Tobin's. "That said, if you suddenly find a reason for staying in Muddy Gap? The job is still yours. The job as is," he clarified. "No promise that I'll get my shit together anytime soon and utilize all this office space as I'd intended."

"Thanks, Ren. I appreciate it."

Renner tapped his pen on his desk. He wore that *I'm about to level the boom* expression.

"What else?"

"I know you've been friend-zoned a lot. I ain't big on handing out advice, especially not advice on women, but there is one thing I wanted to mention."

Tobin tried not to fidget. Or blush.

"You want Jade to see you as more than a friend? Don't act like one. Don't set yourself up to fail. That's not to say be an asshole. Make it clear you're interested in her. And the split second you know she feels the same interest for you? Fucking own it. Take control like it's your due. You ain't the kind of guy who'll push her past a point she's not ready for, but show her that you *are* ready for the next step. Make her believe that once she's in your bed? She won't ever want to get out. Be confident, man. Women dig that."

"So you're saying to pretend to be someone else?"

Renner shook his head. "I'm sayin' you present yourself to be an easygoing, helpful, nice guy. That's who you are. But that's not all you are, T. Show her your intense side. She'll know that's part of you that only she gets to see. That is heady stuff for your woman, my friend. Be that polite, helpful, easygoing guy in public, but when you're alone with her, rip that fucking mask off and be the man she wants ownership of."

He laughed softly. Not out of nervousness, out of relief. His boss had hit it right on the fucking head—that elusive *What am I doing wrong?* that had kept him second-guessing himself.

No. More. "That is the single best piece of advice I've ever gotten, Renner."

"Thank fuck you said that. I'da felt like an ass if you would've stood, tapped the desk and said 'good talk.'"

"I'm gonna do that anyway. But only because I'm done spinning my wheels when it comes to this."

Tobin reached the door, when Renner said his name.

"I owed you. Early on you made me question why I accepted that Tierney wasn't meeting me halfway in our relationship. Demanding she put in equal effort because I deserved it changed everything for us. You deserve a chance to find what's been missing for you."

"Thanks."

## Chapter Nine

❧

"GG. Why don't you have any pictures of me around your house? I know Mom and Dad have sent them to you over the years."

"What do you mean? I have every picture from the time you were a baby up until the ones we took last summer on Cape Cod."

"So where are they?"

"I keep them in albums, so when I get lonely for you, I can flip back through them and remember all of our fun times." GG frowned. "When your dad was a boy, I had pictures of him everywhere. Your grandpa called it the 'shrine to Garwood Evans' and I know it embarrassed Gar whenever his buddies came over." Sadness clouded her eyes. "After I sold the house, I put all those pictures and school things in albums. I continued that tradition with you. Why?"

"When I first got here, Tobin mentioned not knowing what I looked like and that he didn't remember hearing you talk about me . . ."

"Well, girlie-girl, I don't talk about you."

That explained it. Jade had to look away. "Oh."

"That doesn't mean I'm not bust-my-buttons proud of you. Some of my happiest memories are from the times we've spent together. But those memories are mine. They're precious to me. I'm selfish. I don't want to share them with anyone else."

She glanced up at her grandmother. "Really? I thought . . ."

GG took Jade's hand in both of hers. "You thought I was ashamed of you or something? Lord, child, no. Exactly the opposite. But see, this is about me. When women get to be of a certain age . . . all they ever talk about is their dadgum grandkids. They brag on them. Or worse, they blather on about the kids' drug problems, or baby-mama dramas, or complain that their grandbaby-daddy ain't nothin' but a sperm donor. Makes my head hurt. The only reason these women share all of that baloney is to get 'there, there, dear' pats on the hand and assurances from their friends they weren't to blame. Bunch of poppycock if you ask me, because usually they *are* to blame." She shrugged. "Not only that, these same women don't talk about anything interesting because they stopped doing interesting things. They just keep reliving their glory days when they raised their own kids and now they're reliving that time through their grandkids."

"I never thought of it that way."

"These types of women wanna moan and groan about their aches and pains. Or they wanna gossip about other women. They're jealous if a widow has a social life—that mean girl stuff still happens with really old mean girls."

Jade snickered.

"My group of friends—you'll meet the Mud Lilies crew sooner rather than later—and I made a pact that we'd keep our friendship and activities focused on *us*—on the us we are now, not the us from fifty, sixty years ago. I'm an interesting person in my own right, as are they. Sure, sometimes we talk about the grandkids, but mostly, uh . . . no. Sounds selfish, but I gotta say, it sure is fun." She grinned. "It's like we're teenage girls again. The world is wide open to us and we can do anything we want."

Here was her chance to get some answers. "Well, I'm glad for you, but I do have to ask if these friends are . . . a bad influence?"

"Oh pooh. You mean the gun and the jail time? Minor incidents. Besides, they're pretty tame in comparison to some of the other things we've done and haven't been caught for."

"You realize that last statement isn't really putting my mind at ease?"

GG blinked. "Shoot. Scratch that. Forget I mentioned it."

Not likely.

But the real question was how much of it she would relay to her dad.

"Come on." GG stood and pulled Jade to her feet. "As long as you're my captive audience today, we'll sort through some stuff."

As Jade followed her down the upstairs hallway, the barest hint of Tobin's cologne teased her as she passed the open door to his room. Her body heated as she flashed back to being so close to him earlier. She hadn't mentioned her visit to the Split Rock to GG, but Jade had thought of little else.

GG opened up a room that was packed with papers, fabric, art supplies, bags of clothing and stacks of bedding.

"Now, I wasn't gonna show you this, figuring it'd land me on an episode of *Hoarders*, but I've managed to contain my junk collection to this room." She frowned and shot a look at the ceiling. "Well, mostly to this room. There is some stuff in the attic."

There wasn't a single space like this in her parents' brownstone. Clutter was dealt with immediately. So this was pretty cool. She'd get to see remnants of her grandma's life. "What are your plans for all of this stuff? Is it valuable to you?"

"Most of it is odds and ends that I couldn't part with for some reason." She jammed her fingers through her strawberry-colored hair, causing it to stick straight up. "With you listening to me tell you why I kept it and hearing the history behind it . . . maybe it'll be easier for me to let it go." GG wrapped Jade in a hug. "I'm so glad you're here. Not to clean out my room, but to listen to an old broad ramble on. Makes it feel less like work and more a trip down memory lane."

Jade squeezed her grandma tight. The woman was skinny, but there wasn't a frail thing about her. It didn't seem as if she'd aged at all since Jade was a kid. She'd always been unconventional in her approach to life. Jade would give anything to be like that. "I'm happy I finally get to be in your home, GG. I should've come here way before now."

"Oh pooh. If I'm not allowed to have regrets at my age, you're certainly not allowed to have them at yours." She stepped back and smoothed her hands over Jade's hair. "You are such a beautiful girl. Inside and out. So tell me why you ain't got a million boys chasing after you?"

She laughed self-consciously. "I haven't gotten over that whole 'shy' thing, unfortunately. Guys my age want a fast hookup because they're still partying with their bros on weekends, even if they have a respectable job Monday through Friday. Older guys . . . they want to hook up too, but more in a 'let's see if the sex is good enough that I'll consider you long-term-relationship material' and then they grill you on your career plans and if you'd set them aside to have a family."

"It'll make me sound like a fuddy-duddy, but not having sex before marriage was a lot simpler. I got to know him in other ways and he got to know me beyond my killer gams and great bosom."

Bosom. What a great word. Why didn't anyone use it anymore?

"Maybe this is more than you wanted to know about my marriage to your grandfather . . . but we knew there was passion between us from the moment we met. We couldn't wait to get to that wedding night." She smirked. "That was only the beginning for us. We kept those fires burning because neither of us was shy in admitting what we wanted in the boudoir. That wasn't the norm back then, I guess, but it's how we were."

"GG, why didn't you ever get remarried?"

"He was the love of my life. No man I ever met compared to him or what we had together." GG took her hands. "I know you've struggled to find your place in the world. I'm proud of you for the dedication to your schooling and your music."

"But?"

"There's no 'but' just an 'and.'"

"Okay. And . . . ?"

"And what makes other people happy will be different than what makes you happy. You don't have to follow the maddening crowd to find happiness. This whole idea of everyone goin' to college and joining the race to get to the top of the ladder . . . I don't believe the view up there is better than down here."

"You're right. But it's never been my goal to rise to the top."

Her eyes burned bright. "What is your goal, Jade?"

"To live my life happily."

"Were you close to achieving that?"

She shook her head. "Not on any level. Not in my professional or in my personal life."

Why was GG poking her on this?

"A piece of paper given to you by an academic institution isn't what defines you." GG placed her hand over Jade's heart. "This defines you. Some people will tell you to listen to your head. I say poppycock. I say listen to your heart." She pulled Jade into a hug. "I love you. Anytime you need to talk about anything at all, I'm here for you. No judgment."

"Thanks, GG."

"Now you grab the garbage bags from the kitchen and we'll get this place tidied up"

⟨⟩

Jade had finished sealing a box with packing tape, when she heard Tobin call out, "Where are you, Miz G?"

GG walked to the staircase to yell down, "Up here."

The stairs creaked and then Tobin stood in the hallway, eyeing the wreckage. He whistled. "I didn't know we had a tornado touch down today."

"It's been a whirlwind, but a productive one. I can't believe how much we accomplished in just a few hours."

"It looks like you've been productive."

Jade tied a knot in the garbage bag and dragged it to the pile. She put her hand on her belly to quell the fluttery feeling before she met Tobin's gaze.

The way he stared at her—hot and hungry—had her heart hammering.

"Great timing. We could use a break." GG dusted off her hands. To Tobin, she said, "Feel free to haul these bags out to the trash."

"Not a problem."

Good thing GG was oblivious to the fact that Tobin hadn't taken his eyes off Jade since the moment their gazes had connected.

"This cleansing calls for a drink. I'll head down and pour us some champagne." GG patted Tobin in the chest and ducked under his arm as she passed by him.

Jade didn't move.

As soon as they were alone, Tobin stalked her.

The glimmer in his eye sent her pulse tripping. "Two questions for you."

"Okay."

This close to him, Jade noticed a thin white scar, half an inch long above his upper lip. She wanted to taste it. Trace it with her tongue. Kiss it.

"Did you think about me after you left the Split Rock today?"

"I've thought of little else."

"Did you think"—he ran his nose up the side of her neck from the curve of her shoulder to the underside of her chin—"'wasn't it nice of my *friend* Tobin to show me around'?"

That threw her. Despite the heady distraction of the heat of his breath washing over her skin, she managed, "Is that what we are? Friends?"

"No." Tobin braced both his hands above her head on the wall. "The last fucking thing I want to be is your goddamned *friend*, Jade."

When had all the oxygen left the room? Her gaze zoomed from the glint in his eyes, to the sensual curve of his mouth, to the pulse thumping in his throat.

"Know what I want?" he said huskily. "To blatantly break the 'no contact' rule."

She licked her lips. His mouth was right there.

"Say yes." He brushed his lips across hers. Just once. "Admit you want to be a dirty little rule breaker too."

"I do," she said breathlessly. "Like you wouldn't believe."

His teeth gleamed.

Then she found her back against the wall and Tobin's mouth fastened to hers in a scorching kiss.

A blistering kiss.

A dirty, wet, rule-breaking kiss that felt fantastic.

Jade twined her arms around his neck, trying to get as close to him as possible.

Tobin groaned in her mouth and effortlessly lifted her up higher to better align their upper bodies, never relinquishing the kiss.

She loved his show of strength and the way he used it to get what he needed, which was more of her. Digging her fingers into the back of his neck, she held on.

He hadn't let up on the kiss from the first touch of their lips.

Every stroke of his tongue, every stuttered breath, every groan that reverberated down her throat caused her body to become wet and pliant, readying herself for more of him.

His taste, his touch, his scent . . . she was drowning in him.

From just a kiss.

An epic kiss given all the back and forth between them. The heated words. The molten looks. The knowledge that they couldn't have stopped this combustion even if they'd wanted, even if it hadn't been against the blasted rules—not that either one had tried.

Then he dragged his damp lips across her jawline, sending goose bumps from her scalp to her toes.

She sucked in a breath when he sank his teeth into the hollow beneath her jaw.

"Fuck. I wanted you before," he murmured, "but nothin' like the way I want you now." He brushed his lips across the shell of her ear. "Don't retreat after this, Jade. Don't tell me this was a mistake."

"It's not. It's . . ." She moaned when he blew in her ear and she arched into him hard.

"Thank fuck." Tobin made a growling noise and devoured her again in a messy kiss that was ten times hotter because he'd lost control of his lust for her.

After hoisting her up, he'd kept his hands on her behind, kneading and squeezing, never venturing beyond the small of her back.

She wanted those rough-skinned hands all over her. Just when she reached down to bring one of his hands up, he eased back to rest his forehead to hers.

"Why'd you stop kissing me?"

"Because your grandma will be up here at any moment. I'd rather not get caught grinding on you with my tongue in your mouth."

Jade gave him a playful Eskimo kiss. "What are you saying?"

"Now that we've started this, darlin', there ain't no stopping it. But we keep it between us."

"It's better to sneak around and lie about what's going on?" She deserved a pat on the back for keeping her response from sounding bitchy.

"I won't put you in a difficult position with her." He touched his mouth to hers. "And we've been sneaking around since the moment you arrived."

"So this changes nothing."

He pulled back. The intent look in those mesmerizing eyes brought a flush to her entire body. "Wrong. This has changed *everything*."

The bottom stair creaked.

They didn't break apart guiltily. He let her slide down his body slowly, letting her feel the hard ridge of his cock.

"What are you two doing up there?" GG yelled from halfway up the stairs. "It's too gol-durn quiet."

Tobin leaned over the railing. "We were havin' a staring contest. I'm pretty sure I won."

"You wish," Jade retorted, hoping her voice didn't sound shaky. Or breathy.

GG squinted at Jade. "I thought you were coming down for some champagne?"

"I am. I needed to remind your minion to take out the trash sooner, rather than later."

"Hey, I'm not invited to the cocktail party?"

Garnet gave Tobin an arch look. "Were you cleaning out this room and boxing things up all afternoon? Nope. So you're *not* invited to our celebration. Come on, Jade."

As Jade passed by Tobin, he murmured, "We'll have a private celebration later."

But it turned out that "later" hadn't meant later that night.

Tobin received a phone call during dinner, asking for his help rounding up some cattle that'd gotten loose, and he hadn't returned by the time Jade had gone to bed.

❧

The next afternoon, after Jade and GG finished cleaning out the last of the small room, GG insisted on celebrating with champagne. She immediately conked out on the love seat in the sitting room when she made her way downstairs to get a bottle.

At loose ends, Jade started dinner.

Right after she'd slipped the pan in the oven, she turned around only to discover that Tobin was right behind her. "Oh. Hello. You're home early."

"Whatever you're making sure smells good."

"A tomato and asparagus quiche. And a rustic savory tart—a modified version since I didn't find many fresh herbs."

"You been out to Miz G's herb garden and looked around?"

"No. Why didn't she tell me she had one? Where is it?"

"Come on, I'll show you."

She snagged a pair of scissors and a basket from the pantry before she followed Tobin out the back door.

The day had cooled. Late-afternoon sun shimmered across the tops of the trees, sending shards of golden light dancing across the red dirt. Birds chattered and swooped, catching bugs for their evening meal. She'd spent the morning watching puffy clouds building into a thunderhead only to see the tops sheared off by gusts of wind. She'd become so enthralled by the rapidly shifting power of nature that the bedding she'd brought outside to hang on the line had nearly been dry.

Her restlessness had been better today. But she didn't kid herself that was due in part to the hours she'd spent cleaning, packing and hauling garbage.

They'd cleared the backside of the barn when she noticed three separate areas, evenly spread apart and enclosed in barbed wire. Jade was slightly dumbfounded. How had she missed this place? "This is some garden."

"Miz G claims she's doin' half as much planting as she used to."

"Still. It's huge. Which one is the herb garden?"

"The new one in the far back." Tobin pointed to the left. "That one has vegetables—some weird ones, mind you. That one over there"—he pointed to the right—"is flowers."

"I wonder why she hadn't mentioned this. This is like . . . heaven."

"She probably thought you could use a break, bein's you're a cook in the city."

"I am—I was—a prep cook. I chopped and measured and mixed. Not a lot of real cooking."

Tobin shrugged. "Maybe that's why. She doesn't think you can cook."

Jade paused at the gate to the herb garden. "Just because one of her houseguests doesn't cook doesn't mean the other one can't or isn't interested."

"Ouch. But true."

The earthy scents of wet soil and the humidity of growing things enveloped her. Jade picked her way around the plants—nothing had been planted in rows; there wasn't any rhyme or reason to the groupings. She found the tarragon and snipped a few stems. Next she cut a few pieces of orange mint. Luckily GG had left the markers with some of the plants. She mentally catalogued rosemary, thyme, sage, two kinds of basil and parsley, dill, a bay leaf plant, cilantro and . . . what were those growing on the other side, almost hidden beneath the juniper tree?

Holy crap. She jumped back.

The heat from the front of Tobin's body met her backside and he wrapped a beefy arm across her belly as if to protect her. "Did you see a snake? Probably just a garter snake. They're harmless. But up on the ridge you'll find rattlers. Some big ol' boys, so steer clear of that area especially during the hottest part of the day."

"No, I didn't see a snake. I saw . . . those."

Without letting go of her, he leaned sideways. He laughed. "Miz G is growing herself a little ganja."

"Now I know why she didn't mention her herb garden." She took a breath. "I cannot believe my grandmother is growing pot! It's against the law!"

"Maybe she doesn't know what it is and thought it looked like a pretty plant?"

Jade glared at him over her shoulder.

He snickered. "Hell, I couldn't even say that with a straight face."

"This is not funny."

"Yeah, darlin', it is."

Was this typical of Tobin not to take things like this seriously? "Would it be funny if she went to jail? Is it funny that she might be gullible enough to grow an illegal controlled substance for her friends? Can you imagine GG in prison like on *Orange Is the New Black*? Those hardened criminals would decimate her sweet nature. She'd probably get shanked."

Tobin turned her around, keeping their bodies so close his thighs brushed hers. "Whoa. You're goin' full steam ahead and getting pretty far off the track."

She inhaled. Since her nose was practically pressed against Tobin's chest, the clean cotton scent of his shirt filled her lungs. Why did he have to smell so good? "Sorry. I get a little wound up sometimes."

"A little?" he repeated. His gaze zoomed in on her neck. "Your pulse is pounding like a snared rabbit's, sweetheart."

She swallowed hard. "I'm a rule follower, remember? This is breaking a major rule and it makes me nervous."

"Or I'm making you nervous." Tobin dipped his head and placed an openmouthed kiss on the base of her throat. "Goddamn, you smell so freakin' good." He rubbed his cheek across her skin. "I wanna sink my teeth into you . . . right here."

As soon as his teeth connected with the slope of her shoulder, her knees gave out.

"That's what I'm talkin' about," he growled. "Reminding you how it is between us."

"Like I could forget," she said breathlessly. "Were you worried I would?"

"I hoped not. But I planned on giving you a hands-on reminder if you had."

Then she said, "Show me. Kiss me again, Tobin." She slid her hands up his chest and twined her arms around his neck. "Kiss me like you were dying to drag me into your bed."

Jade expected that would drive him to ravish her in a consuming kiss.

Instead, he glided his lips back and forth across hers. Teasing. Tracing the seam of her mouth. Tasting her breath when she opened for him. But he didn't dive in. "Such sweetness," he whispered, "but I know that tongue is tart."

"Yes."

"You want me to suck on it?" He slicked the very tip of his tongue across the bow of her upper lip.

"Please."

"But I want a bite of this first." After a gentle scrape on the inside of her plump bottom lip, he sank his teeth in.

Jade dug her fingers into the back of his neck and moaned.

"Jade? Where are you?" GG called out.

They broke apart with as much guilt as if they'd been caught going at it in the dirt.

*Uh, you* were *going at it in the dirt.*

"Hide under that bush," she hissed at him

"What? No fuckin' way."

"You *will* hide. And don't even think about trying to escape from here until we're back in the house."

Smart-aleck man saluted.

Shamelessly, Jade watched his jean-clad behind after he dropped to all fours and crawled behind the juniper bush—which did not hide his big body at all. Slamming the gate shut behind her, she practically skipped out of the herb garden. "What an awesome herb selection! Not that I got to see more than just the front part."

Was it her imagination or was GG scrutinizing her more than usual?

*Poker face, poker face, come on, poker face.*

Finally GG offered that sweet smile. "You oughta see my veggies. It's a great year for okra. Come on, I'll show you."

By the time they finished the tour and returned to the house, the aroma of the rustic savory tart wafted out from the kitchen.

"You didn't have to make supper tonight, girlie-girl, but I'm sure glad you did. It's quite a treat to have someone cook for me."

"Tobin doesn't cook at all?"

GG snorted. "That man can burn canned green beans. Canned green beans," she repeated. "That stunk to high heaven. After that, I told him I'd feed him. I gotta say, it's been nice cooking for a man again. I forget about such ravenous appetites."

Just then, Tobin stepped past the swinging doors.

His turquoise gaze roved over her slowly and thoroughly, from her mouth to her bare toes.

His molten look when their gazes clashed indicated his ravenous appetite wasn't just for food.

*⌘*

## Chapter Ten

"*T*obin!" Garnet said with a smile that quickly turned into a frown. "Didn't you check the schedule? Tonight isn't your night to eat with me."

"I know. I just came in to see what's cookin'."

Tobin watched Jade's hands as she guided the knife through the perfectly toasted crust, slicing the tart into four equal pieces.

"What are your after-dinner plans, Tobin?" Garnet asked.

"Heading over to Abe's. He's got a two-year-old bull he wants me to look at. He's become as obsessed with diversity in their breeding stock as Ike and Hugh have. What are you ladies up to?"

"I tried to convince Pearl to let Jade come to the range with us tonight."

"Range?" Jade repeated. "As in golf range?"

Garnet snorted. "Do I *look* like I golf? No, it's our gun range night. We only get a limited amount of time. But then again, the sheriff insists we have the range to ourselves after the last scuffle we had with the Gun Club. They challenged us to a shootout and got really ticked off when Vivien beat their best shooter. She won fair and square." Garnet lowered her voice. "Vivien took her smallest-caliber pistol and created a penis at the bottom of the silhouette target. But it was a teeny-tiny penis. And it had no balls." She sighed. "So we won't be invited to their turkey-feed fundraiser this year."

Tobin laughed. He glanced over at Jade.

She stared openmouthed at her grandmother.

"Pretty accurate depiction of one if I remember right." She frowned. "You know, I think I might have a picture on my phone—"

"No, that's okay. I believe you. And I don't know about going to the gun range. I don't want to insert myself where I don't belong."

Jade handed him a plate.

Garnet actually gave him a little push out of the kitchen.

⊷

When Tobin parked in his usual spot in the driveway, he had a moment of doubt. Maybe Jade wanted time to herself. Maybe she'd think it was weird that he'd come back so soon after his meeting.

Tobin exited his truck and breathed in the scents of a summer night. The day had cooled off quickly after the sunset. Out here, air-conditioning wasn't necessary. Just open the windows and let the cross breezes cool everything down.

That's why he'd heard the unfamiliar sound when his boot had hit the top porch stair. He paused. Listened. And he'd heard it again. A drawn-out, mournful wail.

Entering the house quietly, he saw the kitchen lights were off. Two lamps burned in the living room. Light from the sitting room spilled across the wood floor. He moved along the hallway to the small space tucked behind the staircase. You wouldn't even know a room was back there if the door was closed, but it was open and that's where the sounds he'd heard were coming from.

Just then a violent eruption of musical notes exploded into the air. Angry tones, dissonant chords that evoked that gut-twisting feeling of betrayal.

Tobin leaned against the wall and closed his eyes, letting the music wash over him.

The anger and betrayal in the piece gave way to melancholy, long sweet notes rather than fast and furious rapid-fire runs. Gradually the sense of melancholy began to melt away; the tones became brighter, happy little teases, followed by high- and low-pitched short sections that he swore sounded like flirty dialogue between a man and a woman.

Then once again the tone morphed into one of sensuality. A slow tango of rich and steady glides before gradually the strains shortened, creating an urgency that rose and rose until it reached that long, clear high-pitched note. That piercing swell held, and held and held, then in the next moment it spiraled down, becoming a whisper of sweet nothings and ebbs and flows of soft notes.

But the song wasn't done; it had one more deep emotion to pull from those strings—sorrow. Not an angry sorrow, but despair. An almost steady drone of it, with little variation in volume, the kind of despair and grief that comes from loss of love.

That's how the song ended. Abruptly.

Tobin's heart raced. Somehow through the emotions still zinging through his body, he had the presence of mind to speak so she didn't freak out. "Jade?"

First he heard a hollow thud. Then, "Tobin?"

"Yeah."

He heard her footsteps approach and stop.

"I can't apologize for listening in because that has got to be the single greatest piece of music I've ever heard." He took a chance and opened his eyes.

Jade stood across from him, a violin tucked under her arm, a bow dangling by her leg. She looked the same as she had before supper, T-shirt, hip-hugger jeans, bare feet. The only difference was she had pulled back her hair and secured it at the base of her neck.

Yes, she looked the same, but Tobin knew he'd be seeing her completely differently now. This little whip of a thing who could create such intense magic.

She shifted her stance. "Tobin? Are you okay?"

"Nope. I'm completely and utterly blown away by you after listening to you play."

She blushed.

"I don't know anything about music, just what I do and don't like. But that piece? I think I held my damn breath through half of it. And when you finished, I thought about patting my face to see if my cheeks were wet. It was just . . . wow." Tobin shook his head. "How do you do that? Take those notes on a page and churn the emotion and the passion together."

"Practice. Lots and lots of practice." She closed her eyes for a moment and breathed deeply before she looked at him again. "That wasn't meant to sound flip. I've been working on the subtle and blatant variations of that piece for half of my life."

"Is it offensive to say it shows?"

"No." She smiled softly. "It's my go-to piece. The one I play beginning to end, without stopping, even if I screw up a section because even as many times as I've played it, and cried over it and rejoiced in it, and ripped the sheet music up and turned it into confetti . . . every new performance I hear or feel something different."

"Well, I'd say in the aftermath of that I feel like I oughta smoke a cigarette."

She snickered.

"But since I don't smoke, I definitely need a drink." He paused. "Care to join me? If you're done playing."

"Oh, I'm most definitely done. And a drink would be great just as long as it's not beer." She wrinkled her nose and he was completely charmed. "I never developed a taste for it. Especially not in college with warm kegs."

"No problem. Miz G has a decent liquor selection. She's gotta be ready to make the Mud Lilies' signature drinks whenever they ask."

"I'll put this away and be right there."

Tobin stopped in the entryway and used the bootjack to take his boots off. He shoved his socks inside and crossed the dining room to the liquor cabinet. He grabbed the bottle of Jameson and the Chambord. What the hell. He'd try his hand at a fancy cocktail. He poured a shot of Jameson in each champagne flute, a shot of Chambord and topped both glasses off with cold champagne.

"That looks great," Jade said behind him.

"No guarantees 'cause I kinda winged it." He handed her a glass, picked his up and paused to make a toast. "Thank you for sharing your music with me tonight."

Jade touched her glass to his. "You're welcome."

They both drank and looked at each other and laughed.

"You're not spitting it out."

"It's actually pretty good. The raspberry liqueur mellows the whiskey."

"Can I ask you something? Why weren't you a music performance major? Instead of just minoring in it?"

"I'm a great player, but I'm not a fantastic player. I know I don't have that something extra that is obvious in every piece that Joshua Bell, Sarah Chang, Yo-Yo Ma and Itzhak Perlman play." She pointed her glass at him. "I know the life of a musician is ten percent performance, twenty percent practice and sixty percent politics, then the other ten percent . . . that's the fun part. I love music, I love to play, but I realized being a professional paid musician in a city symphony or orchestra could suck the love and the joy out of it. So I play for fun. I was in a wedding quartet at one time. While playing Pachelbel's Canon makes me want to barf—seriously—a wedding is the happiest occasion in the couple's life up to that point and it rocks to be part of it." She took a drink. "Now can I ask you something?"

He hoped he pulled off a nonchalant shrug.

"What part of that piece affected you the most?"

"The section where the loss occurs. There's that steady drone, where I imagined that grief just drowns out everything else."

Jade blinked at him. "That's a very subtle nuance to pick up on, Mr. I Don't Know Anything About Music."

Tobin blushed.

"So did you pick up on it because you've suffered a loss like that?"

"My mom died about ten years ago and that was hard. Her death affected my dad like that. But recently . . ." He paused and swallowed a large mouthful of liquid courage. This wasn't something he talked about. Or rather, this wasn't something anyone in the community spoke of.

"I have two older brothers. I'm not close to either of them. They work with our dad running the ranch and there never was a place for me there. Which . . . doesn't matter. My brother Streeter, he's the closest in age to me. Married his high school sweetheart. They were one of those couples that everyone wanted to be because they were so freakin' perfect? Well, they tried for years to get pregnant. Finally Danica got pregnant. The pregnancy went well. No complications. She gave birth to Olivia, this perfectly healthy darlin' baby girl." Even thinking about this now just tied him up in knots. He knocked back another drink. "Danica always wanted to be a mom so she quit her job to stay home with Olivia. About . . . six months ago, Streeter went home for lunch. He walked into their house, straight into the nursery since that's where Danica always was, and he . . . found her. Danica had killed herself."

"Omigod."

"Olivia was sleeping in her crib. She was six months old. Streeter . . . he just . . . when I heard that sorrowful tone to the music? I wondered if that's what life sounds like to Streeter now. Like I said, we're not close. I check on him every couple of weeks. He says he's fine. Fuck. How can he be fine? He's not fine. But he'd never . . ."

Jade wrapped her arms around his waist and pressed the side of her face against his chest. "Tobin. I'm so sorry. What an awful, awful thing."

"Yeah." It was weird to think this was the first time he'd talked about his sister-in-law's death. In that respect, he was exactly like his father and his brothers. He just shut it down. Didn't allow his thoughts to wander to why Danica had ended her life when she had the life she'd wanted. Why she'd done it in her baby's room? Because she hadn't wanted to die alone? And yeah, it made him a dick, but the fact that her decision forced the man who'd loved her for years . . . to find her that way? No note. No hint she might be depressed, at least as far as Tobin knew. And this was totally morose, but he wondered if in that moment after the shock and loss had passed, if dealing with her death and becoming a single, widowed parent, had turned that love into hate.

"I don't know," Jade said softly. "Maybe your brother doesn't even know at this point."

It hit him then; he'd said all that out loud.

His confusion and heartbreak seemed to be holding on tighter.

And he wasn't fool enough to let go. She smelled good. And she felt good. Soft and yet solid.

Tobin curled his hand around the side of Jade's neck, pressing his thumb on her jawbone, slightly tipping her head back.

Every feature that formed her beautiful face deserved careful consideration. Her dark eyebrows perfectly arched over those expressive almond-shaped eyes. The edges of her cheekbones nestled high in the rounded curves of her face. The wide nose that managed to be both haughty and cute. And then there were those lips. Full and soft, the color somewhere between copper and peach.

She exhaled.

Was it only yesterday that he'd kissed her for the first time? Now he craved how warm and smooth the inside flesh of her bottom lip felt against the tip of his tongue. Now he knew how hot and fast her exhalations were against his mouth.

Tempting to start out with sugar bites, sweet kisses, slowly savoring her until that moment when need and hunger asserted control.

"Tobin?" she said softly. "What are you doing?"

"Memorizing you."

"Why?"

Tobin forced his gaze back to hers. "Because when I close my eyes at night, I want to recall with perfect clarity every nuance of this face."

The interest that flared in her eyes was all the permission he needed.

He brushed his lips across hers. Once. Twice. On the third pass he lingered. The soft flesh tasted like champagne and raspberries. But that was just on the surface. He needed more.

As soon as he slipped his tongue in, Jade opened her mouth to him fully.

Somehow Tobin kept the kiss easy, not devouring her. Allowing her to explore, even as he did the same.

Their bodies migrated closer.

Jade's hand clutched the back of his shirt.

He kept his hand on her face, continuing to sweep his thumb across her jawbone, while he mimicked the motion with his left hand on her hip.

Just when he felt the heat between them expand, Jade broke the kiss.

She rested her forehead on his chest and took long, deep breaths.

Tobin pressed his lips to her temple. Then he nudged her head back and planted kisses down her cheek and over to her ear. Every time he exhaled, she shuddered. He homed in on her earlobe, flicking the tender skin in a carnal preview of his tongue tasting the sweet spot between her thighs. Closing his eyes, he followed the arc of her throat with his nose, breathing in the scent of her heated skin.

That spicy floral scent shot straight to his cock.

"Tobin."

"Shh. Let me."

"Let you . . . what?"

"Learn what you like."

He learned using his teeth made her break out in gooseflesh.

He learned she purred when he pressed soft-lipped kisses below her ear.

He learned sucking the spot above her collarbone sent her body arching hard against his.

The front door slammed.

He learned there was no way they were ever truly alone.

"You have *got* to be fucking kidding me."

Jade stepped back. Her eyes were glazed. Her lips were swollen. She didn't look well kissed; she was halfway to looking well fucked.

"One day soon I'll get to kiss you and touch you without your grandma interrupting us."

"Sorry. Stay here. I'll be right back."

# Chapter Eleven

───❦───

"Jade?" her grandmother called out.

Jade hustled out of the sitting room and into the living room before GG busted them. "I didn't expect you back so soon. How was your night?"

"Crappy." GG plopped on the sofa. "I'm too pooped to even pour myself some bubbly."

Good thing. All the drink stuff was still out in the kitchen, along with two champagne glasses.

Both she and Tobin had been a little reckless tonight.

"Sometimes it's better not to listen to your friends," her grandma announced.

"Is that why you had a crappy night?"

"Yes. Don't ever go in halvsies with anyone on anything either."

"Who are we talking about?"

"Pearl. She hogged the AR-15. I didn't get to shoot it one gol-durn time, which just makes me think I need my own."

Jade nodded like that made perfect sense.

"I need to apologize to you."

"Why would you need to apologize to me?"

"I got to thinking . . . I've been a terrible hostess. Here you are visiting me and I've left you to entertain yourself. We haven't even gone out for a drink or supper."

"That's all right. I know you have a life here, GG. I'm used to entertaining myself." The times she'd spent with Tobin had been beyond entertaining.

"My life of late . . . ain't really been all that fun, to be honest. So I've decided that you and me are gonna make our own fun by taking a road trip to see the sights!"

"Really? When are we going?"

"First thing tomorrow morning. And we aren't planning nothin'. We'll just go where the blacktop takes us."

"You must have some idea of what sights you want to show me."

"I'd love to take you to Jackson, where I raised your dad and spent my married years. But shoot, this time of year it's overrun with tourists, so we'll save that for another time. Maybe in the fall when the aspen leaves are changing and the wildlife is out, getting wild during mating season."

"What are the other options?"

"Yellowstone is at least a weeklong trip if you wanna see the good stuff, so that's out too. I'm thinking we could head over to Devils Tower outside of Sundance. Then head up to Sheridan and take a short tour of the Bighorn Mountains. Beautiful country up there. We'd be gone two days. Of course, you'd have to drive. Them twisty mountain roads ain't for the faint of heart."

Jade didn't have the guts to admit they might be better off with GG behind the wheel.

"What say you, girlie? Wanna have an adventure with your old granny while you still can?"

"You're not old. And yes, I'd love to have an adventure with you." Getting out of the house and seeing the wide-open spaces of Wyoming would be good for her. Plus, she and GG always had a great time on vacation. "What should I pack? Evening gowns? High heels?"

"Oh, you." She flapped her hand. "You've never been the designer-label, live-for-shopping kind of girl."

"Much to my mother's dismay," Jade said wryly.

"Gwen does love her clothes, purses and ankle-breaking shoes. I'm grateful she didn't push that on you, sweetheart. She let you be your own person."

"Not that I know who that person is," Jade said softly.

Naturally GG heard it. "That's what this trip is supposed to be about." She frowned. "The part that's not the spying-on-me-and-reporting-to-your-dad part. The time-off-from-your-regularly-scheduled-life part."

Jade bit her lip.

"I know that anxious look. Spit it out."

"Will I ever be able to crumple up my to-do lists and my compulsion to accomplish something and just . . . learn to wing it?"

GG patted her leg. "That's what we're goin' to find out. So here's the deal. I'll bring my cell phone for an emergency, but besides that? No technology. No GPS. We'll use a good-old-fashioned map. We won't even listen to the radio. We'll leave the windows down and listen to nature. And sweetheart, I won't even allow you to bring a notebook and a pen along, so you can't make a single list."

She laughed.

"Sometimes you gotta force a change. Other times the change happens naturally."

"The forced change applies to me, doesn't it?"

"Nope. It's a mix of both for you." She stood and stretched. "My arms are sore from the shooting range. I'm gonna soak in the tub before I hit the hay. But first I probably better track Tobin down and tell him we'll be gone a few days. Do you know where he is?"

That's when Jade remembered she'd left him hiding out in the sitting room after their hot and heavy make-out session he promised they'd finish.

"His truck is parked out front," GG said.

"I think he went to bed after he came home."

"It'll have to wait until morning then." GG pulled her in for a hug. "Looking forward to sing-alongs with my road trip partner."

"Me too."

"See you bright and early in the morning." She shuffled down the hallway.

As soon as the door to GG's bedroom closed, Tobin exited the sitting room.

"I'm sorry—"

"No worries. If I needed to escape, I could've crawled through the window." He smirked. "Seems to be a theme with you."

Jade twisted her ponytail around. "You'll have two days alone here to remind yourself that I'm not worth the trouble."

The next thing she knew, Tobin loomed over her and his mouth crashed down on hers.

Sweet heaven could this man kiss.

When he finally stopped tormenting her with his skilled lips and the steady pressure of his body against hers, she was light-headed. Her panties were soaked again.

"You're more than worth the trouble, Jade." His callused fingertips skimmed her cheek. "I'll miss you. But I know you and Miz G will have a great time. You both deserve a break. We'll talk when you get back."

❧

Jade's absence for two days left Tobin in a sour mood.

When she'd finally gotten back last night, he'd barely rated a kiss before she'd gone to bed.

Tobin's chores didn't take all that long, so despite his crappy mood, he stuck with his plan to drive to the ranch he'd grown up on, outside of Saratoga.

With part of their acreage made up of forested sections, they'd leased rights for guided hunting groups on their land. Strange to think that's how he'd ended up at the Split Rock originally; his dad had broken his foot and had volunteered Tobin in his place as a guide. Since the hunting party had filled all their tags within the first five hours, he'd expected it to be a one-shot deal. Then Renner invited him back to the Split Rock to celebrate a successful venture. They'd started talking and before the end of the night Renner had offered him a job, including a place to live.

Tobin hadn't asked why the Split Rock started using another location for their guided hunts, but his dad had bugged him about it plenty the first two years.

The scenery whizzed past without him really seeing it, and time dragged as it always did. Almost two hours had passed when he pulled up to the front of the house. Four dogs raced from beneath the shade of the porch to greet him.

The screen door squeaked and his dad and oldest brother Driscoll wandered out.

"Well, well, look what the dogs got treed," his brother joked.

"Yeah, treed all right. They might do some serious damage to me with all these wagging tails," Tobin said dryly.

"Surprised to see you," his dad said.

Tobin shrugged. "I had the afternoon off so I thought I'd see what's up around here. Plus I wanted to get my twenty gauge."

"Whatcha gonna do with the twenty?"

"Just take it to skeet shoot."

"I heard they had a new range in Rawlins," Driscoll said. "Open, so's anyone can come in and shoot."

"Better that than payin' club fees, I reckon," his dad said.

Tobin scaled the steps. "Where's Streeter?"

"Baby is sick again. I swear that kid gets the sniffles and he runs her to the doctor."

"Gotta be hard, not knowing what's serious and what's not. I expect the older she gets the better handle he'll have on it."

"Meantime, I'm doin' his work as well as my own," Driscoll complained.

Tobin stared at his oldest brother. They looked nothing alike. Driscoll had been an early adopter of the mountain man look—he'd had a full beard for as long as Tobin could remember. He'd gotten decidedly more barrel shaped over the years too.

"I gotta git. See ya, Dad." Driscoll nodded at him. "Tobin."

"Later."

Driscoll whistled and two of the dogs jumped in the cab of the pickup. The other two dogs chased the pickup down the driveway.

"C'mon in. I'll grab that shotgun and you can tell me why you're really here."

Tobin followed his dad inside and waited while he retrieved the gun.

"Here it is." His dad lowered into a chair and set a bulky item in an old blanket on the kitchen table. "What's goin' on?"

"It'll sound pretty random, I'm sure. This buddy of mine . . . his family isn't bein' up front about why they've suddenly decided to move his grandma into an assisted living place. She seems okay to take care of herself; there's been no forgetful-type stuff. That reminded me of Grandma Alma. One day she seemed fine, the next you were saying she needed to be looked after. As I kid I didn't understand. Now I wondered if you hadn't told me the whole story. Maybe she had cancer or something."

"Is that what this buddy of yours thinks? His grandma has a disease that his family ain't telling him about?"

"Yeah. Like I said, it got me to thinking."

"That was a long time ago with your grandma. It was one of the few times your mother and I fought, god rest her soul."

That surprised him. "You fought about that?"

"Yep. The guy who ended up buying her place gave her a damn fine offer. She said she wasn't ready to be put out to pasture. But she didn't realize an offer like that wouldn't come along again. So I went ahead and accepted it on her behalf."

"When she told you she didn't want to move?" he said sharply.

His dad squirmed in his seat. "Ma was a great wife and homemaker but she didn't have a head for business. She couldn't see beyond next week's ladies' aid meeting or the spring seed catalogs. I paid all her bills, so she wasn't aware of the spike in propane costs, insurance, taxes and the increases in the cost of living."

*So it was easier to lock her away and let her fucking die than explain that to her?*

"I made the decision for her, like I'd been making most of them for her after my dad passed on. Your mom said my duty to her wasn't an inconvenience. She even went behind my back and asked your grandma if she wanted to live with us. Course, my mom refused. Said she pre- ferred bein' a burden to strangers who were getting paid a pretty penny to care for her than to the family who didn't see her worth. It was ugly. I still say she willed herself to die to spite me."

It had played out exactly as he'd seen it as a kid; his dad had sold her home and shoved her someplace where he wouldn't have to deal with her. "That's not something I'll tell my buddy because that's his night- mare scenario."

"It wasn't the easiest decision to make," his dad retorted.

As much as Tobin wanted to ask what his dad had done with the money from the sale of Grandma's place, he already knew. Most of it went to pay for her nursing home care. And the next year he got a brand- new tractor.

Tobin stood and grabbed the gun. "Yeah, well, I'm sure it won't be an easy decision for us to make either, when the time comes."

That startled his dad, as if it just occurred to him that he'd be beholden to his sons' decisions the way his mother had been beholden to his.

⇜

After Tobin left the Hale ranch, he'd driven over to Streeter's. His dad and brother's attitude toward Streeter concerned him as much as their barbs that Olivia was constantly sick. Streeter's truck wasn't there and no one came to the door. Tobin made a mental note to call him before he left for New Mexico next week.

*Do you really see yourself getting in your truck and driving away from everything familiar just to prove a point that you can?*

His doubts had been getting stronger the past two weeks. Everything from questioning his cognitive ability in an industrial setting to whether he'd saved enough money to live on if he didn't nail the interview and had to go to plan B.

So maybe that was a sign to postpone the interview another week or two. It'd give him two more weeks' worth of wages as a financial cushion. Or a better option was to suggest a Skype interview. That made the most sense, especially if they knew he was still dealing with a family crisis. Besides, what type of company in this day and age expected a potential employee to travel for a job interview?

*A family-owned company like HTL expects it. It was spelled out in the pre-interview process that a face-to-face meeting is mandatory. You signed the paperwork agreeing to their interview parameters.*

His cell phone chirped and he picked it up to look at the caller ID. Not a number he recognized but he answered anyway. "This is Tobin Hale."

"Hello, Mr. Hale. This is Richard Leckband. I'm the employment relations coordinator at HTL in Albuquerque."

Speak of the devil.

Tobin exchanged banal pleasantries about making his acquaintance. The tightness in his shoulders after dealing with his father and now this, multiplied by a factor of ten. Technically he was supposed to be in the HTL offices in less than a week. Chances were good this guy called to confirm appointments and didn't have the authority to authorize an extension.

But it wouldn't hurt to ask . . . would it?

Before Tobin could jump in, the guy said, "The reason for my call, Mr. Hale, is regarding your interview next week. I'm letting you know that interview has been cancelled."

Not what he'd been expecting. "Cancelled? Why?"

"The position you were interviewing for has been filled."

"Excuse me?"

"The position you were interviewing for has been filled," the guy repeated in a monotone. "We hope this schedule change hasn't inconvenienced you."

*Inconvenienced you.* That's how this ended? After a two-and-a-half-month interview process? What would've happened if he'd turned his life even more upside down for a chance at this job?

*How was that even possible?*

He'd given notice to his current employer, for Christsake.

He'd turned down two other job prospects in Omaha and Kansas City.

Maybe it wasn't too late to reapply to those places.

But his heart wasn't in it.

*Because that's not where your heart is these days.*

"Mr. Hale?" the voice on the line prompted.

"Sorry. Just mentally rearranging my schedule since I'll no longer be driving twelve hours to New Mexico."

"We appreciate your interest in HTL. As always employment opportunities are listed on the website. Have a pleasant day."

It was one thing to turn down a job offer; it was another thing to get passed over.

He swung into the Hardee's drive-thru lane in Rawlins and ate in his truck, feeling more adrift than he had in a while. He should head to the Split Rock and talk to Renner about this latest development, but he really just wanted to take off his boots and chill for a bit.

When he pulled into Garnet's driveway, he didn't see her car, but Jade's vehicle was parked up front.

No beautiful strains of the violin greeted him when he entered the house. In the entryway he ditched his boots and socks. Then he peeled off his long-sleeved shirt.

He was so focused on grabbing a beer out of the fridge that he didn't notice Jade sitting at the kitchen table until he'd popped the top off and turned around. "Whoa. Sorry. I didn't see you there."

"That's because I'm hiding."

He swallowed a mouthful of beer. "Why?"

"I'm debating on whether champagne or a big slice of carrot cake would improve my mood."

"Have both." He shrugged. "I won't tell."

"And here's where I confess . . . I already *had* both. Now I have guilt on top of my crappy mood."

When Jade stood and erased the distance between them, Tobin almost swallowed his tongue. She wore boy shorts and a New York Yankees baseball jersey. She looked fucking adorable.

"What made your day so shitty that you're drinking alone?"

"I talked to my dad." She pulled the elastic band from her ponytail and shook out her hair, completely oblivious to him eyeing her with lust. Or maybe she was doing it on purpose. "Why are you drinking in the afternoon?"

"I got a call from the place in Albuquerque."

"What's in Albuquerque?"

Tobin realized they hadn't discussed his leaving—except Jade had briefly mentioned it the night he'd told her the reason he'd agreed to move in with Garnet. But that had been two weeks ago.

*Be honest; it hasn't been on your mind since before you kissed Jade when you figured out the attraction was mutual.*

"A job. I was supposed to interview there next week."

"Why is this the first I've heard of it?" she demanded.

"It's not. You questioned me about me leaving more than once the first few days you were here." He sipped his beer. "Did you forget?" He braced himself when he saw the flash of anger in her eyes because she had forgotten.

"It wasn't like *you've* brought it up since we've been together doing"— she gestured distractedly—"whatever this is."

Tobin lifted an eyebrow. Before he had a chance to respond, she snapped off another retort.

"So why are you telling me that they called you? Because you're leaving?"

"Nope. They called and cancelled the interview."

"Oh. Did they say why they cancelled?"

"They already filled the position. I assume the fact I asked for an extension on my final interview dissuaded them from hiring me."

She frowned. "Why did you ask for that?"

Tobin took a swig of his beer. "You know why."

"No, I don't."

"Fine, we'll play it that way. I asked for an extra week for a family emergency when Miz G asked me to move in. It's been three weeks and I've yet to see a moving van."

"That's because there aren't any coming."

He froze. "What?"

Jade went to jam her hands in her back pockets—something she did when she was nervous—and realized she didn't have pockets, so she fiddled with her hair, which was another show of nerves. "Did I ever tell you that my dad planned to pack GG's house up and ship her and her stuff off? No. That was all my grandma's paranoia."

"But you . . ." He closed his eyes and scrolled through those first few days, when any discussion between them turned into an argument. When he tossed out accusations . . . that she never confirmed.

But she hadn't denied them either.

Fuck. He drained his beer and turned around to set the empty bottle next to the sink, keeping his back to her, bracing his hands on the counter.

How had this gotten so fucked?

*Because you're a fucking idiot.*

"Tobin?"

"What?"

"Talk to me. Please."

"What do you want me to say? That I lost out on an opportunity that would've been great for me because I'm a sucker? That once again, when I thought I was doin' the right thing . . . it turned around and bit me in the ass?" He allowed a bitter laugh to escape. "Don't they always say nice guys finish last? When the fuck am I ever gonna learn that?"

"I'm sorry."

He grunted.

Her hand, soft and warm, glided up his back. "What can I do?"

"Nothin'." Tobin expected her to walk away. He didn't expect her to wrap her arms around his waist and press her cheek into the middle of his back. He closed his eyes and gave himself a moment to remember why he was so crazy about this woman.

This sweetness.

This affection.

This connection.

"I'm sorry," she said again. "I hate that you were caught up in this. I hate that I believed you had ulterior motives when it came to my grandma." Her arms tightened around him. "I really hate that you're feeling one of my very favorite things about you—the fact you are the real deal, a nice guy to the core—is somehow a flaw. It's not." She sniffled. "It's *so* not."

"Jade—"

"Let me finish. As badly as I feel that you missed a chance to put your advanced degree to better use than what you're doing now, I'm not sorry you're not leaving. Not at all."

His heart raced.

"If anyone should go, it should be me. Whatever purpose I was supposed to serve by being here . . . is done. I told my dad earlier today that Grandma is fine living on her own. She has friends. She's part of a community. She has everything she needs right here. You were right. GG doesn't need me or my dad messing that up for her. She doesn't need me for anything."

"I need you." He surprised her as much as himself when he said that out loud.

Jade didn't retreat. "You don't have to say that."

He tried to look over his shoulder at her. "Darlin', why would I say something I didn't mean?"

"Because you're a nice guy."

Tobin slowly turned around. He framed her beautiful face in his hands and bent down until they were eye to eye. "I'm not that fucking nice." Then his mouth crashed down on hers.

The kiss was hot and wet. Fierce. Full throttle from the first thrust of his tongue.

But Jade wasn't passive; she unleashed the tiger, proving her appetite for him was as voracious as his was for her, making the sexiest, neediest fucking moans he'd ever heard.

What little restraint he had snapped.

A kiss wasn't going to be enough. Not now. Not when she plastered her hot, curvy body to his so completely a piece of sheet music wouldn't have fit between them.

He palmed her ass and picked her up, loving how perfectly she fit against him, how easily he maneuvered her petite form, how willingly she gave everything over to him. Even in moments such as this, when his passion held a rougher edge, she trusted him.

Hunger, the likes of which he'd never known, clawed at him. His cock throbbed. His hips began to thrust and grind, searching for hers.

Without breaking the kiss, he pinned her against the first wall they'd stumbled into.

Jade arched into him hard, her arms entwined so tightly around his neck she practically choked him as she fisted her hands in his hair.

Fuck yeah. He wanted her primal passion. This raw mating.

His body bolstered hers, freeing his hands. No gentle caresses. No teasing touches. He shoved his hands under her shirt, searching for those sweet tits. He growled in her mouth when he cupped the soft swells and felt her rigid nipples stabbing into his palms.

She rocked up every time he squeezed the flesh.

Passion heated her skin, filling his lungs with her scent, making him wild. He wanted the taste of her coating his tongue as he thrust into her. One hand twisted in her hair as he used the other hand relentlessly to tug her stiff nipples or stroke her clit.

"Tobin," she said on a soft gasp when he broke the kiss to scrape his teeth down the side of her throat.

When he sucked on the hollow between her collarbone and her shoulder, she shuddered.

"You're so fucking sexy you make me crazy," he gritted out between openmouthed kisses. He lowered her body slightly, aligning the rigid length of his shaft with the notch between her legs.

By the second grinding thrust, he heard "yes, yes, yes" even through the whoosh of white noise in his ears.

Tobin blinked the sweat from his eyes as he flexed his pelvis, his mouth frantic to taste her. To feel her pulse thrumming against his lips in the same fast rhythm as his heart. To yank up her shirt and gorge on the smooth flesh of her chest, feeling her nipples pebble beneath his stroking tongue.

Every time his voice rumbled nonsensical words of need or he whispered words of worship across her damp skin, she trembled and moaned and writhed against him.

Fuck. He wanted—needed—her to come apart in his arms like this. Fully clothed, with nothing but his mouth on her skin and his voice in her ear.

"Jade," he rasped against her throat. "Spread your knees and press up against me."

She gasped when he started to move side to side.

Tobin fastened his mouth to hers, swallowing her groans when he randomly pinched her nipples, keeping her on edge as he alternated sides and the amount of pressure.

He kept kissing her in what had become the hottest kiss of his life. Their mouths open, their tongues searching, their breath shared in short damp bursts. Grinding his cock into her, creating friction exactly where she needed it.

Her body began to shake.

*That's it. Give it to me.*

When the orgasm hit, Tobin pressed her body so tightly against his that he felt the contractions of her pussy—through her clothes and his— as she came undone.

With his mouth on hers and that continual rocking motion, he didn't stand a chance of not following along right behind her.

"Fuck." His head fell back when he started to come, each jerk of his cock a hot burst of pleasure despite the pinching sensation in his balls. He had to slam his hand against the wall to keep himself upright.

Jade's teeth scraped up and down the cord in his neck as he rode out his climax.

He was so damn dizzy . . . and sticky. It'd been a long time since he'd dry humped his way into going off in his jeans, but fuck if it wasn't better than anything he'd had in years.

Their mouths met in a slow kiss, a sweet aftermath of tenderness that left him just as breathless as the driving passion that had ignited between them.

Jade spoke first. "What now?"

"Definitely want more of that." He nipped her bottom lip. "Next time with fewer clothes on."

She nuzzled his ear. "That's the best orgasm I've ever had with or without clothes."

Tobin groaned. "Jesus. Don't tell me shit like that."

"Why not?"

"Because I'll haul your sexy ass upstairs, we won't leave my bed for two days and Miz G will definitely get suspicious."

She giggled.

He loved that sound. He kissed her again and lowered her down until her feet touched the floor. "I've gotta change clothes."

"If you're going to shower I'll wash your back."

"Tempting offer. But I'll just take a whore's bath for now because I have to go back to the Split Rock."

Her eyes widened. "What did you say?"

Tobin laughed. "A whore's bath—same thing as a sponge bath."

"I don't want to know why it's called that." She placed her hands on his cheeks. "Are you going to the Split Rock because of losing the Albuquerque job?"

"Yeah. Renner's been great. I hate that I've been so damn wishy-washy. I gave my notice and a date I planned to be gone only to change it. Twice. Now I have to tell him the interview fell through and I'll still be around for a while."

Jade looked at him like he should define "a while" but he couldn't when he didn't have a clue what might happen next.

He pressed a kiss to her forehead. "I'll see you later."

⟡

Tobin hadn't actually intended on talking to Renner. He knew no one would be in the offices so he could brood alone.

He scrolled through the spreadsheet on his computer and counted up the places he'd applied to that he hadn't heard back from yet.

Six.

But he'd already known that since he'd been gifted—some days he considered it a curse—with a photographic memory. It wasn't something he talked about. People tended to treat him like a freak or expect him to prove it.

His buddy Ike strolled in a little after seven.

"Well, if it ain't my former pool-playin' partner and drinking buddy." Ike spun the chair around in front of the desk and straddled it. "I was out checking the bulls and I saw your truck so I thought I'd stop in." He cocked his head. "Why are you here? I thought you were headed to Albuquerque for an interview."

"It fell through. Today, as a matter of fact."

"Shit, man. That sucks. Have you applied other places?"

"A few."

"Where?"

"A lab in Fort Collins. Another one in Colorado Springs. A family operation in Taos and Salt Lake City. Two places in Wyoming: Casper and Powell."

"You leaning toward any in particular?"

"I was intent on Albuquerque." He shrugged. "Haven't heard from the others. What about you? You doin' much traveling for Jackson Stock Contracting 2.0?"

Ike laughed. "Not yet. Hugh is still getting settled in California. Mostly I think he and Harlow are playin' grab ass until she starts teaching classes, so I'm takin' it easy while I can. Sifting through old contracts and contacts, trying to sort through which ones would be better for me to approach and which ones I'll leave to Hugh."

"What's Riss doin'?"

"Bein' a pain in my rear. Calls me every damn day to update the schedule on when she won't be available because she's takin' cattle to market. Like I'm supposed to keep track of that shit?"

"Aren't you? How else will you know if you've got transport to a rodeo if she's booked the trailer to go to Sioux City to drop off cattle?"

Ike scowled. "I've kept everything in my head for years and didn't need to 'input data' into a computer program just so she can double-check it like a damn schoolteacher grading my homework."

Tobin shook his head. "Dude, don't be one of those guys, okay?"

"One of what guys?"

"One of the old-timers who refuse to change with the times because 'there ain't nothin' wrong with the way we been doin' it'. You're familiar with technology; you used it when you were brokering cattle."

"There's just something about Riss demanding that I conform to her way that rubs me the wrong way." Ike stood. "As soon as you're done with your paperwork meet me at the Buckeye. First round is on me."

❧

But it ended up being more than one round.

Tobin lost count after eight rounds.

He kicked Ike's butt at pool. Four games to one.

Then they switched to darts. Bastard evened the score there and beat him four games to one.

There weren't any more games to bet on at the Buckeye, so they had a drinking contest.

Bad idea.

Sherry, the bartender, called in a favor—and a sober driver to haul their drunken asses home.

## Chapter Twelve

❦

*J*ade was still up at eleven p.m. when two vehicles tore up the driveway.

One pickup was Tobin's.

She watched from the porch as two people hauled a body—a big body—out the passenger side.

Tobin half stumbled between a guy on his left side, and a woman on his right side.

Seeing Tobin's arm draped over the woman's shoulder . . . Jade had a seething moment of jealousy. She wanted to shove the woman aside and warn her to keep her hands off him.

She'd never been a violent person. Hadn't understood that feeling of possession, so this overwhelming need to yell, *Back off, he's mine!* threw her for a loop. Instead, she curled her hands into fists and dropped them by her sides.

The woman said, "Up you go. Left foot. Nope, your other left. Good. Now your right. Left. Right. Left. Just twenty-seven more to go, sweetheart."

Sweetheart?

"*Pissh* off, *Rissh*. Ain't that many steps."

They reached the top step and the woman said, "Where do you want him?"

LORELEI JAMES   134

Jade tipped her chin at the chaise. "At least if he gets sick out here I can hose him and the porch off."

"I ain't gonna get *shick.*"

"Okay, party hearty, sit down first, then slowly turn your body. Hey, can you make sure the head end is up higher?" the woman said to Jade. "He doesn't need to be in full recline."

"Sure." Jade slipped behind the chair and adjusted the pegs until they were almost upright.

"We're gonna let go now, Tobin. Don't roll or you will land right on your fool head, got it?"

"Got it. You're kinda mean, *Rissh.*" Tobin grinned. "I kinda like that about you."

Another spike of jealousy had Jade seeing red and scrutinizing the interplay between Tobin and the redheaded woman.

"I kinda like you too, Tobin, when you're not shitfaced."

"*Sho* you'll go out on a date with me?" Tobin slurred.

The woman's gaze caught Jade's and she rolled her eyes. "I am so going to love rubbing it in your face that you only asked me out when you were hammered, Hale." She stepped away from the chaise and offered her hand. "Hey. I'm Riss. A . . . friend of Tobin's."

"Jade Evans. Garnet's granddaughter."

Riss gave her the oddest smile. "Yes, we've heard all about the beautiful Jade this evening from Tobin. Haven't we, Eli?"

That's when Jade looked up into the face of the long-haired guy who'd shouldered most of the burden of dragging Tobin up the steps. Eli was tall—what was with all these enormous guys in the West?

"Yes, we have heard all about you, Jade. My man Tobin didn't exaggerate." He offered his hand. "Eli Whirling Cloud. Happy to make your acquaintance."

"I'm pleased to meet you also. Thank you for hauling Tobin this far."

"Eh. It was nothin'. He's been DD more often than all of us combined so I owed him. Man's entitled to tie one on once in a while." He grinned. "Though I don't envy him the headache in the mornin'."

Two short bursts of the horn sounded from the pickup and Jade jumped. "Someone's anxious to get going?"

Riss scowled. "That's Ike. Tobin's drinking partner and he can just sit and spin. Why that ornery fucker called me to pick his drunken ass up when he knows I'd just as soon see him—"

"*Shuch* a liar you are, *Rissh*," Tobin announced. "You know why he called you."

"Shut it, drunky," Riss snarled.

Eli sighed. "I'll go sit with Ike."

"I'll be right there," Riss said. After Eli left, she looked at Jade. "I hope you don't think this is weird, but I know how hard it is living someplace where you don't know anyone. So if you get bored and wanna grab a cup of coffee or something, give me a call. Here's my card." She pulled it out of the front pocket of her overalls. "Or if you lose it, ask drunky over there for my number."

After Jade's crappy day, this small offer of friendship meant more than she could express. She said, "Got another card?" When Riss handed her one, she wrote her number on the back. "Now we can keep drunky out of it entirely."

Riss's gaze winged between Jade and Tobin and she smirked. "Good luck with that." At the bottom of the steps she said, "Oh, heads up."

Jade had a split second to register the keys flying at her before she caught them one-handed, like a total ninja. She grinned at Riss and said, "Later."

After everyone had left and she and Tobin were alone, it felt awkward standing next to him as he sprawled on the chaise. Did she just cover him with a blanket and leave him? Did she stay out here and talk to him to try to sober him up?

"*Shorry* you had to *shee* me like *thish*."

"It doesn't sound like it's a frequent thing for you."

"It's not. I mean, I go to the Buckeye 'cause there ain't anything *elsh* to do in this town, but I don't over-imbibe."

"I've heard GG mention that place several times."

"I'll take you there *shometime*." He paused. "*Schratch* that. I *jusht* remembered. You and me—we're not doin' that *shtuff*. And I don't wanna *share* you. Or have *shomeone shteal* you away from me."

Totally sweet sentiment, even if it was the booze talking. "You really are drunk if you think anyone else would want me."

"I want you." Tobin blindly reached a hand out for her. "I want you like fuckin' crazy."

Jade perched on the edge of the chaise after she threaded her fingers through his. She studied his face. With his eyes closed, she noticed his dark eyelashes for the first time—usually she couldn't get past his entrancing eyes. His cheeks were flushed. A silly smirk kicked up the right side of his mouth. Before she thought it through, she leaned over for a closer look at the thin white scar above his upper lip.

"Why can I feel you *shtarin'* at me? Do I got *shomething* on my face?"

"I'm staring because other times when I look at you too long, you turn away." She disentangled their joined hands and ran her fingers down the side of his face.

He sighed and turned into her touch.

"I like looking at you. Everything you feel is right here on this handsome face." She swept her thumb between his eyebrows. "You get a few wrinkles here when you're annoyed. It was a look I knew well those first few days." She touched the corners of his eyes. "You have laugh lines here, which I've seen more and more." She trailed the back of her knuckles down the hollow of his cheek to the faint lines bracketing his mouth. "You have the greatest smile. It's infectious. When you aim that dimpled grin my way . . . I just want to bask in it for a few moments and then feel that smile against my own lips."

"My mouth is yours anytime you want it."

"That's a dangerous promise to make to a woman who's grown addicted to your kisses." Jade followed his scar with the tip of her finger. "What happened here?"

"A fishhook caught me. Bled like a bitch. Hurt like a bitch too. I forgot about it."

"I noticed it right away." She brushed her top lip over the mark. Once. Twice. "I think it's sexy." After softly pressing her lips to his, she eased back to find him watching her with a slumberous gaze.

"You're beautiful." When she opened her mouth to retort, he placed his fingers over her lips. "Not drunk talk, Jade. The truth."

She slid his hand to her cheek and kissed the inside of his wrist.

Tobin closed his eyes and sighed.

"You're about to crash, aren't you?"

"Yeah."

"Sorry I can't drag you up the stairs, cowboy, so you'll have to sleep out here tonight." She stood. "I'll get you a blanket."

"I'd rather you kept me warm."

"Another time. Boots on or off?"

"Off."

She picked up his right foot and pulled on his heel. She repeated the process for his left boot. Then she set both boots at the end of the chaise and went inside to grab a blanket.

When Jade returned a minute later, Tobin had crashed. The blanket didn't cover him entirely and she debated for a few moments about curling up next to him, using her body heat to keep him warm.

But she ended up going to bed alone.

&#x223D;

After the discussion with Tobin after he'd come home from the bar last night, Jade decided to take the bull by the horns tonight.

Geez. She hadn't been in Wyoming two weeks and she'd already reverted to Western colloquialisms.

As the day wore on, she worried maybe Tobin wouldn't return to GG's after work because she suspected he'd be . . . embarrassed about his state last night since that wasn't the norm for him. They'd exchanged cell numbers, but she'd never needed to contact him because they usually interacted in person.

And she planned to get very up close and personal with him tonight. She snapped a selfie and added the text:

I have a surprise for you—make sure you're home before
bedtime so we can break some rules ☺

She forced herself to leave her phone in her room for an hour before she checked it for messages. Tobin's response had come in not five minutes after she'd sent the original text.

No problem. As long as there's no booze involved. But you
probably already knew that . . .

She grinned like an idiot. His sense of humor was just another thing she liked about him.

Tobin didn't show up at GG's until almost ten o'clock. He looked tired but he still made time to chat with her grandmother—which just proved his genuine affection for her.

Jade caught him in the upstairs hallway before he took a shower.

He stopped and eyed her warily. "Hey."

"Hey is for horses," she quipped. "I'm disappointed you didn't say, 'Hello, darlin'' and sneak a kiss."

He smiled. "I've been workin' outside most of the day, so I probably smell pretty ripe. But I'll give you a hello kiss and then some after I knock the dirt off."

They'd gotten used to speaking in whispers when they weren't alone in the house, even when GG probably couldn't hear them from the bottom floor. But there was something more intimate and urgent when they were forced to use that quieter, more intense tone with each other. "I don't care. I need a kiss from you now, Tobin, so I know we're okay."

His gorgeous eyes softened when he gave her a sweet smile. He reached out to smooth his hand down her hair. "We're fine. I'm the dumb-ass for crawling into a bottle last night."

Circling her fingers around his thick wrist, she brought his palm to her mouth for a kiss. "I wish you would've told me you planned to get your drink on."

Tobin feathered his thumb across her bottom lip; his hungry eyes followed the movement. "You would've tried to talk me outta tying one on?"

"No. I would've been your DD, not Riss."

He smirked. "Darlin', that sounds a little like jealousy."

"No, it is jealousy, *a lot* of jealousy." She nipped the fleshy skin at the base of his thumb. "But since you are here with me, burning me alive with that hot, sexy stare, I'll let it slide. Just this once."

Then Tobin was nose to nose with her, his hands curled around her face. "Do you have any idea how fucking hot it makes me that you got jealous over Riss driving me home?"

"You asked her out on a date right in front of me, cowboy. You do remember that, don't you?"

"Vaguely."

"Were you trying to make me jealous?"

Confusion caused him to squint. "I'm crazy about you, Jade. And I hate that I can't take you out and let my friends see just how crazy I am about you."

That was sweet. She didn't think he'd appreciate that sentiment right now, so she waited for him to continue.

"Maybe I had it in my head that if Miz G was hanging around last night when I got home, that if she heard me asking Riss out she wouldn't be suspicious about you and me breakin' the rules every chance we get."

"Seriously? You're going with *that* explanation?"

"No. I'm goin' with the 'I was drunk and didn't know what the hell I was sayin'' explanation." He pressed his lips to hers and held them there for several long moments. "I apologize if that hurt you."

Jade slid her hands across his chest. "It hurt worse to know that you were upset and angry and I couldn't be there for you the way I wanted."

"You wouldn't have liked me. I was a moody dick."

"Will you become a moody dick if I ask you to talk to me about it tonight?"

"No." He brushed his lips over hers. "I'm calmer."

"Good. Meet me on the porch in half an hour."

After he scrambled her brain with a seductive kiss, he shooed her away.

GG seemed distracted and puttered around in the kitchen for nearly forty-five minutes after Jade came downstairs.

*It's almost as if she knows you and Tobin plan to sneak off for alone time.*

Jade chalked that up to paranoia. If GG suspected her grand-daughter and her protector had moved beyond adversaries to more than friends, she'd bring it up. Loudly.

So an hour and fifteen minutes had passed by the time Tobin strolled out to meet her. He smelled divine—a manly kind of clean. He'd swapped out his cowboy duds for a T-shirt, athletic pants and running shoes. His hair had almost dried and she knew he felt naked without a cowboy hat or a ball cap, but she loved how his hair retained some curl when it wasn't smashed beneath a hat. His face and neck were smooth. She reached up to caress his cheek. "I like that you shaved for me."

"One of these days I'm gonna keep the stubble."

"Why?"

"So I can leave beard burn on the inside of your thighs." His wicked gaze hooked hers and he offered her an equally wicked grin.

She imagined his hands curled around her knees as he pushed her legs wide enough to accommodate his massive shoulders. He'd keep his eyes on hers as he teased her with the soft brush of his hair and the rough scrape of his beard as his mouth journeyed higher.

"Don't fucking look at me like that, woman, or I will plunk your ass on this table right now and drop to my knees."

The deep rasp in his voice could be mistaken for a growl.

No. Knowing Tobin, it *was* a growl.

The man was so blatantly sexual she wondered how she'd ever keep up with his needs when they became lovers.

Jade rose to the balls of her feet and kissed his Adam's apple. "You, Mr. Sexy Talk, are distracting me." She grabbed the folded quilt she'd stashed on the chair.

"What's that for?"

"To spread out in the grass so we can talk and stargaze."

Tobin loomed over her and made that rumbling noise again. "By stargaze, please tell me you mean us rolling around on that blanket naked as I make you come so hard that you see stars."

Jade blinked at him and had to bite her tongue against blurting out that it was the best idea she'd ever heard. Instead she stepped back and hugged the quilt tighter. "While I can see that happening one of these nights, it's not tonight, okay? I really think we need to talk."

He curled one hand around her hip and pressed his knuckle under her chin, tipping her head back to gaze into her eyes. "Why is it so important to you that we talk?"

"It just is."

He studied her for a few more moments before he kissed her. "Okay.

We'll talk. But darlin', we are gonna mess around too. If that's not what you want, say so now."

She said, "I want that," quickly enough that Tobin laughed.

"Good." He tucked the blanket under one arm and her under the other. "Lead on."

Jade had found a flat spot away from the compost pile and the gardens where the ground felt more springy than rocky.

Tobin helped her spread out the quilt.

She kicked off her flip-flops and scooted to the middle after Tobin had settled in. The man took up a lot of space.

He clamped a hand on her butt and nudged her closer until her head rested in the indent between the ball of his shoulder and his chest.

They'd never lain down together anywhere, so the fact they just fit this way gave her a funny tickle in her chest.

"This was a great idea," he said and kissed the top of her head. "I like havin' you next to me."

"I like being here with you. Like this."

"It'd be better if we were naked."

"Then we'd get bug bites in weird places."

"Sounds like a fair trade-off to me."

Tobin's left hand was behind his head, and he trailed the fingers on his right hand up and down her back, from her shoulder to the spot where her thigh curved into her butt cheek.

"Not much in the way of moonglow," she said after a bit.

"That makes it harder to stargaze." He pressed his lips to her forehead. "What did you want to talk about?"

Her pulse spiked. She tried to swallow discreetly but of course he noticed.

His hand stilled. "Why are you nervous?"

"Because I don't know how to do this."

"What?"

"Pry into your life. Ask about the job you lost out on yesterday. Ask if you blame me, because if it hadn't been for you moving in with GG, you'd be gone."

"The job wasn't a done deal, Jade. It was an in-person interview."

"But anyone who meets you in person, Tobin, will scramble to hire you."

He grunted. "They didn't give me a chance. Granted, I asked for an additional week before I went down there for the interview. That might've tripped their warning bells. And yeah, I was extremely pissed off and surly about it yesterday."

"Did you blame me?" Jade drew small circles on his chest. "Or at the very least GG because she begged you to stay with her?"

"My first reaction was to get pissed off about it, so there was some blame."

"So there's no chance for that job now?"

"Nope."

"Are there others across the country that you need to get to?"

"I've got other irons in the fire. It's a whole lot of wait and see. Why?"

His eyes were assessing her as she started to respond. "If you have other job opportunities, take them."

"You tryin' to get rid of me?"

"I'm trying to tell you I'd understand if you left, Tobin."

Tobin disentangled himself from her and sat up. "That's just really fucking awesome, Jade."

She rolled to her knees, annoyed that he had his back to her. "I'm trying to do the right thing here, Tobin, after you were essentially wronged by my family. Why are you mad? Because I cost you the job opportunity you really wanted?"

"No, you basically telling me to get the hell out of Miz G's house is pissing me off."

"I didn't say that!"

"Then what are you saying?"

"That I don't want to be responsible for any more of your unhappiness."

Tobin shifted his body so he could look at her. "Whatever gave you the idea that I'm unhappy?"

"You got drunk last night because you were unhappy about losing the job."

"Wrong. You want to know why I got drunk last night? Because I was actually really fucking relieved they called off the interview."

"What?"

"I should've been mad at Miz G, mad at Renner, mad at you. All I've wanted for the last two months was to get the hell out of Muddy Gap. I felt like I'd lost time and opportunity and even a little of myself by not putting myself and my untapped skills out there in the real world. Then you showed up."

Her chest tightened.

"It pissed me off. I had plans, dammit. I knew in my gut if I nutted up and left here that I'd find what I was really looking for."

"Which is what?"

"I thought it was a different career. Or a new perspective." Tobin reached over and twisted a section of her hair around his fingers. "It turns out that it wasn't something I was searching for. It was someone."

"Tobin."

"It's you."

"Me . . . specifically?"

He frowned. "Are you tryin' to tick me off by sayin' that?"

"No. I just . . . This is so far out of the realm of my experience, Tobin. I've never been the type of woman who hears these things from a guy. It gives me a little tickle in my belly, but the kind I can't be sure is excitement or—"

"Disbelief," he finished.

"Exactly. And please don't pretend if the situations were reversed you wouldn't have the same concerns." She paused. "Or maybe women tell you all the time that you were what they were searching for."

Tobin snorted. "Hasn't happened yet."

Jade pushed him flat on his back and straddled his hips. "Are you sure?"

Even in the dark she saw hope flare in his eyes.

"I'm shy, Tobin. I'm happiest not being the center of attention. But that also means I don't take chances when I should. I fear making a miscalculation because my only experience in what *not* to do in a relationship is what I've seen on TV or in movies. You know, where the weird girl blurts out, 'I love you and want to have your babies' after the first time she has sex with a guy? And then he never calls her back?"

"You're worried about putting yourself out there with me?"

"Of course."

"You shouldn't be, Jade. Holding back isn't gonna get either of us what we want, and darlin', I'm not just talkin' about sex."

"I know that. I've been searching too. I didn't know for what, either. Like you, I thought if I worked hard enough maybe the answer would magically appear. But instead . . ." Her heart beat faster and she forced her breathing to slow down before she continued. "Look. I haven't been completely honest with you about something. But it's not like I was hiding it as much as I just came to terms with it myself. I mean, even when I think about telling you this, I want to add little side notes and editorialize."

"Just rip that bandage off, sweetheart. Getting it over with is the best way to do it."

She fiddled with the neck on his T-shirt. "You've heard me mention I had the flu a few months ago? And that was the only time I quit working? Well, that's not true. Calling it 'the flu' was a lie I told myself so I wouldn't have to deal with the fact that I had a mini-breakdown at age twenty-four. It's a lie I told other people so they wouldn't judge me."

"What happened?"

"My roommate's boyfriend moved in, forcing me to live with my parents. I worked three jobs. I had no time for friends. No time for a relationship. Suddenly everything in my life seemed pointless. I was lonely and exhausted and scared my life would never get any better." She inhaled. "I'd fought back against those feelings for about a year until I couldn't fight it any longer. One day I started crying and couldn't stop. I crawled in bed and had to ride it out. It took a week. Then because I hadn't eaten and felt nauseous I convinced myself I'd just had the flu. And I let my life go back to exactly the same way it was before."

He ran his hand up and down her arm in a sweetly soothing manner.

"I know you've picked up on the fact I'm high-strung. I've suffered from anxiety since my mid-teens. I cope with it by doing something productive until it levels out."

His eyes turned thoughtful. "Like rearranging cookbooks?"

She smiled and started running her hand through his hair. "Yes. Or practicing my violin. Or going for a run. Or cleaning. It's not an obsessive-compulsion thing. Just more . . . constant busyness. It's never gotten to the point where it's disrupted my life and I need medication. But it is an off-putting trait."

"What dumb-ass told you that?"

That jarred her. "What?"

"You are who you are. It's part of what makes you . . . you. You're smart enough to know that if your anxiety gets out of hand you get help." Tobin hugged her to his chest. "You really think I'd be judgmental after I told you about Danica committing suicide and none of us having the first fucking clue why she'd do something like that?"

"I didn't think you'd judge me, Tobin, I was trying to explain."

He kissed the top of her head. "Sorry. Keep goin'."

"The first few days here I was on edge. I chalked it up to the change from my constant busyness to having no agenda. But then there was you. Larger than life, suspicious, a little mean, sexy as sin and sometimes so thoughtful I just . . . melted. Little by little I've started to loosen up and discover new things about myself that I wouldn't have known if I hadn't been forced to slow down. You said you were searching for something and you figured out it's me. I'm a few steps behind you. I've been searching for something and now I know that part of it is this place."

Tobin was quiet for several long moments. Then he said, "I can work with that."

Jade tucked her body closer.

Then she shifted her legs along his.

She slipped her arm down across his waist.

The next time she moved, Tobin clamped his hand on her ass and said, "Be still."

"But don't you want to—"

"Hush. Lord knows I love that my woman has a sexy little body and a sassy mouth, but sometimes you just gotta still both of 'em. So just lie here with me and listen."

"To what?" she said petulantly.

"To everything but the sound of your own thoughts and voice, sweetheart. Practice conscious stillness. Can you give it a shot?"

"I'll try."

That's when she noticed the quiet night . . . wasn't really quiet. Bugs contributed a loud hum and buzz that ebbed and flowed. Wind blowing through the tall grass made a whistling rattle. Occasionally the soft *flap flap* of wings whispered above her. In the distance an animal chittered and another answered.

Jade had no sense of time but she was deeply rooted in a sense of place.

Wanting to cement the connection to this moment and to Tobin, she shifted slightly and heard his soft breathing . . . turn into a loud snore.

She waited and heard it again.

Apparently practicing conscious stillness meant something entirely different to him.

So much for her seduction plans.

⁓⁓⁓

## Chapter Thirteen

*A*fter Tobin spent the day dealing with Renner's crappy mood and the resort guests from hell, all he wanted was half an hour of solitude and an icy cold beer.

And Jade straddling his lap, doing that thing where she ran her fingers through his hair over and over. Fuck. He loved that. He hadn't had nearly enough of that last night before he'd fallen asleep.

So when he pulled up and saw the rugs from the upstairs hallway strung up on the clothesline, and Jade whacking the crap out of them with a broom, he knew his evening was about to take a different turn.

Miz G sat on the porch, alternately watching her granddaughter and working on a crossword puzzle. "Tobin, what's a four-letter word for big?"

"Huge?"

"That'll work." She refocused on her paper.

"What's gotten into Jade?"

"Well obviously she's annoyed about something."

"Got any idea what's bugging her?"

"She's pretty high-strung. Could be anything."

Tobin's eyes narrowed on Miz G. "Did you ask her?"

"Nope. And I suggest you keep away unless you've got a hankering to become a piñata."

Torn, he stood there. He didn't want to raise Miz G's suspicions that he and Jade had any kind of relationship, because he knew if he went to her and saw her distressed, he'd wrap her in his arms and try to calm her down.

Miz G's phone buzzed on the table. She scooped it and her paper up. "Sorry, gotta go. My show's on. Then I'm takin' a bath. There's food in the fridge."

As soon as the screen door slammed, Tobin started toward Jade. By the time he reached her, she'd set the broom down.

"Is it safe to come over here?"

"Yes . . . unless you lie like a rug and need a good beating."

He smiled. "I'm a shitty liar."

"Then you're in the clear."

Tobin shot a look over his shoulder before he took Jade's hand and pulled her on the other side of the clothesline behind the largest rug. He cupped her face in his hands, tilted her head back and kissed her.

When she tried to twine herself around him, he stopped. "Be still."

"But I want to touch you."

"I want that too. But not yet. Right now I want you to close your eyes, put your hands by your sides and let me kiss you. However I like, for as long as I want."

"Okay."

But when his lips slid over hers, she leaned into him to chase his mouth.

"Jade. I'm serious. The only thing I want you to think about is this."

"Why?"

"Kissing you is a singular pleasure."

"It's the *only* pleasure because we're not having sex."

Didn't that sound testy?

Instead of ignoring it like he wanted, he met her gaze. "Wrong. Kissing you is a singular pleasure because everything in the fucking world disappears for me when we're mouth to mouth. Last night you told me about your struggle with anxiety. Let's try dealing with it this way and see what happens."

Her irises were nearly black as her gaze darted between his eyes. "This is not your issue, Tobin. It's mine. I need to learn how to deal with it on my own."

"No, darlin', you don't." He sidled closer to her. "We are together and that makes you mine. I take care of what's mine. From the smallest things to the biggest. Now close your eyes and pucker up, baby, 'cause I am gonna rock your world."

That brought the first smile he'd seen from her.

Tobin pulled out all the stops, using every seductive trick he'd learned, seen or wanted to try. He nibbled, licked, teased. Then he switched it up, interspersing bursts of tongue-tangling passion with lingering smooches.

And when she became perfectly pliant, he stopped.

She peered at him from beneath lowered lashes. "Now what?"

"Do you trust me?"

"Yes."

Made him feel ten feet tall when she answered that with no hesitation. "Did you go for a run today?"

She shook her head.

"Then that's next. Get your gear on."

"Seriously?"

"Yep." Tobin grinned. "Go on. Get movin' and get those endorphins riled up."

That defiant chin came up. "And if I don't?"

"You could go back to beating the rugs."

"I'm done. They're bug-free now."

"What happened today that brought about this beatdown?"

"I saw a spider crawl under the rug in my room."

He crossed his arms over his chest. "Really."

"I really hate spiders."

"So why are the rugs from the hallway and bathroom out here too?"

"Because I had to move them to vacuum. Then I got totally creeped out there were more spiders hiding under all the rugs so I decided to air them out."

Tobin eyed the cans of Lysol and Febreze lying on the ground next to a large pair of tongs and an industrial-looking rubber apron. Maybe this *was* only about spiders. "How'd you get the rugs outside?"

She pointed. "I tossed them out the bathroom window and dragged them over here."

"With the tongs."

"I wasn't going to *carry* them out and take a chance one of those sneaky hairy buggers would make a break for it."

They'd gotten offtrack. "If you're done, then quit stalling and get ready."

"Why are you making me run?"

"Because your grandma is home."

She frowned. "That matters . . . why?"

He crushed a handful of her hair in his fist and clamped a hand on her ass. "Because if we were alone I'd fuck you until your body was covered in sweat, your legs went weak and you couldn't breathe. Then you'd forget all about the spiders."

"Oh."

"Running or sex. Same results, different actions. I prefer one action over the other but it ain't like we have a choice tonight."

"True." She backed away from him. "But you'd probably fall asleep anyway."

He stared at her. "Was that a shot at me for last night?"

"Do you think?"

Smart-ass. "I had a long damn day plus I'd woken up with a hangover that morning."

"You were snoring."

"That just means bein' with you is the most natural thing in the world and I relaxed enough to let my guard down."

She laughed. "Right. I wanted to get your *pants* down."

Fucking hell. Could his untimely nap have factored into her anxiety today? "Jade—"

"No time to talk, cowboy. I've gotta work up a hard, hot sweat. Too bad you can't watch and learn."

Her sassy little ass twitched at him as she walked away.

Now she'd done it.

It was on.

Ten minutes later, Jade stepped outside in a pair of running shorts and a matching spandex tank top. She jogged to the end of the driveway and turned left.

*Watch and learn, my ass.*

Since he had access to a fitness facility at the Split Rock, he had a duffel bag of workout clothes in his truck. He told Miz G he forgot something at work and he had to run back there. He hopped in his truck and took a right at the end of the driveway. He parked in the pullout and changed into his running gear.

He paced on the gravel road for another ten minutes before setting the fitness program on his watch and heading out.

Tobin caught up to her about a mile and a half into the run. He didn't smile, or wave, or stop to chat; he just blew past her as if she'd been standing still.

Of course Miss Competitive kicked up her pace to try to match his.

*Good luck with that.*

But he did slow down slightly, allowing her to almost catch him.

*Almost.*

Then he put on a burst of speed, leaving her in the dust.

When he hit the two-mile mark, he slowed and ran backward, watching her huff and puff as she tried to keep up. This time he did let her reach him. "Nice evening, isn't it?"

She was so winded she just grunted.

And he could tell it annoyed her that he didn't seem out of breath at all.

"How far do you usually run?" he asked.

She held up four fingers.

"You're at the halfway point."

Jade braced her hands on her knees, leaning over to catch her breath. "How. Far. Do. You. Run."

"Six miles, sometimes seven, depending."

She panted. "Show. Off."

"The elevation here is killer," Tobin offered. "That could be what's slowing you down."

Jade lifted her head. "Why did you follow me?"

"Your challenge of *watch and learn* wasn't an invitation?"

"You suck," she wheezed. "You're not even breathing hard."

"My job at the ranch is physically demanding so I'm in better shape than I look."

"No lie there." Jade gave him a once-over and her gaze lingered on his chest. "But that isn't an answer as to why you followed me."

"I thought we could race back. The winner gets the choice of oral sex or regular sex. You know, to make up for me falling asleep last night."

"I'm not racing you, Tobin."

The panic in her eyes made him want to kick his own ass. "Darlin'. I was joking." He skated his hand up her bare arm, over her shoulder and cupped her neck in his palm. He stroked his thumb along the edge of her jawline.

Jade closed her eyes for a moment and leaned into his touch. "Sorry. I just find this a little weird."

"What?"

"You demanding that I go for a run and then following me. If we're trying to keep this relationship under wraps for a little longer, us both being gone and then us both showing up at GG's in exercise clothes will raise her suspicions."

"Jade. Give me some credit," he chided gently. "Your grandma knew you went for a run, right?"

She nodded.

"About fifteen minutes after you left, I told her I had to go back to work. I drove to the pullout a quarter of a mile up the road, changed clothes and ran to catch you." He grinned. "Smart, huh?"

"Very. But I hate we're going to such extremes to see each other when we're living in the same house. Our rooms are next door to each other. We could be sneaking into each other's beds every night and GG wouldn't know."

"Jesus, Jade. Are you trying to make my dick hard?"

She smirked. "That's my right—my job—as your girlfriend."

His eyes searched hers. "Is that how you see yourself?"

"Well, we're not friends. We're not lovers—yet. The word 'companion' makes me think of a dog. The word 'partner' sounds like a business relationship. So what other word is there?"

*MINE*, roared into his head.

Yeah, that declaration would likely freak her out.

"I can admit I liked it when you called me your woman. So if you don't like the word 'girlfriend,' then you could, ah, call me that if you want." She stepped back and tried to shove her hands in her back pockets, forgetting that she didn't have any.

That nervous mannerism got to him, because she shouldn't be uncertain of this. He sure as fuck wasn't.

*Then why don't you nut up and tell Miz G you're falling for her granddaughter?*

"My woman," he said, almost to himself. His gaze roamed over her face, this beautiful, sweet, smart, determined woman who'd brought him such happiness in a few short weeks. Every time he looked at her, he experienced a feeling damn close to euphoria.

And why should he have to hide that from the world? From the people in his life who mattered to him? Tobin wanted everyone to know that Jade was his. His to touch, his to hold, his to tease, his to cherish, his to belong to. His to make long-term life plans with. Because that's where this was headed.

"What is going through that head of yours, cowboy?"

"Tryin' to figure out the best way to tell your grandma that you're my woman."

She smiled. "With GG timing is everything."

"True. This might be a little tricky. We have been sneaking around since day one, darlin'. I don't want her to feel like an 'old fool' because that'll set her on a tear. I don't want her to think I've disrespected her by living in her house and takin' advantage of you."

A beat passed and Jade got right in his face. "That's why you haven't invited me into your bed or tried to sneak into mine, isn't it? You are mindful of how GG would react if she caught us rolling around in the sheets naked."

He blushed. Fuck. Had he ever blushed this hard in his life?

"Tobin Hale. I adore you for so many reasons." She trapped his face between her palms. "But your respect for my grandma is at the top of the list."

"Jade—"

"You will listen to me heap praise on you for a few minutes and then you can go back to that 'aw, shucks, it wasn't nothin' gentleman-cowboy mindset."

His heart kicked hard.

"I've never met a man like you. You are helpful, thoughtful, mindful, respectful and wonderful—not just to GG but to me. You don't pander, you don't assume, your pride isn't enormous or easily bruised. You are stubborn, but you're also sweet. You're patient . . . until you're not."

He smiled because she had taken that exactly as he'd intended.

"I could tell you that you're smart—but that's redundant. I could mention that you're a hard worker—but that's also a given. I could tell you that you've transcended the term 'nice guy'—but you're too humble to take the compliment. I could tell you that everything about you—your big muscled body, your handsome face, your intense eyes, your sexy mouth, your ropy forearms that I'm obsessed with, your broad shoulders—just does it for me in a bad, bad, bad way, but I'd rather show you."

Tobin couldn't think, he couldn't speak, he couldn't fucking breathe when she looked at him and let him see the truth of everything she'd said, right there in her eyes.

Jade pulled his face closer, using her mouth with erotic intent. When she finally allowed their lips to part, she whispered, "And then there's that." She nuzzled the hollow below his ear. "You've maintained tight control over the passion that's such an innate part of you." The hot, openmouthed kiss she dragged down his throat caused his entire body to tremble. "No more containment, Tobin."

"How did you know?"

"Because like recognizes like."

He groaned.

"So when we become lovers, no holding back."

"For either of us." Tobin tilted her chin up. "Which means the first time we get naked and sweaty together can't happen here."

"Agreed. Let's check into a seedy motel."

"Christ. I'm about to throw you over my shoulder and sprint to my truck. We can be in Rawlins in half an hour."

"I want a whole night with you, Tobin. No interruptions. Just us—"

"And a case of fucking condoms."

She laughed. "I'll leave you to set it up."

"How's tomorrow night?"

"I'm officially meeting the Mud Lilies tomorrow sometime." She folded her arms together in front of her. "But that shouldn't take all day and night."

The sun had dropped and so had the temperature. Tobin rubbed his hands up and down her arms. "Cold?"

"A little."

"You want my shirt?"

"You'd be bare-chested?" The gleam in her eyes was unmistakable. Then she blinked. "I couldn't control myself if you were half-naked, so . . . better not."

"Let's head back." Tobin threaded their fingers together and they strolled down the dirt road, hand in hand. "Wanna hear something corny?"

"Sure."

"This is why I sent you on a run."

"So you could chase after me?" she teased.

"So we could hang out together away from the house. I like talking to you. I want to know everything about you."

She turned her head and kissed his bicep. "That's not corny. We haven't had a normal courtship, have we?"

"Courtship." He snickered. "You have been spending all of your time with Miz G. That sounds like something she'd say."

"I did have coffee with Riss today," Jade pointed out.

"How'd that go?"

"I like her. She definitely isn't shy, which is what I need in a friend. Someone who pushes me just a little further than I would myself. She asked me to join her book club."

Tobin lifted an eyebrow. "Riss is in a book club?"

"I guess she's been part of it for three years. They meet at different members' houses in Casper. It sounds like an eclectic group. I'll have time to read the book before the meeting next month."

Jade had no trouble keeping up with his longer strides. Their joined hands swung between them. Her ponytail bobbed from the spring in her step. But she didn't say anything for what seemed like an eternity.

When he couldn't stand it anymore, he tugged her against his body. "Spill it."

"This is going pretty fast."

"That's the speed you like."

She smiled. "True. It just seems like a lot of promises between us and we haven't had sex yet."

"Oh. That's the problem? You think we'll be sexually incompatible and this will all fall apart?" Tobin fused his mouth to hers and kissed her.

And kissed her.

And kissed her some more.

By the time he relinquished her lips, she clung to him.

He put his mouth on her ear. "Are you wet?"

"Very."

"And I'm hard as a fucking post, so yeah, I don't think sexual incompatibility is gonna be an issue for us, darlin'. But I'll tell you what . . . I'll prove it. Tomorrow night. I'm getting us that motel room."

"Okay."

Tobin smirked. "I thought you might say that. Let's head back before the mosquitos eat us alive."

## Chapter Fourteen

❦

Jade fussed with the pitcher of lemonade.

"Girlie, why are you so nervous?" GG asked.

"Because you know that's just the type of person I am."

"Oh pooh."

"These women are your friends. Your best friends. I want to make a good impression on them."

"Why? Because I don't give a hoot if they like you or not. I like you." GG squeezed her from behind. "I love you, Jade doll. You know that. I've managed to hold them off for two weeks, but they ain't havin' none of it anymore."

"Why did you wait so long?"

GG moved to stand in front of her. She adjusted the lace collar on Jade's blouse. "I wasn't sure how long you'd be here. Heck, I wasn't sure how long I'd be here since I imagined moving vans showing up out of the blue."

That was the first time GG had said that to her directly. Jade put her hand on her grandmother's shoulder. "Where did you get that idea anyway? Dad never said anything to me that that was his plan." She paused. "Did he threaten you with that?"

"It's kind of a blur, to be honest. I heard, 'blah blah blah, you shootin' off guns and blah blah blah, can't trust you not to do crazy stuff and blah blah blah, you oughta be someplace where someone can keep a better eye on you.'"

Jade frowned at her. Something didn't fit. "GG. That is a long ways off from what you told Tobin. Like miles and miles away."

"Well, sweetheart. Tobin is one of them kind of protective men. You mess with someone he cares about and he sees red. He acts first. His first action was to move in here to make sure that no one could move me out. What was I supposed to say? No? There is no sayin' no to that man."

*Don't I know that.*

She let her hand drop and turned away so her grandmother couldn't see the heat staining her cheeks when she thought about how thoroughly Tobin had . . . ravished her. That wasn't a word she'd ever thought would apply to her, but it did in this case. The heat in his eyes, the hunger in his mouth, the greed in those big hands, the intuitive way he made her completely unravel. She'd never experienced anything like it.

"Jade? Is everything all right? You've been distracted the last day or so."

She manufactured a smile before she turned around. "I'm just muddling over my life choices."

"The world is wide open to you, sweets."

"I never know what to think when people say that. What does that mean? It's not advice. It doesn't give me a direction."

"Oh goodie." GG rubbed her hand on the outside of Jade's upper arm. Her eyes twinkled. "I've been waiting to play this what-if game with you."

Jade remembered Tobin muttering about "what-if" being useless words when put together.

"What if money wasn't an issue? How would you spend your days?"

"I don't know."

GG frowned. "That's not how this game works."

"I know. But I get stuck on that question every time because believe me, I've asked myself. And to be honest? That's how I ended up with a degree that I can't use to make a living. I still love those time periods in history. But it wasn't a smart answer to that question."

"Dadgummit. You're making too much sense. We'll move on. Where do you see yourself living? In New York City?"

"It's the only place I've ever lived."

She shook her finger in Jade's face. "Again. Not an answer."

"This is why I'm struggling, GG. I don't have answers to any of these big life questions."

"Sometimes when you find one thing, everything else slips into place. Maybe that one thing is a dream job. Or finding a place to set down roots. Or having friends who get you like no one else. Or finding a man you can build a life with. If you learn nothin' else from this trip, girlie, I hope you discover that havin' it all is a lie. Havin' only one thing? One good thing that's yours? That's what you need."

Jade fought the urge to cry. This was how it'd always been between her and GG. She knew when her granddaughter needed sage advice. She knew when she needed fun. She also knew when she was being a brat and deserved a kick in the patootie. She'd never forget the time GG had shown up in New York, walked into Jade's room and announced no granddaughter of hers would ever be a snob or take her parents for granted.

Gravel crunching in the driveway brought her focus back to the here and now. She sidestepped the couch and walked along the edge of the room to the picture window. She lifted the curtain and peeked out.

Two vehicles had pulled in. One was parked out front, but the other was . . . backing up to the barn?

"Jade! You were raised better than to lurk from behind the window," GG chided. "Do me a favor and grab two extra rolls of toilet paper out of the supply closet upstairs. The bathroom on the main floor is out."

Five minutes later, Jade paused at the top of the stairs. The Mud

Lilies were congregated inside the front entryway and they all looked up at her arrival on the scene.

Talk about being put on display.

GG waited at the bottom of the staircase, beaming. "Jade, honey, come down here and meet my friends."

Plastering a smile in place, she started down the stairs. Nerves kicked in overtime and she fought the urge to giggle. Or to wave like a beauty queen. Or to throw her leg over the handrail and slide to the bottom.

None of GG's friends said a word as she made her descent.

But once her foot hit that last stair tread, they were on her.

"Omigoodness, look at you! Aren't you just the cutest thing ever?" a stylish redhead gushed. "Bernice. Look at her hair! Isn't it gorgeous?"

A stout woman moved in next to the redhead. "It is pretty. A little more texture than I expected, but the color is exceptional."

A tiny, birdlike woman floated closer. "Oh, sweetie. I love that you're petite like I am."

Jade didn't point out that she had almost half a foot on her.

"Hush up, Tilda. She's not that small." A woman in an honest-to-god beret and olive green camo stepped forward. "Since none of them have bothered with formal introductions, it looks like it falls to me again. The redhead? Vivien. Next to her is Bernice. She's interested in your hair because she owns a salon. You met Tilda the petite. Behind me is Maybelle. She's the society reporter for the *Muddy Gap Gazette* so make sure to clarify that anything you don't want in the paper is 'off the record.'"

Jade peered around camo woman to the reporter. Was she wearing a . . . muumuu?

"And I'm Pearl," camo/beret lady said in a booming voice.

"It's so great to meet you all finally."

Silence stretched as they studied her.

It felt like she was facing a firing squad.

"Would you like refreshments? GG made lemonade. If you'll all have a seat—"

"We're your granny's BFFs so there's no need to fuss over us," Pearl said.

"Although it is appreciated," Maybelle said. "But I believe Tilda is helping Garnet out in the kitchen today. That'll free you up to spend some personal time with us."

Jade looked to GG for guidance but she'd already disappeared into the kitchen with Tilda.

Vivien slipped her arm through Jade's. "Garnet tells me you've been working in the garden quite a bit."

"There's such a variety of flowers and herbs. I could spend all day outside."

"Let's take a stroll out there, shall we? And see what you've been up to?"

She froze.

They knew about the pot plants. Maybe she'd been right all along; maybe the marijuana belonged to these women and not GG.

And now *they* knew that *she* knew about it.

Crap.

Vivien led her down the porch steps with Pearl, Bernice and Maybelle following close behind.

Were they taking her outside and away from GG to warn her to keep her mouth shut?

Maybe she could feign ignorance. Not everyone knew what marijuana plants looked like.

*Set the stage now.*

Jade faked a laugh. "I'll admit that being a sheltered city slicker, I didn't know what ninety-nine percent of the plants were." There. That sounded plausible.

But Vivien didn't steer her toward the gardens; they headed to the barn.

"This is making me a little nervous, ladies."

"The only reason you should be nervous is if you're feeling guilty about something," Bernice said.

"No. She might be nervous if she's got something to hide," Pearl retorted.

Maybelle opened the barn door and Vivien shifted sideways to step through first.

After the bright sunlight, Jade had to close her eyes for a moment. When she reopened them . . . well, she couldn't believe what she was seeing.

"This is some kind of a joke, right?"

## Chapter Fifteen

❧

*Tonight's the night . . .*

Tobin had that Rod Stewart song on the brain all damn day.

*No. You've had naked, sexy time with Jade on the brain all day.*

Finally they'd have uninterrupted alone time.

He'd planned everything for a perfect romantic night.

A candlelight dinner at the Chez Majestique in Casper.

A stroll through City Park.

Then spending the rest of the night fucking like animals in the suite he'd booked at the Radisson in downtown Casper.

He'd even slipped Teddy a hundred bucks to do the first cattle check, so he and Jade could have a leisurely morning together, hopefully with room service and shower sex.

But the very first thing on his agenda was scrubbing off the day's grime. Then he'd pack a bag and try to sneak out of the house without it becoming the Inquisition.

It threw him to see Miz G sitting dejectedly on the front steps.

He slid out of his truck, his arms and legs aching. An eight-mile run coupled with his day of heavy lifting hay bales had him moving more slowly than usual.

"Why so glum, chum?" he said to Miz G.

"Do you ever wonder if your friends are laughing at you behind your back? If they tell you one thing to your face and then turn around and act a completely different way?"

"Friends . . . meaning your friends? The Mud Lilies?"

"Yep."

"What have they done now?"

"I'm not sure. It started when they all stopped by today to meet Jade." The back of his neck prickled.

"I went into the kitchen to get refreshments. When I returned to the living room, everyone except Tilda had disappeared. I asked where they'd all gone and Tilda gave some vague response. Then she whipped out the new Pyramid catalog and my brain sort of went offline. I love that dadgum catalog."

"What kind of catalog is it?"

"They specialize in fantasy knickknacks, them fancy historical clothes, signs with inspirational sayings, jewelry up the wazoo, Celtic stuff. So I started flipping through it. By the time I got to the last page, an hour had passed. An hour in which I shirked my hostess duties. The ice cubes had melted in my lemonade, and the cherry crisp I'd warmed up in the oven had become hard as a brick."

Tobin made what he hoped passed for a sympathetic noise.

"So I'm looking around and wondering why my friends needed time alone with Jade."

That got his attention. "What were they doin'?"

"Talking, they said. But Tilda had let it slip they'd been in the barn. What in the blue blazes were they doin' in there?"

"Did you ask them?"

"Of course I asked. But those women are masters at deflecting. They asked me if I'd seen anything in the catalog worth buying and it was like a trained dog response." She slapped her knee. "I tell you, from here on out I'm goin' cold turkey. No more catalogs."

"Did Jade tell you what they talked about?"

"Nope. She was pretty quiet afterward. She's shy and she gets over-whelmed. They didn't take that into account when they were talking to her."

"How long ago did this happen?"

"They left . . . maybe two hours ago."

"Where's Jade now?"

"Out in the garden. She's been out there forever."

No wonder he couldn't get a hold of her. "Why don't you go inside and salvage some of that cherry crisp. I'll try and talk to Jade about it."

"Be nice," Garnet warned and rolled to her feet.

"I'm always nice, Miz G."

As soon as she shuffled into the house, Tobin removed his hat and ran his hands through his hair. After he brushed the worst of the hay dust off his clothes, he cut around the edge of the porch and headed toward the gardens.

He found her sitting on the stone bench in the corner, her forehead on her knees, her arms wrapped around her shins.

"Jade?"

She jerked at the sound of his voice and jumped up.

Tobin froze.

What the hell had happened to her today?

Bits of dried grass were dangling from her hair.

Her face was filthy, save for the tear tracks that zigzagged down from the corners of her eyes to her jawline.

Her T-shirt was streaked with dirt. As were her jeans.

He tried for a light approach. "Did you forget to tell me you're trying out for Ladies' Mud Wrestling Night at the Prickly Cactus?"

That's when she burst into tears. "Don't you ever say the word 'mud' around me again, Tobin Hale, or so help me, I will—"

He had her wrapped in his arms before she finished.

Her entire body shook. That scared the fuck out of him. He squeezed her tighter and pressed his lips to the top of her head, breathing in the sun-warmed scent of her hair.

When Tobin tried to discreetly wipe away the dried leaf that had gotten stuck to his lip, Jade wiggled until he let go of her.

That's when he realized she wasn't crying from distress but from fury.

He noticed the shovel lying next to a pile of dirt. His gaze moved across the ground, zeroing in the other new holes. She'd taken a different approach to her frustration instead of beating rugs into submission.

"Talk to me, sweetheart. What happened today?"

"I don't think I can talk about it when I just want to yell about it!"

Tobin propped his hands on his hips. "Go ahead. Ain't the first time you've yelled at me and it won't be the last."

Jade glared at him for several long moments, as if she didn't believe him. Then she let fly.

"I'm so, so, so, so mad!" She'd picked up the shovel and punctuated each *so* by stabbing the metal tip into the ground. "How dare they? Seriously? I don't care if they are worried about GG's health—that was *not* the way to go about finding out if their concerns are justified! Did they really think if GG had confided in me that I'd break that confidence just because they're her friends? No, no, no, no." More ground stabbing.

He stayed mum and let her rant.

"Not to mention they brought my dad into it and asked a bunch of questions that are none of their business. And if they're such good friends of hers, then they should know that my grandmother has a habit of exaggerating. With her, it's always worst-case scenario and then she has a hard time remembering what's fact and what she's embellished."

No argument there, but Jade's diatribe still didn't make sense.

"Plus, they also have to know that if Garnet Evans is backed into a corner she comes out swinging every time."

*Like grandmother, like granddaughter.*

"And look out if you wrong her because there's no way you can ever make it right again."

Jade took a minute to breathe.

Tobin watched her, completely . . . turned the fuck on at seeing this side of her. Yeah, he knew she was pissed off, but goddamn. This fierceness was hot as hell. Not that he'd share that with her right now—he valued his balls, thank you very much. But he'd much rather see her all het up, screaming mad, than watch her weeping and wringing her hands.

This was how she ought to deal with her anxiety issues. Get a fucking shovel and beat it into submission. Not that he'd tell her that right now either—he'd mention it later. When she wasn't wielding a weapon.

"And you know what else?"

She wasn't talking to him, as much as at him, but he answered anyway. "What?"

"Those results are skewed. They're inconclusive ninety-nine percent of the time. And I don't think they even knew what they were doing anyway. So the whole thing was an exercise in futility. Unless their motivation was to test me. Not only to see how mad I'd get, but if I'd tell GG about their scheming ways, knowing full well that it would hurt her."

"Jade. You're talking in riddles, darlin'. Tell me exactly what Miz G's friends did today."

She aimed that stubborn chin at him. "They hooked me up to a lie detector machine."

Tobin's jaw nearly hit the dirt. "What?"

"Oh yes, that's right. First thing today, GG's beloved *friends* squired me away to the barn and practically strapped me into a chair so I could privately address their . . . concerns. By taking a lie detector test."

"How the fuck did that even happen?"

"They claimed they had something to show me. And I went along with it." She frowned. "At first, when we were walking outside and they started asking me how much time I'd been spending in GG's gardens, I worried they were trying to get me to admit I knew about the pot plants and intended to warn me off. But they didn't care about that at all. They demanded to know when Dad and I planned to lock Garnet away, where we were stashing her, if we were selling off her assets. Not only that, they accused me of encouraging GG to hide her health issues from them—which isn't true because she's healthy as a horse. But really, that isn't their business! If GG wanted them to know something so personal, she'd tell them. Then they asked me a bunch of other stuff, but by that time I was so angry I blanked it out.

"The last thing I remember before I grabbed the shovel and came out here was their suggestion that I didn't mention our 'conversation' to GG. Ever." She blew out a long breath. "Which I actually agree with because GG would be so hurt if she knew what they'd done today. She was so excited for me to meet them and these women are such a huge part of her life . . . I mean, they didn't cause me physical harm. And I get that they were probably acting out of love for her, but they should've used a different approach." Jade looked away, but not before he saw her firm her trembling chin. "I am not the enemy. That's how they treated me. So that's how I ended up out here, channeling my frustrations. But the longer I've been out here digging holes, the angrier I've gotten."

"Baby, I don't blame you for being upset."

The Mud Lilies had done some crazy shit over the years . . . but this crossed the line.

"Let's go back to the house and figure out—"

"No. I can't be around GG right now. She'll know something is wrong." Her eyes narrowed. "Promise me that you won't tell her any of this."

"Jade—"

"Promise me that you won't bring any of this up with her at all."

"Fine. I promise." This was so fucked. He scrubbed his hands over his face. "So now what? You'll just stay out here and dig holes until dark?"

"Probably." Jade made a growling sound. "And I'm really mad that this—no, that *they*—ruined our plans for a whole night of hot sexy times."

What? Fuck that. "Jade. We can't let them—"

"Too late, Tobin." She held up her gloved hand. "I'm feeling a little ragey and a lot stabby, if you haven't noticed. And even when I'm not mad at you, I *will* take it out on you."

"I'm a big guy, tiger. I can take whatever you dish out." He had an image of her completely wild. Her silken hair a tangled mess as she rode him. Her teeth at his throat. Her fingers digging into his chest, his ass, his shoulders, the tops of his thighs . . .

"Omigod. Seriously? Lose the hard-on, buddy."

His gaze reconnected with her face, but Jade was eying his groin. "You're backing out of our plans for tonight?"

"Yes. First of all, I don't want to leave GG alone. You saw her. She knows something is up, doesn't she?"

He nodded reluctantly.

"We've waited this long. I want the focus to be completely on us. No distractions. No interruptions."

"All right."

"Can you set it up for tomorrow night?"

"No. I'm goin' to a bull sale in Nebraska with Abe Lawson tomorrow at noon. It's an overnight trip. I won't be back until the next day."

"This sucks."

The anger he'd kept in check rushed through him. "We'll talk more after I set some things straight."

"With GG? But you promised you wouldn't say anything!"

"To your *grandma*. But I made no such promise about the rest of them. And this shit? Not gonna fly with me, Jade."

"But—"

"It's wrong, they know it's wrong and I have a personal stake in it because it affects you."

❧

Tobin figured the ladies would reconvene at Tilda's house since it was closest to Garnet's. To retain the element of surprise, he parked his truck on the road and hoofed it up the driveway.

He knocked loudly on the screen door and then stood off to the side. Polite behavior was too ingrained for Tilda not to answer, but he sure as hell wasn't giving her a chance to slam the damn door in his face.

When she said, "Who's there?" and he stepped into view, she yelled, "Run, ladies, we're busted!"

But it was too late; Tobin barreled into the dining room. He said, "Nobody move." Since Vivien and Bernice were already up and out of their chairs, he pointed at them and said, "Park it."

"Tobin. What a nice surprise," Miz Maybelle said with wide-eyed innocence. "Could I get you something to—"

"Nice try, Miz Maybelle, but you sit back down." He motioned to Tilda. "You too. And that had better not be a damn Taser behind your back, Pearl," he warned. "You do *not* want to piss me off any more than I am right now. All of you. Hands on the table."

Pearl sighed. Her Taser hit the wood table with a clunk.

Bernice followed suit by dropping a pair of scissors that had been fashioned into a shiv.

Vivien's small-caliber Walther pistol gleamed as she set it down.

Tilda's pocketknife made a slow spin.

Miz Maybelle was the last one to show her hand, which contained . . . another Taser.

"Is that it? Or do I need to frisk the rest of you for firearms too?" Tobin demanded.

"We all have permits to carry concealed," Pearl sniffed, "so I don't suggest you try it. You won't like what you find."

Jesus.

"Fine. I will cut to the chase. What in the hell were you thinking forcing Garnet's granddaughter, who is a guest in her home, to take a lie detector test today? A test which you conducted without Garnet's knowledge and for all intents and purposes without Jade's consent?"

They all exchanged looks, as if they were asking each other . . . *How do we play this?*

"Huh-uh. You look at *me*. Not each other. Because you all knew what you were doin' today was wrong, yet you did it anyway, so don't give me any bullshit crocodile tears." He slammed his hands on the table. "But Jade's tears were very real."

"Jade was crying?" Tilda said with horror.

"Of course she was crying. Her grandmother's best friends, who she met for the first time today, subjected her to a freakin' *lie* detector test. She took that to mean that you all think she's capable of emotionally hurting her grandma, which couldn't be further from the truth. And you grilled her on other personal things about Miz G that are very much not any of your business." He got in Vivien's face. "You have a granddaughter. How would you feel if all your friends descended on her, dragged her out to the damn barn, hooked her up to a machine and asked her a bunch of questions?"

"Well, when you put it that way . . . no. I wouldn't be okay with it."

"Vivien!" Pearl snapped. "We're supposed to stick together."

"What Pearl said," Miz Maybelle chimed in. "This was a group decision."

"But Jade was crying," Tilda said. "Not to mention none of you were in the house with Garnet. She has no control when it comes to that magazine. And to make it worse . . ." Tilda's chin wobbled. "She was picking out gifts for us!"

"This is why she was not allowed in with us when we were asking Jade questions," Bernice scoffed. "She's a soft touch."

"If you'd just been *asking* her questions, you'd've done it in the house over lemonade and cherry crisp." His angry gaze moved from Bernice, to Miz Maybelle, to Pearl, the ones who seemed to be the least apologetic. "And where in the hell did you get a lie detector machine anyway?"

All eyes zoomed to Vivien.

"I found it by the side of the road."

"Bullshit."

She shrugged. "That's my story and I'm sticking to it."

Miz Maybelle smirked at Tobin. "Don't you want to know what Jade said about *you* during the lie detector test?"

"Why would you ask her about me?"

Bernice snorted. "Because even before you showed up here, raging like an angry bull because you think we done your lady wrong, it's obvious you have the hots for her."

"Jade said some pretty juicy stuff," Miz Maybelle said slyly.

*Wrong. Your interference today ensured there'd be nothing juicy going on tonight.*

Vivien rolled her eyes. "It is not juicy, Maybelle. Jade said Tobin's kisses were juicy."

"No, she admitted his body was juicy," Pearl argued. "Like she drooled whenever he took his shirt off."

"Are you sure she didn't say juicy when he took his pants off?" Tilda asked.

All eyes swiveled to her.

"What?" she asked indignantly. "I just wanted clarification since I wasn't there."

Jesus. He oughta grab the fucking Taser and turn it on himself.

"So why are you here?" Bernice asked. "To make sure we don't spill the beans to Garnet that you're sneaking around with Jade?"

"I'm here to make sure you never mention this incident to Miz G, because it would break her heart."

They all nodded.

"That's it?" Pearl asked suspiciously.

"No, that's not it. You're each gonna do something really fuckin' nice and special for Jade. And yes, I'm mad enough that my language is warranted, so deal with it."

"What kind of special things are you expecting us to do?" Vivien asked.

Dammit. Just as he started to berate himself for not thinking this through, an idea clicked. "You're gonna talk to your buddy in Casper— the one who runs the music department, or the symphony or whatever it is—about the talented young woman living outside of Rawlins. A violinist with a degree from Columbia who is looking to connect with other musicians in the area."

Vivien's eyes turned shrewd. "This is a serious favor, Tobin. "

"Oh, I know. But trust me. When you hear Jade play? You'll thank *me* for doin' you the favor because the woman is an outstanding violinist."

"Since when is Jade going to be living here permanently?"

Tobin flashed his teeth at her. "Since she and I became serious."

It might've been the first time he'd shocked them all into speechlessness.

Vivien cleared her throat. "I'll get right on it."

Next he leaned in front of Bernice. "If Jade wants a full salon treatment, you'll give her the works. No charge."

Bernice squirmed. "How about at a reduced rate?"

"How about if I tell your husband about the birthday spanking you got—onstage—at the Lumberjack Jamboree strip show in Casper two months ago?"

"Does Garnet tell you everything?"

"Just the blackmail stuff," Pearl grumbled.

Tobin faced her.

She threw up her hands. "You got nothin' on me, Hale."

"Not yet. But I have my suspicions about what *you've* been up to."

The woman all but looked at the ceiling and whistled innocently.

"So, Pearl, I expect when I ask for your cooperation, in whatever capacity I need it, I won't have to ask more than once?"

"Yes, sir."

Smart-ass. Tobin eyed both Tilda and Miz Maybelle.

Tilda smiled brightly. "Since Jade will be one of Wyoming's newest residents, I'll take her out to lunch and introduce her to my great-niece, Elise, who just moved to Rawlins herself last month from Oakmont. She's a very lovely girl and she doesn't know anyone around these parts either."

"Why'd she relocate to Rawlins?" he asked skeptically.

"Oh, you know, change of scenery."

"Uh-huh. Try again."

"Good lord, Tobin. You are a hard man to please when you're looking after your woman."

He raised a brow—and . . . Tilda cracked.

"All right. Elise's boyfriend is in prison, but she swears he was set up—"

Tobin held up his hand. "Scratch that lunch date. The embroidery stuff you do," he said to Tilda. "Make her something nice that she can frame and hang on the wall. Or better yet, offer to teach her how to do it. She really digs that kind of craft stuff but she's never had a chance to learn."

"That is so sweet," Tilda said.

Tobin focused on Miz Maybelle.

She folded her arms across her ample chest. "I don't care how much trouble I'm in with you, Tobin Hale, or how much you love them; I am *not* divulging my prize recipe for molasses cookies to Jade or anyone else."

"I'll give you her recipe," Bernice offered. "It ain't all that secret."

"Bernice!"

"Well, hon, it's not really a secret when you're jotting it down on cocktail napkins at the Blue Lantern in exchange for free shots," Vivien said gently.

"Shoot. I'd hoped I'd dreamed that." Maybelle looked at Tobin. "What's my punishment?"

"You used to fish with your husband, right?"

"All the blasted time. Why?"

"Do you still use your equipment?"

She shook her head.

"Jade's never been fishing and I'd like to borrow your equipment to see if she likes dropping a line before I buy her rods and reels."

A long beat passed before Miz Maybelle said, "Fine. At least someone would be getting some use out of it. It's just been gathering dust since Mr. L passed on."

Tobin might've missed it if Tilda hadn't pointed at Maybelle, discreetly wiping her eyes with a tissue. He crouched down. "If it has sentimental value to you—"

"It does." She looked up with watery eyes and sniffled. "That's why I'm so happy to let you use it."

"This is the last thing I need from all of you. I'm goin' out of town for a couple of days. Please let me and Jade tell Miz G that we're together on our own time frame."

"Don't wait too long, sonny," Pearl warned. "We're old. We might forget it's supposed to be a secret."

"Especially if we're drinking," Vivien pointed out.

"And if you like it, you should put a ring on it," Bernice said with a smirk.

After a round of laughter and fist bumps, they started singing.

Yep. He definitely should've Tasered himself.

*Chapter Sixteen*

❦

"*J*ade!"

She jumped and the can of coffee in her hands slipped and crashed to the floor.

Vivien picked it up and eyed the dent in the can before swapping it out for a new canister and setting it in Jade's cart. "Sorry, I didn't mean to scare you."

*Right. You already did that.*

"I'm used to dealing with my hard-of-hearing friends. I tend to speak loudly, or so I've been told." Vivien studied the items in Jade's cart.

Coffee, a package of fudge-striped cookies, a small box of dish-washing detergent, the latest issue of *Cosmo*, a carton of yogurt and a small container of Nutella. Jade might as well have a neon sign on the front of the cart announcing THIS WOMAN IS SINGLE! The only clichéd items she was missing were a bottle of cheap white wine and bag of cat food.

That's when Jade noticed Vivien had nothing in her cart. "I'll let you get started with your shopping."

When Jade moved forward, Vivien blocked her exit. "I'm happy I ran into you. Garnet's order from the Beauty Barn came in. You can swing by and pick it up from Bernice."

"I'll let GG know. I'd hate to deprive her of a visit to town." *Fool me once*... Although every one of the Mud Lilies had apologized for the "misunderstanding," Jade wasn't going anywhere near them without backup.

"It'll just take you an extra five minutes," Vivien said breezily. "And Garnet will be so appreciative. I'll just text her real quick and let her know you're picking it up."

Jade watched as Vivien whipped out her phone, typed out a text and sent it.

A *ping* sounded.

"Garnet said thank you. So I'll just wait up by the checkout counter and you can follow me to Bernice's."

No manipulation there. But what could she say? More importantly . . . what could she do to get out of it?

*Make your own backup plan.*

Jade smiled. "I have a couple of other things to grab first."

Vivien said, "Take your time."

Jade rolled her cart to the next aisle, pretending to look for something as she pulled out her cell phone and sent a text.

JE: Are you around?

A couple of seconds later, a reply showed.

Yes. What's up?

JE: How long would it take you to get to Bernice's Beauty Barn?

Why? Fair warning that I'm not the pedicure type.

JE: Can you meet me there? You said if I needed anything
just to ask . . . remember?

Fine. Be there in 20.

After checking out, Jade tossed her bags in her car and followed Vivien
to Bernice's Beauty Barn, secretly snickering that she'd driven a block.

The scents of permanent wave solution and coffee hit her as soon as
she walked inside. And what a coincidence; Miz Maybelle, Pearl and
Tilda all just happened to be watching Bernice cut another woman's
hair. A gorgeous woman with flowing blond locks who could have had a
starring role in shampoo commercials.

The Mud Lilies stood up, one by one, and hugged Jade, as if they
were the best of friends.

Bernice removed the cape from her customer with a flourish and
said, "All done, sweetheart. In and out in under an hour, as promised."

"Thanks, Bernice." The blonde unfolded from the chair—of course
her clothes were as gorgeous as the rest of her—and stopped in front of
Jade, offering her a brilliant smile and her hand. "You're Garnet's granddaughter?"

Not said in a snarky manner at all, so Jade's hackles came down a
notch. "Yes. I'm Jade Evans."

"So pleased to meet you, Jade. I'm Harper Turner. I used to have a
nail studio in the back, so I've known your grandma for years."

"I'll tell her I saw you. I'm here *briefly*"—she emphasized the word—"to
pick up an order before my groceries melt."

"The only perishable thing you bought was yogurt. And honey, that
stuff could go bad and who would know the difference? It already tastes
like sour milk," Vivien said. "Which is why we know you have time to
chat with us for a bit. No need to run off."

Jade laughed. "I remember how our last chat went, so you'll understand if I decline."

Harper's eyes narrowed. First on Jade and then on each one of the Mud Lilies, who all managed to pull off *we wouldn't harm a fly* smiles.

"We're damn proud of Harper," Bernice said, putting an arm around Harper's shoulder. "Hardest-working woman you'll ever meet. She stuck around this tiny town at the expense of pursuing her own dreams to raise her youngest sister until she graduated from high school. Now Harper owns a clothing company up at the Split Rock—and *whoo-ee* does she have some nice stuff. So nice she ships it all over the world."

"And she hooked herself a hot cowboy," Tilda added.

"I remember when you couldn't wait to get out of Muddy Gap. You said there was nothing here for you."

"Sounds like someone else I know," Jade muttered. She thought her comment went unheard amid the chattering about Harper's hot husband and even more adorable boys, but Harper looked at her quizzically.

"How long are you visiting?" Harper asked.

Silence as all eyes swiveled to Jade.

"It's up in the air at this point."

"You and Garnet should swing by the store. Between that, the ranch and our three sons, my husband Bran and I don't get out at all anymore."

"I'm sure GG would love that."

Harper and Bernice walked to the register. Harper kept trying to sneak looks at her.

*Yes, I realize I don't look like my grandmother or anyone else around here.*

But maybe her ethnicity wasn't the curiosity. Maybe Tobin had mentioned Jade since it appeared he worked with Harper.

As soon as Harper sailed out the door, Bernice rubbed her hands together. "So, Jade, to make up for the 'misunderstanding' the other day, I'm offering you a free makeover. Hop in the chair, sweetheart, and I'll get started."

"It's sweet of you to offer, but I have plans today so I'll just grab GG's order and be on my way." Maybe it was ridiculous, but Jade's gaze scanned the area for tie-down straps.

"Nonsense. Every woman needs a pick-me-up now and then."

Jade started to back away. "Not me. I'm good. I had a style update before I left New York."

"Come on, it'll be fun! We'll stick around to offer our input," Miz Maybelle said.

"Input" from a woman who wore a muumuu and had added a fake bun to the back of her head complete with red lacquered chopsticks? Not a confidence booster.

"Have you ever considered cutting your hair short?" Tilda asked. "That Twiggy looked so hip."

Who was Twiggy? It sounded like a dog. The one thing Jade had going for her was her hair, so a chop job definitely wasn't happening. "I think—"

"I'm in charge." Bernice grabbed a new cape off the stack. "Don't listen to them. Let's get you situated in the chair."

"But—"

"Lord, you're looking at it like it's an electric chair."

"Can you blame me?"

The door slammed open and a voice boomed, "What in the hell is going on in here?"

Jade practically did a herkey she was so happy to see Riss.

"Riss. What are you doin' here, girl?"

"Hello, Aunt Bernice."

"Aunt?" Jade repeated.

"Yep. Not that she claims me." Riss put her hands on her hips. "Jade and I had plans today. She texted that she was stopping here for a minute and it's been fifteen so I thought I'd see if you were trying to force her into a makeover or some damn thing."

Bernice bristled. "Just because *you've* never had a makeover doesn't mean other women aren't interested in one."

Riss rolled her eyes. "Jade is beautiful. The only thing she's interested in is a margarita."

"In the middle of the afternoon?" Vivien asked.

"I'll pretend I haven't seen *all* of you totally tanked at the Blue Lantern before noon—on more than one occasion," Riss shot back.

"Those were special celebrations. And the mimosas they serve during their pork festival pack a wallop," Miz Maybelle said.

"Regardless. Jade and I are headed to Rawlins."

"To the Blue Lantern?" Vivien asked.

"Nope. The Prickly Cactus."

"That is not a nice place for nice girls," Tilda said with a sniff.

Riss smirked. "Which is why I'm a regular there. Later, ladies. And Aunt Bernice." She held the door open for Jade.

As soon as Jade was out of view of her watchers, she hugged Riss hard. "Thank you, thank you, thank you, a million times. I started to worry they were going to strap me in a chair again."

"Again?" Riss said. "When was the first time?"

"Not important now. I am so ready for a margarita. Or five."

"Same. Follow me into town. I gotta stop and buy a different shirt since this is the only one I have with me and there's a streak of cowshit across the girls."

Jade's gaze fell to Riss's chest. Sure enough, she saw a brown smear. "Does that happen a lot?"

"In my line of work? I'd consider this a clean shirt day."

"Good to know."

"You seriously ready to get your drink on? Cut loose a little, Wyoming-style?"

"Yes. I need a reminder that I'm twenty-four, not eighty-four."

She grinned. "Call Garnet and tell her it's a pixie dust night for you."

"Pixie dust?" Jade repeated.

"She'll know what it means. She'll also know not to panic if she doesn't see you until tomorrow morning." Riss dropped her sunglasses over her eyes. "Stick close. I sorta speed."

Great.

❦

In Rawlins, Riss stopped at the farm and ranch supply store.

Jade wasn't a shopper, but she didn't have high expectations about the clothing selection in a place that sold chickens and tractors, so the section dedicated to women's ranch and leisure wear was a happy surprise. Especially when Riss decided they both needed barhopping clothes.

Riss outfitted Jade in a tight button-up with swirls of glitter across the chest—that actually created the illusion of cleavage—and boot-cut jeans with rhinestones on the back-pocket flaps. Instead of cowboy boots, Jade selected a pair of funky flip-flops with a three-inch wedge heel covered in western beads and medallions.

"Lookit you, New York. Totally countrified."

Jade took a bow. "I owe it all to you."

"Come on. My turn. I'm here, I'm stocking up."

And stock up Riss did—in record time. Within ten minutes she'd tossed two frilly shirts, five basic tank tops, identical in style but different colors, and a pair of jeans into her cart.

At the checkout stand, a woman coming in the front doors stopped and said, "Larissa?"

Riss muttered *fuck* before she plastered on a smile. "Hey, Dodie! Long time no see."

"I'm surprised to see you shopping."

"Don't tell my mother," Riss said in a pleading tone. "I still have nightmares about that prom dress."

"I've kept your other secrets, haven't I?" The apple-shaped and apple-cheeked woman—who looked to be in her late fifties—focused on Jade. "Who's your friend?"

"Sorry. Dodie, this is Jade Evans. She's Garnet's granddaughter. Jade, this is my mother's cousin, Dodie."

"It's a pleasure to meet you," Jade said.

"Dodie is the head cook up at the Split Rock," Riss said. "She's been there since the place first opened, right?"

"Right."

"There've been some changes with Hugh leaving. How's everything going up there?"

Dodie sighed. "Hectic. We're at full capacity through the summer. Everyone in every department is stretched thin, so we're all tired and cranky. Naturally that's when Lou-Lou gives notice, claiming she's developed a bulging disc. I don't care that she's my cousin. I wanna throttle her."

A calculating look settled on Riss's face. "It sucks that you're short staffed. Lou-Lou . . . she wasn't the baker?"

"Only thing she baked was her brain. Besides, we don't make baked goods in-house; we order them from an artisan bakery in Casper. Lou-Lou is a prep cook."

"You're kidding! What a coincidence. Jade was a prep cook in New York City."

*Shut it, Riss.*

"You don't say." Dodie's eyes turned shrewd. "Are you just here visiting?"

Everyone asked her that. And it hadn't come up between her and Tobin since the night they'd gone for a run. "I'll be staying longer than I planned."

Riss hip-checked Jade. "That's because she's hooked herself a gen-u-wine Wyoming cowboy and she's in love."

"Riss!" Jade felt her face and neck get fiery hot. If Dodie had been at the Split Rock since it'd opened, then she probably knew Tobin pretty well. Hopefully Riss wouldn't share that.

"We *are* hiring, if you're interested. It's only part-time. The shift starts early in the morning and prep is usually done by eleven."

"Oh, Jade is familiar with early morning shifts. She mentioned that she had to get up at three a.m. to catch the subway to her job that started at the ungodly hour of four thirty."

"Good lord, I can't even imagine that!" Dodie said.

Riss started tossing the items from her cart onto the conveyor belt. "Great chatting with you, Dodie. We've gotta scoot. But Jade will be in touch."

"I hope so."

Jade paid for her purchases and didn't say anything to Riss until they were outside. "What was that?" she demanded.

"Serendipity," Riss deadpanned.

"No. Seriously. I am not going to work at the Split Rock! Even if they are hiring."

"Why not? You are qualified."

"Because it would be weird if I said, 'Hey, Tobin, by the way, now I'll be working at the same place as you! We can live in the same house and work together. Maybe we can even carpool!'" She slammed the passenger door.

Riss rolled her eyes. "Whatever. But at least ask him about it, okay?"

"I think he's mad at me because I cancelled our date after . . ." *I had a mini-meltdown after the "misunderstanding."*

"I'm not worried. You shouldn't be either. Especially not after what you told me the other day." Riss looked at her watch. "Cool beans. We're running ahead of schedule. Follow me to the truck stop."

During the drive, Jade flashed back to the first conversation she'd had with Riss over coffee. Normally Jade had problems connecting with people. She worried about saying the wrong thing or looking like a nerd, so she erred on the side of not saying much at all. But Riss just blew right past her defenses from the moment they'd sat down.

"So what type of guy do you usually go for?" Riss had asked.

*Big, built, with a beautiful smile and a skilled mouth.*

"I don't know that I have a type."

"Liar." Riss laughed. "Level with me. What's going on between you and Tobin? Because he babbled incessantly about you when he was hammered last week."

"He also asked *you* out on a date," Jade reminded her.

"Not seriously. It's sort of a joke between us."

"You have no interest in him? At all?"

"Only as a friend. Don't get me wrong, Tobin is a great guy."

"But?" Jade prompted.

"But he's almost . . . too good, if you know what I mean. He's like a freakin' Boy Scout. Polite, thoughtful, kind. He always does the right thing, even if it's not the best thing for him. That's not the kind of guy who's a good fit for a woman like me. I'd sour him sooner rather than later and he deserves better."

"Tobin and I have been messing around," Jade blurted out. "And trust me; that man is no Boy Scout when he's got that mouth in motion."

Riss blinked at her. "How long has this been going on?"

"It's been this back-and-forth thing since the day we met. We haven't . . ." Jade blushed.

"What's the holdup? I know Tobin's in total lust with you since he freakin' *told* me that himself."

"The holdup is that we're living with my grandma."

"So? Give me a legit reason why after granny goes to bed that you shouldn't be climbing that man like a tree and letting him bang you like a coconut."

She snickered. "Interesting imagery, Wyoming."

"You're stalling. Come clean, New York, on why you're not getting down and dirty with him every chance you can."

"Fine. Tobin isn't a fling kind of guy."

"And you're worried he'll want more than a fling?"

"I could end up hurting him if I say 'screw it' and start screwing him. I don't want that. And I live in New York."

"Tobin knows where you live, dumb-ass," Riss said crossly. "And I . . ." She paused and smacked the table. "Omigod. *I'm* the dumb-ass. You're not the fling type either, are you? If you start this with him, chances are good you'll fall for him too and it'll—"

"Be too late? I think it already is . . ."

◆━

Loud pounding on the car window startled her out of the memory.

Riss grinned and opened the door. "Grab your stuff and let's do this thang."

As they crossed the parking lot, Jade said, "We're really getting ready at a truck stop?"

"Not a lot of female truckers. So the women's bathroom is super-duper nice since it's hardly ever used."

An hour later they walked into the Prickly Cactus looking as *hot as a prairie fire*—Riss's words, not hers. The joint was a total dive, filled with kitschy western memorabilia—what little Jade could see of it since the only light in the place came from the neon bar signs. They found a table in the middle of the bar area and set it up as their base since it wasn't quitting time for the blue-collar patrons.

"Another hour and this place will be full." Riss smirked around the straw in her margarita. "The cream of the crop will come to us."

"So you're here . . . ?"

"To get laid? Yeah. Pretty much. Been a while. How about you?" She leaned in. "Please, please, please tell me that you and Tobin have done the nasty like five times a day since the last time we talked."

"No. We're still trying to get the timing right. The night it was sup-posed to happen it didn't. I haven't heard from him at all today . . . so he's probably mad or something. I don't know."

"Did you tell him what you wanted?" Riss asked.

Jade sighed. "I'm used to hanging back and waiting for someone to approach me."

"I think you'll be surprised at how many times you get hit on tonight. Babe, you've got to know that you're—"

"If you say exotic looking, I will karate chop you."

Riss choked on her drink. "Fuck, woman. You are funny. I'd totally do you if I was a lesbian."

She laughed.

Guys started coming in one after another. First they'd order a drink, then they'd look around.

"Okay, show time," Riss said.

## Chapter Seventeen

 ⌖

$\mathscr{T}$obin mumbled to Garnet on his way past her.

A long-ass day in the truck driving back from Nebraska meant a shower was an immediate necessity. He took his time cleaning himself up, so when he emerged from the bathroom twenty minutes later, Garnet had resorted to pacing in the hallway.

She stopped and pointed at him. "It's about time."

"I didn't use all the hot water, I swear."

"I know that. I need to talk to you about something. So after you're decent"—she gestured to the towel—"come into the kitchen because we have to talk. Make it snappy. Time is wastin'."

He slipped on a clean pair of jeans and a T-shirt. He'd plugged his dead cell phone in before hitting the shower and quickly checked his messages.

Three. From . . . Riss? What the hell?

The first was a selfie of Riss and Jade in a bar.

His stomach cartwheeled at seeing Jade's sweet smile. She just did it for him. On so many levels.

He squinted at the next shot. Jesus. Was that a picture of Jade's ass? He enlarged it. Oh yeah. Jade's ass in tight jeans with sparkles on the butt that just made him want to sink his teeth into that curve below the pocket.

But why had Riss sent him a picture of Jade's backside? Judging by the way Jade stood, she had no idea her friend was secretly snapping pics of her butt.

In the third pic, a guy had his hand on Jade's shoulder. The time stamp on that one was half an hour ago.

Tobin texted: Where are you?

RT: The Prickly Cactus . . .

Garnet appeared outside his door. "Tobin, I really need to talk to you."

"Make it fast, Miz G. I'm on my way out."

"Jade called me."

Tobin whirled around. "When?"

"Earlier. She's out with Riss and she told me not to wait up."

"Christ."

"She's an adult entitled to her fun. Heaven knows I resist when anyone tries to end my good times. I just worry because she's never had much use for a pixie dust night."

He remembered the one time he knocked back a few pixie dust shots. Or maybe he should say, he didn't remember—the next morning he woke up naked on his deck with a sunburn in places the sun don't shine. Ever since that incident, the Mud Lilies referred to a night out making questionable decisions a pixie dust night.

"So I need a huge favor." Garnet twisted her gnarled fingers. "Make sure Jade is all right."

"How, Miz G?"

She blinked. "By spying on her, of course."

"Not happening. I'll check on her to make sure she's not doin' anything illegal like *some* people who tend to get carried away on pixie dust nights. But whatever else she's doin'? Ain't your business. Got it?"

"I hate when you shoot down my ideas with logic."

Tobin smiled. "I know. You'll be all right by yourself? I probably won't be back tonight."

"Where are you goin'?"

*To get a tiger by the tail.*

His grin told her that wasn't any of her business either. "Have a good night."

She stomped her foot. "Dadgummit. You oughta be taking me along."

"Nope." He touched her nose as he walked past her in the hallway. He could only handle one Evans woman at a time.

Tobin made a call as soon as he turned onto the main highway.

Ike picked up on the second ring. "T, what's goin' on?"

"Riss and Jade are drinking at the Prickly Cactus."

"Are you kiddin' me?"

"Not even a little."

"Hang on." Ike muffled the phone but Tobin still heard some background noise. "I've gotta go, sugar." Then thirty seconds later, he heard, "On my way."

"See you in a few."

⮑

Tobin had worked himself up pretty good by the time he'd reached Rawlins.

Ike leaned against the side of the building, looking disheveled. "Hey."

"You been in there yet?" *Does Jade have some asshole's hands all over her?*

"Nope. Waiting for you."

"Let's go."

"Ah ah ah. Not so fast. You lookin' for a fight?"

Tobin shook his head. "Doesn't mean some dumb fuck won't give me one."

Ike muttered something about dental insurance as Tobin brushed past him.

The look on Tobin's face kept the bouncer from stopping either of them.

The music wasn't overly loud yet. There weren't as many people inside as he'd imagined, and most of them waited at the bar. Tobin scanned the tables for a sign of her.

Bingo.

His elation at seeing Jade didn't extend to the half dozen guys hanging around the table. If the bar area wasn't so swamped, he might have ordered a beer and observed the situation for a bit before approaching.

Instead he marched right up to her, inserting himself between her and the guy about to lose his fucking hand for putting it on her.

When Jade saw him, she smiled. "Fancy meeting you here."

"I was in the neighborhood."

"Liar," she stage-whispered. "We live in the same house and I haven't seen you in our neighborhood for . . . two days."

"I had to go to Nebraska, remember?"

She licked the rim of her glass.

Fuck. That tongue. "You look gorgeous."

"Riss taught me how to get dolled up cowgirl-style."

He ran his knuckles down her cheek. "I can teach you to ride cowgirl-style."

She laughed. "You are in rare form tonight."

Riss whooped and stepped right between them. "Hey howdy, Tobin. Fancy meeting you here."

He snorted.

"This doesn't seem like your kind of place."

"It's not."

"The ambience is lacking." She cocked her head. "Are you here to listen to the band?"

Tobin didn't look away from Jade. "Nope."

"The drink specials end at nine, so maybe you oughta toddle on over there and get us a round."

"Sure. You want another one of those?" He pointed at Jade's glass.

"I'd love one."

"Make it two," Riss said. "And buy fuckface a beer. He looks annoyed to be here."

Ike flashed his teeth at Riss. "Annoyance is my permanent expression around you."

"I thought you were just constipated."

"Be right back." In the fifteen minutes it took for drink service, Tobin watched three different losers approach Jade. None of them stuck around, thank fuck.

Back at the table, when everyone had drinks in hand, Riss raised her glass for a toast. "To friends, lovers and foes; may they not be one person."

With each sip of her margarita, Jade inched closer to him.

He tamped down his impatience over how long before they could get the hell out of here.

"So, Tobin, dude, I'm afraid I have to put you on the spot a little," Riss said.

Fucking awesome. "About what?"

"Why you aren't considering coming to work for Jackson Stock Contracting? When I heard you've sent out resumes to other places?"

He felt Jade's curious gaze on him and Ike avoiding his eyes. "Might be awkward with Renner."

"That's it?"

"No."

"Then what?"

"I'm looking to do something different. You guys are running on a tight margin and there's no money to pay me. I'm sorta fond of not livin' in a homeless shelter and panhandling."

"But you do have another commodity, don't you?" Riss pressed on.

"Not one that'll pay me."

"So the bulls . . . BB's offspring. You own them?"

What was she getting at? "Yeah."

"How many?"

"Four."

"See? That's four potential—"

"There's the word that means nothin'. Potential," he complained. "Zero plus potential? Still equals zero."

"Semen collection is out?" Riss asked.

"Without a state-of-the-art facility and the ability to offer buyers something they can't get anywhere else? Yes. Zero potential for profit. Huge potential for a huge building with . . . oh, an arena in it."

Ike laughed and held his bottle up to touch Tobin's.

Jade looked confused.

Tobin nudged her. "Fun stuff, huh?"

"I have no idea what you guys are talking about."

"Funny. Neither does Riss," Ike said.

Riss flipped him off. Then she flounced off and Ike followed her.

Tobin put his arm across the back of Jade's chair. "I'm happy to see you out having fun."

"Riss is hilarious. Vivien tricked me into going to the Beauty Barn and Riss rescued me." She groaned. "I was so happy to escape that I left GG's order there."

His gaze turned sharp. "Tricked you? How?"

"I think she followed me to the grocery store. Then she claimed GG's order was in or something. I called Riss before I left the grocery store so I had a backup plan. And good thing because Bernice had decided to treat me to a makeover—whether I liked it or not."

Shit. That was not what he'd asked her to do.

"How did you know I was here?"

"Miz G told me when I went home to change. She said you were out havin' a wild night with Riss."

"And you thought you'd check up on me? Or GG sent you to check up on me?"

"I'm here of my own accord, Jade. I'm pretty sure you know that. But darlin', if you need proof . . . well, pucker up. That seems to work best for us."

Jade's focus dropped to his mouth. "Maybe later."

Oh, definitely later. "You don't look like you've been knocking back shots."

"I've had four margaritas in three hours. Why would you think I'd be doing shots?"

"Miz G said it was a pixie dust night. That's what pixie dust is, darlin'. A very potent shot. After one, you're dancin' on the tables. After two, you're *under* the table."

She wrinkled her nose. "Good thing I haven't had any."

"Very good thing." He angled his head closer, letting his mouth touch the spot below her jaw, then he moved into her hairline and inhaled the scent of her. He growled, "Christ you smell good."

"I can't think when you whisper in my ear like that."

"That's our problem; we both think too much."

Jade's hand landed on his chest. "Is that what you've been doing the past forty-eight hours since our plan for alone time bit the dust? Thinking?"

"I'm a man of action. I have a plan in place and a place for us since I've thought of little else the past forty-eight hours. You can feel how hard my heart is beating. And if you moved that sexy ass closer, you'd feel how hard my cock is."

"Tobin."

"Would you like to get out of here?" Maybe it made him sound desperate. But fuck, he was damn near desperate for her.

She pushed his face away with the side of her head. Then she placed a single, soft kiss on the pulse point on the side of his throat. "Yes."

*Thank fuck.*

When Tobin eased back to kiss her, she pressed her fingers over his lips.

"Not until we're truly alone, okay? No interruptions this time."

He uncurled her fingers from his shirt and kissed the center of her palm before clasping her hand in his and pushing to his feet.

Riss and Ike were standing by the bar.

"We're taking off."

"Have fun. Text me later, New York." Riss scowled at Ike. "Feel free to hit the road too, since you weren't invited."

"Am I scaring away the dirtbags you planned to get down and dirty with, La-riss-a?"

"Dirt washes off. I'll take that over your asshole behavior any day, Ike."

"Really?" Ike leaned closer to her. "Hate sex can be really fuckin' hot. Don't you think?" But he might as well have said, *Don't you remember?*

Riss said, "I don't think about things I hate, douche bag. Ever."

"Do I need to warn security there might be a bloodbath?" Tobin asked.

Ike said "yes" the same time Riss said "no," and even Jade rolled her eyes.

Tobin led Jade through the crowd, forcing himself to take measured steps and not break into a sprint.

Once they were outside, he spun and hauled her against his body, tilting her head back to get at her mouth.

The tart and sweet taste of her exploded on his tongue. He kissed her with hunger, greedily swallowing her soft groans.

Jade broke the kiss first. "I want more than this."

"So does that mean you won't be pissed that I rented a room for tonight before I walked into the bar?"

Those beautiful eyes locked onto his. "You did?"

Tobin swept her hair back from her face. "I didn't want you drinking and driving."

"Is that the only reason? You were concerned for my safety?"

"No." He laughed. "I'm a nice guy, but not *that* nice."

"But you are prepared like any good Boy Scout would be."

He got right in her face. "I'm no Boy Scout."

"Prove it."

His mind was a maze of lust as he towed her toward his truck. The two-block drive to the motel happened in the blink of an eye, and they stood outside room 118 as he jammed the keycard in the slot and the green light flashed.

Once they were inside the dark room, he realized they'd lost that urgency.

Leaving the lights off, he slipped her purse off her shoulder and tossed it aside. He pushed her up against the door, twining one hand in her hair and burying his face in her neck, letting the spicy floral scent of her skin take him back to that moment where desire overruled common sense.

Jade didn't wait for him to make the first move. Her mouth found his and she slipped her hands beneath his T-shirt, her cool fingers trailing up, over his abdomen, pausing at the top of his rib cage to stroke the cut of muscle that defined his pectorals.

Gooseflesh erupted from her erotic caress. He kissed her harder, absolutely on fire for this woman. His hand drifted down the center of her torso, gravitating toward the buttons that kept her bare curves beneath his greedy hands. "Jade," he panted against her lips, "baby, we've gotta lose some clothes."

"You first."

He retreated only far enough to pull the T-shirt over his head. Then his mouth returned to hers and he fumbled to unbutton her blouse as she trailed her fingertips up and down his sides, from the base of his armpit to the waistband of his jeans.

That continual, sensual touch kept him on edge more than if she stroked his cock the same way.

Tobin tugged the tails of her shirt out of her jeans and pulled her away from the door to strip it off her completely, leaving her in just her bra. In the dark, he traced the satin straps down to the lace-edged cups. "I want to see you." He blindly reached out to the wall until his hand connected with the light switch.

Fluorescent light flooded the room like they'd stepped into a grocery store at midnight. He quickly shut it off. "How about we go to plan B?"

"Does it involve us getting naked?"

"Uh-huh." He peppered kisses along her collarbone. "And sweaty too."

"I'm in."

He smiled against her throat and wrapped his fingers around her upper arms. He shuffled backward—almost as if they were dancing. Once his calves hit the bed he sat on the edge. "Stay just like that for a second." He reached the lamp on the nightstand. One quick twist and softer light illuminated the room. Then his hands were on her again. Jade was so compact he could almost span her waist with his big hands. "Kick your shoes off."

After Jade took off her heels, her chest was nearly at his mouth level.

Tobin slid his hands around her sides and up her back to undo the clasp of her bra.

She shrugged her shoulders, letting the bra fall halfway down, but with the angle of her head, her hair covered her chest.

"Jade. Move your hair so I can see you."

"There's not much to see," she said softly.

He swept her hair over her shoulder. Her breasts were on the small side, but perfectly shaped. In the center of that gentle rise of smooth caramel-colored skin was a dark brown nipple. "Hell yeah, that's what I want." He urged her forward and opened his mouth on her nipple, closed his lips around it and sucked.

"Oh my god."

He used his mouth, his hands, his teeth on those sweet little tits, until she writhed and arched and whimpered.

Everything he did to her, she said, "Yes, more!" He thought she might've had a tiny O with the way she squeezed her thighs together.

Tobin dragged openmouthed kisses down her belly and unbuttoned her jeans. He murmured, "Off," and helped her shove them down her legs to her ankles.

Jade smoothed her hands over his hair and tipped his head back to look into his eyes. "Tobin. Why are you shaking?"

"Tryin' to keep myself from tossing you on the bed and fucking you hard enough to break the bedframe."

"I'd like to see you try." She bent down and kissed him. Hungrily. Greedily.

When he was out of breath and filled with the taste of her, she backed off.

Keeping her eyes on his, she reached between them and flicked open the button on his jeans. "Off." She immediately sidestepped him as soon as he stood.

Tobin watched as she pulled the bedcovers back and stretched out on the white sheets, clearly waiting for him. First he took out his wallet, removed a condom and flicked it at her.

She caught it, held it between her teeth and waggled her eyebrows.

Crazy woman. He grinned and shed his pants.

Jade's eyes zeroed in on his dick. Her mouth dropped open and the condom fell out. "Tobin. Is that what women mean when they say, 'He's hung like a horse'?"

Jesus. He blushed. Then he felt stupid for it and crawled across the mattress above her. "I haven't had any complaints. But how about we go to plan C?" He rolled onto his back and brought her on top of him, body to body with his cock pressed between them. He curled one hand around the back of her head and squeezed her ass with the other as he kissed her.

Jade's stiff posture relaxed as he fed her slow, drugging kisses. She lowered her knees to the mattress, creating space between them so she could get to his cock.

He silently breathed a sigh of relief that she wasn't shy. But if she kept stroking him like that, they'd have a repeat of the hallway incident. Trailing his lips to her ear, he rasped, "Put the condom on me."

She pushed upright, ripped the package open and rolled the latex down. She checked out the wrapper and mouthed "Magnum" before tossing it aside. Flattening her palms by his head, she smiled shyly. "Got any ridin' tips, cowboy? Because I've never done it this way."

Sweet baby Jesus she was killing him. "Do what feels good. And I'm very good at takin' direction, so don't hesitate to tell me exactly what you need."

"Same goes." Jade scooted back and took him in, inch by inch.

Tobin kept his hands on her hips, letting his thumbs track across her hip bones as that wet heat enveloped him. He gritted his teeth when she stopped a couple of times and pulled back, because she was really fucking tight. And, well, he wasn't small.

The look of concentration on her face? Seriously beyond adorable. When she'd finally worked him all the way in, she did a fist pump and slumped across his chest with a sigh.

"You okay?"

"I think so. I like how it feels. I just need a moment."

He lifted her head off his chest so he could kiss her. The kiss began with just a pass of his lips over hers. A side-to-side glide that he mimicked where they were joined. Nothing overt, just subtle movement.

Jade whispered, "Yes," against his mouth and the kiss got a little hotter. More tongue, more panting breaths.

Then his fingers drifted up and down her spine, stopping to squeeze her ass or caress the dimples in the small of her back.

She rolled her body up over his and kissed him harder. Opening her mouth fully, her body started to set a rhythm. Once the pace increased, she moved her hands to his chest for leverage as she pushed back onto his dick.

*That's it, baby. You got this.*

Tobin closed his eyes. Fuck. That felt good. Especially when she added a clenching grind on the downstroke. All the tightness increased around his cock and he could feel her getting wetter and his balls drew up in response.

Whoa. Not yet. It'd been a while for him but he wasn't gonna blow this fast.

Sweat dotted his body, and he'd run through the periodic table of elements when Jade stopped moving completely.

Softly, she said, "Tobin?"

He looked at her. "You okay?"

"Help me. It feels good, but awkward. I don't know what I'm doing wrong."

"Hey, tiger. You're not doin' anything wrong, let's just fine-tune it a little, okay?"

"Thank you."

She kissed him so sweetly that when she started to retreat, he growled and clamped his hand onto her head to keep her in place. Using that kiss to crank the heat back up between them so they were both panting when he said, "Scoot back some and push up."

She batted her hair out of her face. "Like this?"

"Yep." Tobin rose up far enough to latch onto her nipples, one with his mouth, the other he twisted and pulled with his fingers.

"Oh, I like that."

"I can tell." Jade had started moving faster, creating more friction, driving his cock deeper.

Did she have any idea how sexy she looked? With her hair swirling around them, her teeth digging into her bottom lip, her eyes closed, one hand clutching his head as he alternated between sucking on her neck and her tit.

"Tobin. I'm . . ." Her expression changed and she rocked her hips with shallow strokes, again and again until her body shook and she shouted, "Yes, yes, yes, yes, that feels so good, don't stop, oh please . . ."

Tobin couldn't hide his grin. So Jade was loud in bed. He kept kissing her neck, nuzzling her and caressing her as she came down.

Then she pushed him flat to the mattress and devoured him with hot, wet kisses. Her lips migrated to his ear. "Tell me what'll get you there."

Immediately, he rolled her beneath him.

She blinked those golden eyes and smiled. "Agile *and* hung. I like that."

He pecked her on the mouth and rested his forehead to hers. "Are you sore?"

"Not yet, I'm still delightfully tingly. Why?"

"I need it hard and fast."

"Tobin, I'm not fragile."

"Guess we'll test that, won't we?"

Jade hooked her legs around his hips and nipped his neck. "Come apart for me, cowboy."

Tobin took some of his weight off her as he began sliding in and out. It also allowed him to watch his cock disappearing into that tight pussy.

Fuck yeah. He liked that.

He picked up speed, bottoming out on every thrust.

She used that sassy little tongue on his neck, and her hands were on his chest, thumbing his nipples.

That combination sent gooseflesh straight to his balls.

Despite the cool air blowing in the room, sweat escaped from his hairline and ran down his spine.

He plowed into her harder, not as close to the edge as he thought he was. But it felt too damn good to stop.

Jade's lips brushed his ear. "Yes. Like that. You're going to make me come again."

When her body tightened around his, he let go, pumping into her with enough force to rattle the bedframe. So lost in the rush of release, he barely heard her cry out before she muffled the sound in his chest.

After he'd stopped shuddering in pleasure above her, her mouth reconnected with his. Between sweet and teasing kisses, Tobin managed to roll to his side so he didn't crush her.

"Okay, that was awesome."

Tobin laughed. "Yeah it was."

"But we'll probably have to invest in some lube from here on out."

He nuzzled her temple. "This wasn't a onetime thing for you? Crossing 'banging a cowboy' off your list on your Wild West adventure?"

Jade scooted up and got in his face. "It's not a onetime thing for me, any more than it is for you. We can at least be honest that neither of us is into casual one-offs. Or at least not very often."

"More often than I'd like in my younger years."

"Recently?"

He shook his head. Then he curled his hand around her jaw. "This didn't happen because you were convenient. This didn't happen because I'm tryin' to manipulate you around to my way of thinking with Miz G. This happened because you've fired my blood since the moment I set eyes on you. And I like you." He stroked the corner of her mouth with his thumb. "We clear on that?"

"Yes."

"Good." He pressed his mouth to hers. "Be right back."

In the bathroom Tobin ditched the condom. He took a leak. He washed his hands and face and wet a washcloth with cold water. Exiting the bathroom, he found Jade beneath the sheet.

She eyed the washcloth suspiciously. "What's that?"

"How sore are you now?"

"A little."

Which probably meant a lot. "This will help." Tobin pulled back the sheet and said, "Spread 'em."

"You're joking."

"Nope." He waited.

Finally she slid her heels out and said, "Whatever."

He placed the cloth between her legs and muffled her shriek with his mouth. When he was relatively sure she wouldn't take a swing at him, he ended the kiss and looked into her eyes. "Better?"

"Yes, but it's cold."

Tobin crawled in bed, gathering her into his arms. It surprised him how quickly and easily she snuggled into him. "If it gets too cold, I'd be more than happy to warm you up with my mouth."

"I'll keep that in mind." Jade drew circles on his chest. "How many condoms did you bring tonight?"

"Just one."

She lifted her head and looked at him. "Really?"

He grinned. "Nope. Got another one in my wallet."

"Boy Scout," she teased.

"Optimistic," he volleyed back. "As much as I'd love to spend the night over you, under you, behind you, seeing how many times I can make you come, it'd kill the mood to see you wincing."

"Has that happened before?"

Even as he wondered how honest he should be, Jade said, "Truth between us always, Tobin."

"All right. I've had a few women only want me for my cock; that never lasted long. But one time I stripped down and the chick I was with looked at my groin with complete horror and told me to get my 'meat club' the hell away from her."

"Meat club? Seriously?"

"Yeah."

"Meat club," Jade repeated. Then she started to giggle.

He loved to hear her giggle; it might've been one of the happiest sounds in the entire world.

"Sorry, I shouldn't be laughing," she said, still laughing. "I'll pipe down before you club me with your—"

Tobin put his hand over her mouth. "Don't even *think* about sayin' it."

She snickered off and on for the next little bit. Then she yawned.

"Want me to shut off the light?"

"Mmm. But come right back where you were. I'm so comfy like this."

Once they were twined together in the darkness, Jade said, "This didn't happen because I wanted a wild cowboy sex tale to brag about to my friends in New York. It didn't happen because I was bored and lonely—I live with that every day so that's nothing new. It happened because something about you sucked me in, Tobin. The more time I spend with you, the more I like you."

He kissed the top of her head. "Thanks."

As he drifted off she whispered, "And now I'm pretty fond of your meat club too."

"Now you're in for it." Tobin tickled her until she shrieked.

Then he kissed her until she twined herself around him again.

Sleep didn't come as easily the second time when she said, "How will we explain this to GG? Or is this something we keep to ourselves for a little longer?"

"I don't know, darlin'. I truly don't. Can we talk about it in the morning?"

"I suppose. But I'm not really tired anymore."

"Me neither."

"Do you want to watch TV?"

"We haven't done that, have we?"

"That's because we're not allowed in the same room." Jade snickered.

"We're definitely breaking all the rules tonight."

After a bit, Jade murmured, "Being here with you like this? The ultimate pixie dust night."

Tobin fell more than a little in love with her right then.

## Chapter Eighteen

Jade woke up alone the next morning.

She stretched and smiled, feeling so well . . . rested. And deliciously sore in all the right places.

Man. Tobin definitely knew how to use that rocket in his pocket. She couldn't remember the last time she'd had two orgasms in one night. Two and a half orgasms if she counted that mini O when he'd sucked her nipples. Guys overlooked her breasts since they weren't big, bouncing mounds, but her breasts were so sensitive that she could get off just from a hungry mouth and clever hands. And the sexy cowboy had both of those.

As she dreamily relived everything that happened last night, she realized being in bed with Tobin had been fun. And intense. And adventurous. She definitely wanted more of him—of this—but where did they go from here?

The door clicked, the knob turned and Tobin walked in, balancing two cups of coffee on a tray in one hand and a plastic bag draped around his other wrist. He smiled at her. "Mornin', tiger."

"Good morning, slick."

"Here I went out and got us coffee and a few toiletries and I can tell by your eyes that you thought I'd bailed on you first thing."

She blushed. "Busted." She scooted up and held out her hand for the coffee, sending the sheet sliding down to her hips. "I am happy you didn't take off."

Tobin leaned over and kissed her lips, then bent down even more and brushed his mouth across her exposed nipple. "Drink your coffee and get dressed before I ditch my clothes and crawl back in with you."

"That condom burning a hole in your pocket?"

"Yep." He handed her a cardboard cup, but his eyes were on her chest. "Maybe I've got time for a little taste of you."

"Go. I'm getting dressed."

Tobin ducked into the bathroom.

Jade found her clothes—she'd be doing the walk of shame into GG's house. She snagged her purse off the floor and fished out her brush. After a few detangling passes, she pulled her hair into a low ponytail at the base of her neck.

Sipping her coffee, she looked around the room. Pretty basic. Strange to think this had been the first time she'd checked into a hotel with a guy for the express reason to have sex.

*Don't forget watching TV.* Which she'd loved. Snuggled up to Tobin's big body. He constantly had to be touching her and she could easily become addicted to it.

The bathroom door opened and Tobin stepped out, that clean soap scent trailing behind him. "I got you a toothbrush."

"Thanks. What about hair spray?"

Those beautiful eyes of his sparkled. "Sorry, babe. I bought some but I used it all. Takes a ton of product to make my hair look this damn good every morning."

She smiled. "I like your hair. As if you couldn't tell by how many times I pulled it last night."

"No complaints from me about that."

"My turn." Teeth brushed, face washed, she left the bathroom to find Tobin frowning at his phone. "Something wrong?"

"Did you get a text from Miz G about both of us bein' on a conference call with her at eleven this morning?"

"I haven't looked at my phone since last night." She dug it out of her purse and punched in the access code. "I got the same message." Jade looked at Tobin. "Maybe someone saw us racing off to the motel last night and tattled on us."

"Could be."

"If that is the case, what are we going to tell her?"

"You regret what happened?"

"Not at all. Do you?"

"Not a single moment. So if I had my way? I'd sit Miz G down and tell her that we're involved."

"That's it?"

Tobin smirked behind his coffee cup. "I might warn her to buy earplugs since you're loud in bed."

"Tobin!"

"Well, babe. You are. And it's hot as hell so I'd never tell you to pipe down."

"Great. Now I'll never be able to have sex in GG's house."

He raised an eyebrow.

She didn't buy that lame argument either. She changed the subject. "Do you have to go into the Split Rock today?"

"Ike is filling in for me. So we're goin' grocery shopping before we head back to Muddy Gap."

Jade groaned. "I went shopping yesterday and just remembered I left a carton of yogurt in my car."

"We'll have to swing by and pick up your car after the store."

"Why can't you go to the store without me?"

"I always go to the store by myself." He tugged her against him. "It's lonely, it sucks and if I have a chance for a hot woman to be strolling beside me? I'm takin' it."

She studied his handsome face.

"What?"

"How is it that a man who looks like you is still single?"

Tobin blushed. "Jade. You're sweet. But I'm not exactly a guy that turns women's heads."

"You turned mine." She stood on tiptoe, letting the stubble on his chin abrade her lips because she loved how it felt. "So I'll go to the store with you because I know how much it sucks to shop for one. But know what's worse? Eating out by yourself every night."

His eyes softened. "You end up doin' that a lot, sweetheart?"

"Honestly? Yes. More than I liked. My roommate had a boyfriend and I never wanted to be one of those people that always tags along. I have other friends, but again, I felt weird calling up and saying 'Hey, wanna hit the soba noodle joint on East Twenty-third because I'm tired of eating takeout in front of the TV?'"

He pressed his lips to her forehead. "Loneliness is loneliness regardless if you're in a city surrounded by millions of people or out in the middle of nowhere surrounded by tumbleweeds and cows."

So how did she explain she felt less lonely in the few weeks that she'd been here than in the past two years at home?

"Can I say something totally sappy?" he murmured in her hair.

"Sure."

"I like you even more now that I know you understand that."

Her arms snaked around his neck, allowing her to maneuver his head so she could get at his mouth.

Tobin hadn't soothed her with sweet and gentle kisses. No, the man utterly seduced her, feeding her long, deep soul kisses that stirred something inside her she hadn't felt for a very long time.

Hope.

&#x269C;

Being Tobin's lover meant he treated her differently in public. He held her hand as they crossed the grocery store parking lot. He touched her frequently—not in an overtly sexual way, though. But she did catch him watching her with that dark look of desire in his eyes. Then he'd blink and that intensity would be gone. Clearly she'd merely scratched the surface with him in the weeks they'd known each other, and she couldn't wait to dig a little deeper to see what else she'd discover about him.

He pushed the cart and seemed to have a set path in his head.

"Did GG give you a grocery list?" she finally asked him.

"She doesn't need to anymore."

"Why? It's the same every week?"

Tobin shook his head. "It rotates every three weeks. This is the list she gave me the first week I moved in."

"It's on your phone or something?"

"Nope. I memorized it."

Jade peered into the cart. There were already fifty items in there. "How many—"

"One hundred and twelve items this week. Make that one hundred and thirteen if we buy lube here. But I'm leaning toward stopping at the drugstore so I can buy a case of condoms too."

Her head whipped around. "A case?"

He crowded her against the shelves of crushed tomatoes. "A case to start with and we'll go from there."

"Tobin, you're intimidating me."

He bent down and placed an openmouthed kiss on the pulse point on her neck. "No I'm not. You're as excited about our sex-fest as I am."

"Sex-fest?"

"Yep." His lips traveled up to her ear. "Hot, sweaty, dirty, sweet, fast, slow, quiet, loud, raunchy, fun . . . I want to try it all with you. And when

I look in your eyes, tiger, I see the same curiosity and longing I know you see in mine."

"It should annoy me that you read me so well."

He chuckled. "But you're already compiling a list of things you wanna try, aren't you?"

"Here's a dash of cold water. We're living with my grandmother. It'd be embarrassing for all of us if she waltzed into the kitchen and found you on your knees licking—"

"Tobin?"

He straightened up and offered her a devilish smile before turning around.

"Celia! Lady, I haven't seen you in forever."

Jade took two steps away and immediately Tobin's arm came around her shoulder.

The blond woman flicked a quick glance at them before spinning around to say, "Brianna Lawson. Get back here right now."

A pigtailed little girl of about five raced back, her shoes sending out bright pink flashes of light with every footstep.

"Mama! Up!" a girl with curly, dark hair strapped into the shopping cart yelled, and lifted her arms into the air.

"Nice try, but you're locked in for a reason." She pointed at the little girl. "Hands on the cart."

"Okay, Aunt Celia."

The woman looked at Tobin and stepped around her niece. "It has been a while. I don't get out as much as I used to. Seems my husband's goal in life is to keep me knocked up."

Tobin acknowledged her baby bump with a chin dip. "How you feelin'?"

"Happy."

That answer surprised Jade. She'd only heard pregnant women complain.

"Last week when I saw Kyle he mentioned . . . twins?"

She smiled. "Oh yes. Two for the price of one this time. Holt is start-ing on the addition next week so it's done before calving starts. What a zoo that'll be." Then she focused on Jade. "I'm sorry; I'm usually not so rude." She offered her hand. "I'm Celia Gilchrist. This hooligan is my niece Brianna and this is my daughter, Ashlyn."

"Jade Evans. Nice to meet you."

Celia cocked her head and her long braid swung to the side. "Evans. Garnet's granddaughter?"

"Yes."

"I heard—"

A loud stomp sounded out followed by an equally loud, "Hey!"

Jade glanced down at the freckle-faced, pigtailed girl who studied her suspiciously. "Hello, there."

She said, "*Hola*." When Jade didn't respond right away, she sighed. "You look kinda like her but you don't talk like her."

*This ought to be interesting.* "Who?"

"Dora the Explorer. She's on TV. She speaks *Español*."

"Sorry to disappoint you, Brianna, but even though I am Hispanic and Asian I don't speak Spanish or Chinese. I was adopted as a baby so I just speak English."

"I could teach you *Español*," she offered.

"How kind of you to offer. Thank you." Jade looked at the girl's aunt, but her focus winged between Tobin and Jade.

"So . . . what's goin' on with you two? Did I see PDA in the grocery store?"

Tobin grinned. "Yes, you did. We're new at this couple thing. In fact we haven't told Miz G yet, so is there a chance you can keep it on the down low?"

"I can, but Kyle gossips like the Mud Lilies and there's no way I'm keeping something this juicy from him." She smirked. "'Bout damn time you got a woman of your own, Tobin."

Jade saw Tobin blush again.

"Just keep Kyle from telling Sherry, until me'n Jade get this squared away, okay?"

"Okay. But you know Mr. Romantic will be grilling you at the Split Rock first thing Monday mornin'."

"I figured."

Just then the little girl let out a bloodcurdling scream and started kicking her legs against the shopping cart.

"That's my cue to go," Celia said.

"Can you handle all this by yourself?" Tobin asked. "Do you need help with loading the groceries or the kids in your truck?"

"You're thoughtful to offer, T, but I'll be fine. Kyle can help me once I get home." She smiled at Jade. "Nice to meet you."

"Same here." Then Jade waved at Brianna. "*Adios.*"

She grinned ear to ear. "*Adios.*"

Tobin stole a kiss as soon as they'd walked away. "Let's get this done so we don't miss Miz G's conference call."

Jade put her hand on his chest. "Back up. We got sidetracked."

"From?"

"From you telling me how you know all the items on GG's week one grocery list."

He lifted his cowboy hat and ran his hand over his hair. "Here's a little-known fact about me. I have a photographic memory."

"For real?"

He nodded. "It's not something I talk about because people either think I'm lying or they act as if they have the right to test me. Like I'm some kind of lab monkey that should be happy to perform on demand."

Jade stared at him.

"What?"

"I don't know if I've ever been so jealous of a person in my entire life. Do you know how handy that would've come in for me? When I had to memorize a Shostakovich piece and twenty pages of a Kabalevsky concerto in the same week?"

Relief crossed his face. "It came in pretty handy for mapping genomes and DNA sequences. It still does for the genetics work I'm doin' on the side."

She poked him in the sternum. "See? That's another thing I didn't know about you that Riss mentioned last night."

"I'll make you a deal. I'll bore you with my genetics research for a short time if you'll play your violin for me."

"You sure we'll even have time for that with this 'sex-fest' plan of yours?" she teased.

"My research will make for great pillow talk after we've rocked the mattress because it'll definitely put you to sleep." He ran his knuckles down her jawline. "Your musical selection will be foreplay because I'll want to jump you after you're finished."

Jade smirked. She had a tango to play him that was pure sex on strings. "You have yourself a deal."

❧

Since Tobin refused to let her pay for any groceries, she informed him she'd stop at the drugstore and stock up on sex-fest supplies. And it was really cute when he blushed and wrote down the brand of condoms that fit him.

By the time she arrived at GG's house, he'd already hauled everything inside.

They were each lost in their own thoughts as they put away the groceries.

Jade's phone rang first at the appointed time. "Morning, GG."

"Hang on, sweetheart, I've gotta loop Tobin into the conference call. Dadgummit. If I remember how to do this."

"Tobin is right here. I'll put you on speaker." Jade pointed at him.

"Mornin', Miz G."

"Can you hear me now?"

Jade rolled her eyes.

"Yes, ma'am, I can hear you fine. Can you hear us?"

"Jade," GG said. "Say something. Something nice," she warned. "None of that bickering crap. I don't have time for it."

Nervous, with no clue what to say, she broke out into the chorus of "Wannabe" by the Spice Girls.

"Stop!" GG said, way too loudly. "I get it. You can hear me."

Tobin scrawled out *WAY TO BE DISCREET* in Sharpie across the newspaper that had been lying on the table.

Jade snatched it out of his hand and smacked him with it.

His grin promised retaliation.

"Okay, kiddos, listen up. Me'n Pearl are in Denver waiting to board a plane to take us to Fort Lauderdale."

"What? Why?"

"She got one of them last-minute cruise deals. And we made a pact that if this one ever came up again, we'd drop everything and go."

"Go where?" Jade demanded.

"The Panama Canal."

"When did this come up?" Tobin asked.

"First part of the week. Pearl didn't know if there'd be cancellations until yesterday. She found out last night. Since neither one of you two were home, I just packed my stuff and we left at five a.m."

"GG, are you sure this is safe? And it's not a scam?"

"Oh pooh, girlie. I've been around the block a time or two. This is a once-in-a-lifetime trip for two old-timers like me'n Pearl. Might be our only chance to do it."

"How long will you be gone?"

"Three weeks. We're both too cheap to spring for international phone service, so we'll be out of touch until we're back in Los Angeles."

She cleared her throat. "But my trip don't change nothin' for either of you, you hear me? Tobin, I don't trust that son of mine not to see this as a golden opportunity to get me packed up and moved out, so I still need you there, keeping an eye on Jade so she's not pulling any funny business while I'm gone."

Jade's gaze connected with Tobin's when he said, "Trust me, Miz G, I will keep a very close eye on your granddaughter."

"Thank you, sonny. Now, Jade doll, you still there?"

"I don't know, GG. Maybe I'm up to my elbows in all sorts of funny business."

"Now, sweetheart, don't be like that. I know you're only following your daddy's orders. That's why you cannot let on that I'm on vacation, okay? You just keep on keepin' on like I was there. And with all the stuff in my garden getting ripe, well, I'll need you to put up some beans, pickles and okra. Peppers too. Maybe some pear chutney."

She froze. "Put up? What do you mean? Like bag them up?"

"No. I mean pick 'em, clean 'em, and can 'em."

"What? I don't know how to do any of that stuff!"

A pause. "You don't?"

"No!"

"Well then, it's past time that you learned, doncha think?"

Jade's jaw dropped.

Tobin laughed.

"I put the rest of the Mud Lilies on notice that they're to come over and check on you once a day to make sure you haven't killed each other. Blood is damn hard to get off the walls. You gotta paint over it to get rid of it."

*Don't ask how she knows that, just let it go.*

"Miz G, Jade and I are reasonable, responsible adults. We don't need your retired friends to babysit us. In fact . . ." Tobin sauntered forward and stopped right in front of her. He hooked his index finger beneath her chin and swept his thumb across her bottom lip. "It'd be best if they steered clear and let us hash this out in our own way."

Oh, that dangerous, sexy look in his eyes set her panties on fire.

"Shoot, we're starting the boarding process, so I gotta go. Be good the next three weeks. Both of you."

*Click.* She ended the call.

"Not a chance," he rasped as he took the phone from Jade and chucked it on the counter.

"Not a chance . . . what?"

"Not a chance in hell that I'm gonna be good. I plan on bein' very, very bad. Starting right now." Tobin put his mouth on her ear. "Take off your jeans and brace yourself against the counter."

Her head fell back and she whimpered when he started nibbling on her neck. Her nipples, her belly, her thighs had already gone hot and tight with anticipation.

Tobin freed her hair and smoothed his hands over her head. "Jade. Darlin'. Jeans off. Now."

"I can't think straight when you talk to me like that."

"I'll get you started." He popped the button on her jeans. Somehow those thick fingers got a hold of the zipper tab and pulled it down. Then he slid his hand down her abdomen, his fingers slipping beneath the denim and lace underwear, over her mound.

She gasped when his middle finger pressed against her clit.

"Fuck. You're already wet."

"I've been wet since the grocery store."

He groaned. "Don't tell me that."

She turned her head and let her tongue taste the skin below his strong jawline. "You'd rather I . . . ?"

"Take your goddamned pants off so I can put my mouth on this pussy and test your wetness myself."

Her sex clenched and of course he felt it.

"You like that."

Blushing, she angled forward trying to dislodge his hand as she worked her jeans down her legs.

He backed off only when she needed to kick her jeans aside. Then he dropped to his knees.

Jade's belly rippled as she looked down at Tobin's head. His hair seemed to be ten different colors of brown with russet, blond and burnished gold highlights that made it difficult to classify. When his mouth touched her belly button, her stomach rippled again.

"I never would've pegged you as a lace thong type." His rough-tipped fingers traced the band running from her hip bones to her lower back. "I figured you'd be either funky bikini bottoms or those sexy boy shorts."

"Disappointed?"

"Nope." Tobin wound the lacy band around and around his finger until it got uncomfortably tight on the right side of her hip and started to pull up between her legs. He tipped his head back and locked his gaze to hers. He said, "Are you?" and jerked hard so all she heard was *riiiiiip*, and then her thong dangled from his fingers.

"God, Tobin. Are you trying to see if you can make me come without you even putting your mouth on me?"

"You liked that too," he murmured. "Take off your shirt so nothing blocks my view when I'm watching you come."

Her shirt hit the floor.

Those big, callused hands skated up the outsides of her thighs. "Spread your legs and hold on to the counter." As soon as he had her in the position he liked, he opened her sex up with his thumbs, exposing the sensitive inner tissues to his gaze, his soft, short exhalations and his tongue.

Oh. That tongue.

Just the very tip circled her clit, then he flattened it as he slid it down the contour of her mound until his searching mouth found the source of wetness and he started to lick her. Lap at her. Making greedy, hungry, growling noises. Then he stopped and she could see his shoulders heaving. He turned his head and planted a soft smooch on the inside of her left thigh with warm, sticky lips.

Jade's fingers tightened around the edge of the counter as she watched him, her heart thudding in her throat and chest. Her pulse throbbed differently between her legs, almost in anticipation for the next touch of his tongue or whisper of his breath.

"Jade, baby, I can't."

She swallowed hard. "You can't what? Go down on me?"

Tobin's head snapped back and he looked at her. "What? Wait. You think I don't want to . . . ?" His groan vibrated everywhere and she trembled. "I was gonna try and take this slow, but fuck, woman. This pussy tastes like fucking candy. I just want to lick you, suck on you and bite you until you give me more of that sweetness as you're bucking against my mouth."

Reaching down, she gently pushed his hand away. Then she grabbed a fistful of his hair and used it to pull his head back. "Time for plan B. Follow me."

Jade heard him groan behind her and she put an extra swing in her hips as she pushed through the swinging doors and entered the living room. She sat in the middle of the couch next to the bag containing the condoms and lube.

As soon as Tobin cleared the door, she scooted to the edge of the cushion, with her feet on the edge and her knees spread wide. She threw her arm above her head and said dramatically, "Have your wicked way with me, however you like. Somehow I shall endure your thorough tongue-lashing."

Then Tobin was on his knees in front of her. He trailed his fingers across her pussy from her clit to her opening and back up. "Jesus. You're pretty here too."

Feeling . . . ornery and like they'd lost some momentum, Jade held three fingers up in front of Tobin's face.

"What's that?"

"The number of orgasms I need for you to gain admission to this ride."

His eyes gleamed. "You throwing out a challenge, tiger?"

She reached out and traced his lips. "Only because I know I'll be sore after you bend me over the couch and fuck me. So make me sore with this clever mouth first, slick."

"That's the first time I've ever heard you swear."

"'Fuck' is not a swear word in this context. It's an action word, and it's really the only one that adequately describes what you're going to do to me, isn't it?"

"Stop talkin' and start moaning."

Tobin hadn't been kidding that he couldn't go slowly.

Her first orgasm came in under two minutes. He dragged his mouth up and down her slit a few times, then he settled his flicking tongue and suctioning lips directly over her clit until she came unhinged, her body giving up a gush of wetness.

Tobin's mouth was sliding everywhere as he built her up for orgasm number two. Licking, sucking, a tease here and there, but mostly he feasted on her relentlessly. Right at the moment when her legs began to shake and all the blood seemed to flow hot and fast to her pussy, and that burst of tingles radiated out from behind her tailbone, he shoved two fingers into her opening.

That shot her straight into orbit.

Instead of the pulsing and throbbing being synchronized, the orgasm rolled over her in waves. The inner tightening of her muscles, the *throb throb throb* of her clit, back to his stroking fingers coaxing more of those long pulls and then his mouth squeezing out three slower throbs.

When her legs still trembled in the aftermath, Tobin nuzzled that delicate area between her hip bones as he tenderly caressed her.

Jade had squeezed her eyes shut both times he'd worked her into a frenzy. So when he showed her a gentler touch, she opened her eyes to find

Tobin peering up at her. He was just . . . all man. From the brooding set to his lips to his rugged profile. She reached out to trace the hard line of his jaw.

He trapped her arm against her knee and kissed the inside of her wrist. "You are so fucking sexy when you let go. I can't even describe what a fucking rush it is that you give yourself over to me completely, knowing you come undone from what I do to you, knowing that it's real because I can feel it. I can taste it."

"Tobin." His honestly floored her.

"So fair warning, baby, now that I know how it is between us? I'm gonna want you more that I already did. I'm gonna want it all the fucking time." He scraped his cheek up the inside of her wrist. "Does that scare you?"

"Only if you don't give me a choice. But that's not you. Or else you would've used that second condom last night without a second thought."

He smiled. "Yeah, I showed remarkable restraint. Lucky for you I don't have to do that right now."

"Very lucky for me. But I'll warn you. I've never hit three oral Os in one night."

"I'll remind you, babe, that it's not night. And I could stay here all damn day with this sweet pussy in my face."

"That position isn't strangling your poor cock?"

"A little. Every time you come and make that sexy fucking moan, it's raring to go to get you to make that noise again." He licked up her slit. "And again."

The thought of all that power and passion unleashed on her . . . she couldn't wait.

Tobin slowed the pace. His kisses on her clit were fleeting, making her arch hard for more contact with his mouth. Which he denied her. He sucked her pussy lips. Wiggled his tongue all the way inside her. He didn't take her to the edge and back off. Instead he drove her to that edge one lick at a time.

Finally he ramped up the pace. He swept the stubble on his chin back and forth across her swollen clit. Sometimes that bristle was soft. Sometimes it wasn't. But that quick sting quickly melted into pleasure.

Then Jade had drifted back into that place where *please please please* became a mantra as her body inched closer and closer to that state of pulsating bliss.

At some point Tobin had started swirling his wet thumb over the pucker of her ass, and that gave her an entirely new sensation to focus on. So she didn't notice at first when the abrasion of his beard on her clit increased and stung more than tickled.

But she started to squirm, and he used his free hand to keep her hips pinned against the couch. Then she held her breath with every prickly pass and became light-headed.

Just when she thought she couldn't take another sharp pain, Tobin opened his mouth over her clit and sucked softly, adding the random lash of his tongue.

Jade came hard—harder than she'd ever come in her life. A kaleidoscope of shifting patterns and shapes danced behind her eyelids, twirling her around into a white vortex of nothingness, where the only constant was the roaring in her ears and the accelerated beat of her heart.

When every inner and outer muscle and tendon and tissue stopped twitching, she opened her eyes.

"So fuckin' hot," Tobin murmured against her belly. He snatched the bag from the drugstore and dumped out the box of condoms and the lube. After pushing to his feet, he kept his eyes on hers as he ditched his jeans and boxer briefs and rolled on a condom. One flick of the cap and he had the lube open.

Was there anything sexier than a confident man stroking himself?

Maybe a sexy, naked man gritting out, "Need to fuck you now. Get to the end of the couch and bend over before I lose my ever-lovin' mind."

"Maybe you should lube me up first."

Tobin squirted a long thick line of lube down the seam of his first and second finger. Then he gently pushed those fingers inside her, swallowing her gasp at the cool temperature of the lube.

He kissed her, pausing only to add more K-Y.

"You taste like me," she said softly.

"I smell like you too. I might not wash my face for days."

She blushed. And wasn't that just stupid. The man had his fingers inside her and she was uncomfortable with him telling her how much he liked the way she tasted and smelled.

He eased his fingers out and pressed the tube into her hand. "Keep it close in case we need more."

She nodded and ducked her head, allowing her hair to cover her face.

An awkward moment passed.

Then Tobin's rough palm skated up her arm. He brushed her hair over her shoulder. "Second thoughts?"

"No." She took one step back. And another. "Just wondering which couch. This one is too low." She pointed. "That one is too high. So which one is just right?"

Tobin lunged for her. "Oh, this one will do just fine." He spun her around and put his hand in the middle of her back, until her chest rested on the cushions and her butt hung over the edge.

Jade pushed up and looked over her shoulder at him. The look of lust he wore for her . . . pretty heady stuff.

He widened her stance, and his hand shook as he smoothed his hand over her butt. "I wanna take a bite outta this ass."

"Maybe next time."

The head of his cock prodded her opening. "Lower your hips. There, that's it."

She bit her lip as he pushed in.

And in.

And in.

And in.

"Christ. So tight. You okay?"

"I don't know yet."

His withdrawal had her handing him the lube.

"More is better."

Whatever Tobin did made it better—much better.

After a few slow deep strokes, he ground out, "Jade. I have to move."

And then he did.

Chills erupted when she stole another peek over her shoulder. There was some serious power behind the way those lean, muscular hips could thrust and pump.

His grip increased and he said, "Fuck. Fuck me."

Which Jade took to mean she should drive back onto him harder.

"Yeah. Like that. Sexy little thing. You movin' like that is makin' my dick harder."

She smirked.

"Ain't gonna last. Too good."

*Slam. Slam. Slam. Slam. Slam.*

Tobin threw his head back and roared.

She watched the cords in his neck strain as his orgasm overtook him. The ropy muscles and thick veins in his forearms popped up like a topographical road map as he clutched her hips. His chest heaved as he tried to suck in air. Biceps, triceps, pectorals, all glistening and quivering. And she really wished she had a mirror to watch his glutes flexing.

He exhaled and opened his eyes.

"Worth the price of admission?"

"Smart-ass." He leaned over and peppered kisses up her spine. "Let's crawl in bed for a few hours and figure out how else we're gonna spend these three weeks together."

## *Chapter Nineteen*

⤜⤛

*I*t was weird napping during the day.

It was really weird napping with a woman.

A naked woman.

A naked, snuggly woman.

Tobin brushed the hair out of Jade's face and ran his hand down the side of her body, stopping at the curve of her ass.

She stirred against him and made a little moan.

Fuck. He loved how vocal she was.

Her soft lips teased his pectoral as she rubbed her nose and cheek across his chest. "For you being so hard here, you sure make a great pillow."

"Glad you think so. It's yours anytime you want."

Jade shifted to look at him and smiled shyly. "Hi."

He grinned at her. "Hey, baby."

"I don't suppose we can laze in bed all day."

"We can do whatever you want."

She ruffled his chest hair with her fingers.

"Something on your mind?"

"Two things actually."

He waited, forcing himself not to freak out, but in his experience, shit like this never went well for him.

She sighed. "I've always been a geeky orchestra girl with her nose buried in a book. Hot guys never noticed me. I'm not saying that to get sympathy or anything. It's just something you should know."

"Why? I don't see that it matters now because I've more than noticed you."

"You've got mad bedroom skills, plus confidence and charm. I don't know if I can keep up. So I want you to be honest with me if I . . . disappoint you."

He counted to ten. "Seems like you wanna do this now, so we'll do it now and be done with it for good."

"Done with what?"

"Old baggage. Old exes."

"I also said you had mad bedroom skills, but you didn't pick up on that," she retorted.

Tobin grabbed a handful of her hair and tilted her head back. "You did see how hard I came, right? You heard me. You watched me. So you've got some mad bedroom skills yourself, baby."

She smirked. "Fine. Dish on the exes and then I'll feel superior about the women who were too stupid to keep you."

He smiled and kissed the top of her head. "I was a virgin until I started college. The first girl I slept with became my girlfriend. We dated maybe six months. She wanted more of the date-type relationship, going to movies or out to eat or events at the college. When we were alone she just liked to cuddle. Her saying that to me—a horny eighteen-year-old guy—was way fuckin' worse than bein' friend-zoned. At least in that zone there's no body-to-body contact. Her snuggling into me, rubbing on me sometimes all night? I hated that she assumed I'd be okay with junior-high-type physical contact."

"So did you get wild on Sorority Row after that?"

"Never as much as my buddies thought I should. I liked the idea of being with one person. My next semi-serious relationship was in grad school. At first we had a lot of sex, but then . . . Then we didn't do anything but study and she'd bitch about her parents. The longer we were together the less sex was part of our relationship. Then all she ever needed from me was a rubber ear." He cringed. "I pulled the ultimate dick move and told her if she bought a rubber cock then she wouldn't need me at all."

Jade snickered. "And that was the last time you saw her."

"Yep. I moved home after getting my master's. While I was waiting for my life to begin and for the job offers to start pouring in, I started seeing a woman a few years older than me. She taught third grade in Saratoga. We clicked and started making plans—life plans. But she didn't want to leave Wyoming so she encouraged me to only apply for jobs within driving distance. So I turned down a great job in Omaha."

"She asked you to turn it down?"

"I tried to do the mature relationship thing and discuss it with her first, but she said if I wanted to be with her then I should be willing to make sacrifices. I ended up working at the Split Rock part time and serving as a hunting guide the rest of the time. I don't know why I trusted her or believed that we were building something permanent. She owned a house but she wouldn't let me move in with her. Instead I had to live at home which fucking sucked. We didn't ever hang out with her friends or her colleagues. She didn't want to meet my buddies. She kept me a dirty little secret. Within two days of the school year ending, she broke it off with me. Evidently I was a placeholder until her real boy-friend was released from jail. She took off on the back of his bike." He released a nervous laugh. "I've never told anyone that story."

"Really? Why not?"

"Because I was her fuck toy and it makes me sound like an idiot."

"Were you in love with her and broken-hearted when she left you?" Jade asked softly.

"No. That's the thing. I was pissed at myself for having shitty judgment. After that? I decided hookups were best even when I always wanted something more meaningful."

Jade remained quiet a beat too long.

"What are you thinking about?"

"You being a fuck toy. I hate that for you."

Tobin tipped her head back. "But?"

"I don't want you to treat me the opposite. I'm petite . . . and you're big all over. Bigger than I imagined. But you don't treat me like I'm fragile. You haven't so far. However . . ." She drilled her finger into his pectoral. "I don't want any set schedules. You, Mr. Math Genetics dude, looking at the clock, thinking, 'It's been eight hours. Maybe I should wait another two before we go at it again.'"

He blushed. He saw himself doing that very thing.

"Here's a scenario. I'm finishing the dishes and you're . . . having a frosty beverage in the living room. It's been four hours. Then you think of something or maybe you're watching porn on your phone and you get hard and you want to fuck. Do you, one: yell 'Babe, it's go time' over your shoulder, or do you, two: come up behind me in the kitchen and whisper, 'Are you sore?'"

"None of the above." Tobin rolled on top of her. "First off, if I ever yell 'Babe, it's go time' and I'm expecting to get laid? Punch me in the nuts. Seriously."

She laughed. "Deal."

"Secondly, you aren't gonna be doin' dishes while I'm sitting on the couch drinking a fucking beer. You wash and I'll dry or whatever. Then maybe when we're almost done with the dishes, I hook the towel around your neck and pull your body against mine. Maybe I tease you until you're ready to blow. Maybe I finger you until you're wet and making those sexy little gasps. Maybe I grab the lube out of the junk drawer because I've started stashing it all over the damn house, just in case"—he grinned—"and I strip you down to skin, right there. After I hoist you onto the counter and I'm kissing you everywhere, my mouth lands like here"—he dragged his finger along her collarbone—"or here"—he pressed his thumb into the pulse point at the base of her throat—"or all the way along here"—he started at her earlobe and followed the curve of her neck across her shoulder.

Jade's breathing turned choppy.

"As I'm doin' all that tasting and licking of your skin on the top, I've shoved my pants down, squirted lube on my cock and have your hot cunt aligned perfectly so I can slam into you with one snap of my hips. I fuck you however your mouth and body tells me you need it. Fast. Slow. Deep. Shallow. After you come screaming my name and I get off pounding into your tight pussy . . . I don't think either of us will remember if I asked you if you were sore."

"There's a sink full of dishes down there right now."

Tobin laughed and kissed her. "I'll file away 'fucking on the kitchen counter' as a future possibility."

"I like the lube-all-over-the-house idea. Since it's just us and we can be spontaneous."

"I'll start carrying it in my front pocket."

"Good. And let's skip the condoms. I have the implant so we're covered for pregnancy. I haven't had sex with a real live penis since my senior year in college so no VD."

"Same." He brushed his mouth across hers. "No condoms from here on out. And since I gave you my assorted sexual backstory . . . give it up, tiger."

"It's so typical and boring. High school boyfriend punched my V-card midway through the summer before college. So we had sex like . . . maybe six times. It always seemed rushed."

Tobin made a mental note to slow things down next time.

"He chose Stanford; I stayed in New York and went to Columbia. We broke it off before he left. No bitterness or drama. I dated here and there. A lot of group dates. Some one-on-ones. I didn't have sex again until my sophomore year. We were together about a few months. We didn't have sex all that often. The dorms are small and privacy was a joke. It felt skeevy taking a date to my parents' house so we could screw. I had a few hookups after that. My dry spell began after I graduated and continued until I met you." She nipped his chin. "So it's been stellar so far. Hot motel sex. Walk of shame in the grocery store. Amazing oral and a trip to pound town before noon. A refreshing nap and some cuddling." She shrieked when he poked her in the ribs. "And I'm still sprawled naked in the early afternoon, with the hottest, sexiest, sweetest guy I've ever been with."

"You and me are gonna have some fun these next three weeks."

Jade studied him but she didn't say anything. He noticed she did that a lot. Carefully measured her words before she spoke. Was that a trait of her shyness? Or because she was so methodical from her musical training?

Then she smiled and scraped her fingers in his facial scruff. "I like this."

"I can stand it about one day and then it's gone. It gets too itchy. Especially when I'm outside and the sun is beating down on me and I'm sweating. Then dirt gets trapped in the damp hair and I'm ready to tear my face off."

"You were right. I liked how it felt on the insides of my thighs."

No artifice. Just . . . Jade.

"I am hungry. Let's go make lunch."

He set his hand on her shoulder after she scooted to the edge of the bed. "Hold on. Before you said you wanted to talk about two things. What was the other one?"

"We can talk about it downstairs. No biggie." She stood and stretched.

"You look good naked all stretched out like that, tiger." One glimpse of her ass and that glorious fall of hair and he'd already started to get hard again.

Jade whipped her head around, sending her hair flying. She peered over her shoulder, gifting him with a coquettish look. "You can do me like this . . . my palms flat on the wall above me, my feet spread, my hips"—she performed a stripper-like pelvis roll—"however you want to position them with those big rough hands."

Holy fuck. Playful tiger.

Hot tiger.

His dick definitely approved.

Then she tossed her head and spoke to his groin. "Food first, big guy. Then we'll play."

Yeah. His dick definitely approved.

❦

After the sandwiches were made and the fruit sliced—Tobin was ridiculously happy that Jade remembered to pour him a glass of milk—they sat at the smaller table in the kitchen.

"All right, cowboy. What would you do with your three weeks if I wasn't here?"

Tobin swallowed his mouthful of roast beef goodness. "I'd masturbate a lot. Watch some TV. Go fishing." He took a swig of milk. "What about you?"

"I'd practice."

"For what? A concert or something?"

She shrugged. "Practicing is just a habit I've had my entire life. Some people do yoga or journal or sketch. I practice. I have more sheet music than most school systems, which is embarrassing to admit." She set her sandwich down. "I'd try and figure out what I want to do for a job. I haven't been employed in my field of study at all since graduation." She looked at him as if it pained her to admit that.

"Welcome to the club, darlin'. I've been ridin' the range as a hired hand for the past six years. And before I went full time at the Split Rock, for almost a year I worked part time as a baggage handler and errand boy. Not much need for a master's in reproductive biology when I'm opening gates and spreading hay."

"Well that shot down my little whine-fest. Here I thought I was special."

He laughed. "I'd love to make us both feel better by saying a lot of grads never utilize their degrees, but I happen to be surrounded by folks that are doin' just that. Janie, the Split Rock GM, went to school for hospitality and business management. Tierney, Renner's wife, has like four advanced degrees in finance, business and economics. She runs all the finances for the Split Rock and the cattle company. Plus, she has her own financial consulting business, which to be honest? I don't even know what that means except she knows how to make money and other people pay her to show them how. Then there's Fletch, the local veterinarian. He performs surgeries and all that medical stuff he went to school for."

"So why didn't you end up at a research lab someplace?"

"Good question. Jobs were really tough then. Not that it's that much easier now. I'd spent time in Brazil during grad school and developed the mind-set that I just wanted to be home. In Wyoming." He rubbed the back of his neck and laughed. "I don't know where I thought I'd get a job. Not a ton of research facilities out on the prairie. So I didn't look real hard for work beyond the state border. Which means, I'm pretty much a dumb-ass."

Jade covered her hand with his. "Don't say that. My parents encouraged me to get my master's and I couldn't fathom why I'd want an advanced degree in a subject that wasn't employable with a basic degree. I still love history. Still love that time period. So I can play music from the Renaissance era and tell you all about the history, the politics and the literature from then. It is excellent cocktail party talk." She smirked. "If I was the type who actually spoke to people at cocktail parties, instead of hiding in the corner wondering if my shoes look okay with my dress."

He laughed. She was so refreshingly honest. But not mean. And not pitiful. "We might've met at a cocktail party like that. I'm not petite enough to hide in corners, so I have the opposite problem. Everything seems scaled down when you're used to wide-open spaces. Then I'm bumping into shit with my big boots and knocking things over. And it was ten times worse in Brazil because I don't speak Portuguese."

For the next hour they talked about bad job interviews and prima donna professors. Of how practicality can crush passion. Of triumphs and disappointments. He told her about the applications he'd filled out and his worry that with the rapid advancements in the field that even just six years out of school, his education might be outdated.

After they put away the lunch fixings, Jade washed the dishes and he dried. Miz G had a dishwasher, but he preferred standing next to Jade, sneaking in little pats on the ass or a quick kiss.

She was equally affectionate. Standing close enough to make sure their bodies touched and some part of her hand or arm connected with some part of his even when she handed him a soapy plate.

With her, the getting-to-know-you stuff flowed more naturally than he'd ever dreamed. But Jade became introspective as she wiped down the counters and table.

When Tobin returned from taking out the garbage, she was leaning against the doorjamb of the back door, gazing across the yard. He curled his body around hers, resting his chin on the top of her head. "Whatcha thinking about?"

"Canning. If GG really expects me to do it, do I buy a book? As much as I'd like to ask her friends for help . . ."

"I'm not much help either. When it cools off let's head out to the veggie patch and make lists of what there's too much of." He brushed his lips across her temple. "Because I know how much you love your lists, darlin'."

She laughed.

"Something else on your mind?"

"Yesterday when Riss and I were in the ranch supply store, I met Dodie. And she said Lou-Lou the prep cook had given notice, so Riss just blurted out that I had experience as a prep cook. Dodie told me to fill out an application."

Tobin turned her to face him. "Is that something you're interested in?"

"I actually liked working as a prep cook. I'm used to getting up early. It's a part-time position . . ."

"Jade. Sweetheart. You should definitely apply."

She studied his eyes. "You wouldn't mind if we worked in the same place? I mean, it's not the same job. Obviously I won't be out chasing cows. But we'd be in the same area. That wouldn't feel like I was trying to insert myself into every part of your life?"

"Let's see . . . how do I phrase this?" He moved in closer to her. "My life would be a million times better if you were in every single part of it, every minute, of every day."

"Really?"

"Scout's honor." He smooched her lips. "Apply for the job if you want to. Don't apply if you're worried that working there will stress you out."

She fiddled with the collar on his shirt. "Then I'm going to apply."

Tobin tempered his initial response to whoop and holler and spin her around. But this was such a good sign that she was taking steps to stay here for a while.

*Isn't it ironic that four of the six job applications you've sent . . . are for positions out of state?*

He wouldn't think about that now. "Do you want me to bring you an application since I'm there every day anyway?"

"Sure. And maybe put in a good word for me?"

"Jade. Janie and Renner would be thrilled to have a former New York City cook working in their kitchen." He tucked her hair behind her ear. "Tell me you're excited about spending these next three weeks together."

"I am."

"I've got big plans for us." He pinched her ass and she squeaked. "Not all of them will revolve around you bein' naked."

"Now I'm dying to hear what you're planning."

"Next weekend I'm takin' you fishing."

"Why?"

Tobin laughed. "Because I like to fish. Maybe you will too. Lots of couples end up with common interests."

"Great. We'll go fishing together. Then at some point over the weekend, we'll make popcorn and watch my favorite movie."

"Please tell me it's *Die Hard*."

She wrinkled her nose. "No, it's an opera."

"Like . . . ?" Fuck. He couldn't name a single opera.

"It's *La bohème*, a Puccini opera. The Italian edition is subtitled."

Great. "We could go dancing too."

"I'm not a very good dancer," Jade said. "But I'm not bad at tennis."

"I hate tennis. What about horseback ridin'?"

She thought about it. "I'll try it. But since you were born with reins in your hand, that means you have to do something I'm good at. Which in this case is cooking. You have to learn to make one thing."

"Fine. There is one other point to mention. You're in my bed every night."

"Like that'd be a hardship. But I'll warn you . . . I'm a light sleeper with insomnia."

"How about . . ." He pinned her hands by her sides and used his teeth on the back of her neck. "I wear you out. We could go for a run every night. Then you'll sleep."

"You have the best plans." She rubbed her ass into his groin. "Or we could skip the couple activities and just fuck."

"That works for me." Tobin scooped her up, tossed her over his shoulder and raced up the stairs.

✄

Two days later, Tobin sat at his desk at the Split Rock messing around with possible dam matchups for BB, the bucking bull from hell. He'd had good luck breeding him so far.

His cell phone rang and he answered it absentmindedly. "Hello."

"May I please speak with Tobin Hale?"

"Speaking. Who's this?"

"Chris Gowden. I own the LME Corporation in Casper. You sent in a resume and we'd like to meet with you in our offices, if you're still interested in an interview?"

Holy shit. "Yes, sir. I am."

"Excellent. When would be a convenient day and time next week?"

"I can be in Casper after two o'clock any day."

"How about Monday?"

"That would work. Thank you. I'm looking forward to it."

"We are as well. See you next week."

Tobin hung up and slumped back in his chair.

Wow. He had an honest-to-god interview.

He couldn't wait to tell Jade.

And what did that say? That she was the first person he thought of when it came to sharing good things and bad.

The irony of the situation didn't escape him—he'd finally bucked up and sent out resumes so maybe he'd have a shot at finding a woman he could settle down with . . . and the most beautiful, talented, amazing woman he'd ever met was currently living in the same house with him and sharing his bed.

Since his computer was up he headed to the LME website to re-familiarize himself with the company.

Started doing business last year. So, unproven. He kept reading. Not unproven. The owner had partnered with the guy who started the bovine IVF company in Powell. But that partnership had ended and he'd begun his own company.

Interesting that LME had a different focus.

But then again, dissenting opinions on how to move forward were usually what ended business partnerships.

*That issue had ended plenty of relationships too.*

⤬

The next evening Tobin was naked, sprawled on his belly, his mind drifting and his body sated after Jade had tried out her riding skills— which were excellent—but she was such a perfectionist that she kept asking for a do-over. Like he'd ever say no to that.

This living together stuff was fucking awesome. Not just the sex part . . . but it was a serious rush to have Jade under him, or on top of him, or bent over the closest piece of furniture, anytime he wanted.

His tiger was as obsessed with him as he was with her. They couldn't be in the same room and stay on opposite sides for longer than five minutes. They held hands through supper. Her place was on his lap when they watched TV. He loved going upstairs with her every night. He loved watching her getting ready for bed. He loved the moment when she wrapped herself around him. He loved the sense of completeness when he woke in the middle of the night and Jade was still right there, holding on to him.

She drew squiggles up and down his back. "I talked to my mom today."

*Don't panic.* "Yeah? How'd that conversation go?"

"It was . . . hard. I can't really talk to her about you. So I listened as she chattered on."

"How many times did she ask you when you were coming back to New York?"

Jade sighed. "Five. And since all my restaurant uniforms are in my closet at their house, I don't know the best way to ask her to send them to me. I know you said Dodie doesn't wear a uniform, but I want to be prepared in case I have to wear one."

"Does that mean you're sticking around and not heading back to New York even to pick up your uniforms?"

She stopped abruptly and jerked her hand free. "After all I've told you? After how incredible it's been between us? You still think I have the ability to walk away from this? If your answer to any of those questions is yes . . . then why am I even looking for jobs?"

"Whoa. Hold on. I'm looking for a job too. And whenever I bring this topic up, you distract me with hot sex and it gets shoved under the bed—which is about the only place we haven't fucked."

"Is that a complaint?"

"Yes."

Her eyes widened.

Shit. "I mean no. But bein's I have an interview in Casper next week, it is something we need to talk about."

"So talk."

"I am in a transitory position, Jade. I have five job applications that I haven't heard back on. What happens if the place in Taos offers me a full-time job? Would you stay here or go with me?"

"Would you *want* me to go with you?" she retorted.

Tobin didn't even hesitate. "Yes."

"There's your answer. Yes, I'll go with you. No matter where that might be. It's not like I'm unemployable and you'd have to support me."

"Maybe I'd like to support you."

"There's every man's dream. To have a freeloading girlfriend."

He kept his temper in check. "I don't give a shit about any man's dreams but *mine*. Maybe it makes me a fucking throwback, but I'd be happy as hell to take care of you. I'd consider it a damn privilege."

"A privilege. Seriously?"

Tobin slipped his arm beneath her and rolled until he was on top, with her arms pinned above her head. "Okay, we'll do this a different way. I've waited a long damn time for you to come into my life. And it would make my dick hard and fill my chest with macho pride if every time I looked at you, I knew I was the guy you trusted to *be* everything you need. Not give. Not buy. *Be.* That's what I consider taking care of you."

Jade snared his mouth in a hungry kiss. "Be what I need right now, Tobin. Take me to that place where it's just us."

"I am so lost in you." He buried his face in her throat, waiting for her to hook her legs around his hips, so he could drive inside her and take them both to the only sure thing, to the only place that really belonged to them.

# Chapter Twenty

❧

*J*ade had just ended her cell phone call when she heard a series of short horn blasts. She wandered onto the porch and saw a van in the driveway.

The door opened and Riss jumped out, wearing a mechanic's suit—a grease-smeared mechanics suit.

She grinned at her crazy redheaded friend. "To what do I owe this visit?"

"I need booze. Is there anyone else here?"

"Just me."

"Good. Bring the hooch. I've waited long enough for you to share the down-and-dirty details about you and Tobin."

"Come up and snag a seat. Preferably not a cloth one because it looks as if you rolled in oil."

"Sat in it is more likely." Riss plopped down.

"How about some hard cider?"

"Perfect. Got any cigars?"

"Just Cubans."

Riss's eyes went wide. "Are you fucking kidding me?"

"Yes. Sorry. I couldn't resist."

"Jerk."

Jade brought out the bottles of cider, wondering if she should've grabbed snacks.

"Relax, New York. Booze in bottles with no glasses is how we prefer to be served in the West." She held her bottle out. "Cheers."

"Cheers."

Maybe being nosy went with that mind-set too, because Riss immediately said, "We're drinking buddies, shopping buddies and I baited the hook for your hookup with Tobin, so, sweet cheeks, you owe me some dirty deets."

"Baited the hook," Jade repeated. "What did you do?"

"Snapped a picture of your ass in your new cowgirl jeans and maybe a pic of men surrounding said ass in the bar and sent it to your man."

Jade laughed. "You *are* a good friend."

"Tell me one juicy thing."

She swigged from the bottle. She'd never been great at doing stuff like this.

*Here's your chance to change and you don't have to pretend you're as tell-all as the* Enquirer.

"All right Riss, I'll confess . . . I've always sucked at swapping confidences. Especially about sex. But you asked, so I'll give it a shot. *One* juicy thing? But, gosh, there are so many."

"You suck."

She laughed. "There is one thing that sticks out in my mind and is so much more obvious than any others." She set her elbows on the table. "Tobin is hung. Like, not a little hung, like 'holy mother that is the big daddy of all dicks' hung."

Riss spewed cider. "Shit, Jade. Warn me next time." She blotted her face with her sleeve. "Okay. He's hung. Does he know how to work the oversized equipment?"

"Oh yeah."

"Damn. Now I'm wishing I would've gone out on a date with him."

"Too late."

"Staking your claim already?"

"Absolutely."

"Good for you." She held the bottle over for another toast. "How's granny feel about the two of you doing the deed in her house?"

"GG went on a last-minute cruise with her buddy Pearl. So she doesn't know that Tobin and I got together. She's under the impression that we don't like each other."

"How long is she gone?"

"Three weeks."

Riss whistled. "You two are gonna get used to playing house and then what happens when granny comes home and doesn't like it?"

"I don't know." Jade drummed her fingers on the table. "For the first time in my life? I'm living in the moment."

"Attagirl. That's how I live every moment of my life."

"I don't believe that." When Riss's brows drew together, she backtracked. "I didn't mean for that to come out so harsh. I meant you're part of a business, so you can't just say, 'I don't feel like delivering these baby cows today. I'll leave them in the semi while I go to the movies.'"

"Baby cows are called calves, New York. I schedule runs, but they have to be worth my time. I know guys in this business who barely break even. That's why I walked away for a few years." Riss leaned back in her chair. "What about you?"

"I did fill out an application for the prep cook job at the Split Rock."

"Tobin was okay with that?"

"Very okay."

"Told ya. You'll love it up there. Everyone who works there does. Multiple part-time jobs are the norm around here. Most people have more than one job."

"What else do you do besides drive stock transport and . . . ?" She gestured to Riss's overalls.

Riss grinned. "Why yes, I am a lube jockey. Thanks for asking."

"You work on cars?"

"I'm not a mechanic. I change oil. It's not a full-time job. Guys with families to feed get priority over me. I'm good with that."

"Maybe it's clichéd to ask, but are you happy?"

"It's been a long time since anyone has asked me that. Most days? Yes. Would I be happier if I was twenty pounds thinner, if I could upgrade from my dumpy trailer? Thinner . . . eh. A better living environment is already on my list of improvements."

"Scenario one: lube jockey boss says, 'Riss, I need you full-time. This is your salary. It's enough that you can quit transporting stock completely.' Scenario two: Ike says, 'Riss, I need you full-time. This is your salary. It's enough that you can quit your lube-jockey job.'"

"Which do I pick? I'd work for Jackson Stock Contracting." She scowled. "It means working with Ike all the freakin' time, but I'd still take it."

"Why?"

"Although the job is the same, the people are different. I'm not in the same place. With the lube jockey job . . . it's stable. That's all some employees look for, so they're a better fit, which is why I have no problem bein' part-time." Riss stretched her legs out. "So how'd we get on the hard-hitting life stuff and not the 'how hard did you hit that' sex stuff?"

"You poking me about my future plans." Jade smirked. "But it does have relevance. I had an interesting call right before you got here from the Casper Symphony director."

"No shit? What did he want?"

"To know if I plan to be around for the season and if I'd be interested in auditioning."

"Would you?"

"Maybe. Would it be worth it? The money is lousy in music performance in New York; I can't imagine it'd be good here."

"But you have to look at it as an opportunity to make local contacts.

If you meet other musicians you could end up in a quartet with them. That's a paying gig. You meet someone else whose kid wants lessons? That's a paying gig."

"True."

"Since so much shit is up in the air right now, I'll throw in my two cents. I'd take you on as a roommate if everything with Tobin goes to the dogs."

"Thanks, Riss. That means a lot."

She finished her cider. "Now if you could learn to play that violin like a fiddle . . . you'd have your pick of gigs in Western bars across four states."

"You do know there's no difference between instruments, right? They're the same. Even Itzhak Perlman calls the Stradivarius he plays his fiddle."

Riss shrugged. "It's something to keep in mind. Because it sounds like music is where your heart is."

"It's where my skill is; I've been playing since I was four."

"What's your college degree in again?"

"History with concentration in medieval and Renaissance studies."

"Dude."

"I know, right?"

"Well, it is unique. Maybe one of them online colleges are looking for someone to teach classes." She snapped her fingers. "You know what I just remembered? Theresa, a chick in the book club? She works at the Casper Community College. She could totally put you in touch with someone in the right department. We'll ask her about it at book club in two weeks."

"That sounds awesome." She grinned at Riss. "Has anyone told you today that you're brilliant? And generous?"

"No. But the guy with the '67 Chevy told me I had great tits."

The breakneck way Tobin's truck barreled up the drive . . . Jade knew he had a one-track mind: getting her naked as soon as possible.

He hopped out of the cab and headed toward her at a good clip. He only slowed slightly when he saw Riss. "If it's not my favorite stock transporter. How are you, Riss?"

"I'm jealous my buddy Jade can ride the cannon you're packing in your pants anytime she wants."

Silence.

Jade couldn't look at Tobin.

And she sort of wanted to kill Riss.

Then Tobin laughed. "Your loss, darlin'."

"Congrats for hitting the genetic lottery." She held her fist for Tobin to bump—which he obliged. Riss laughed. "I think Jade wants to crawl under the table right about now."

"Or smack you with the chair like on World Federation Wrestling," she grumbled.

"Tobin understands that as my new BFF, you and me are sharing some stuff."

"A minimal amount of the naked stuff," Tobin warned Jade.

"No worries. She didn't go into detail." Riss started down the steps and blew Jade a kiss. "I'll call you later in the week."

Jade didn't look at Tobin until Riss was in her van. "Are you mad that I had girl-time sex chat?"

"I guess it's better that you told Riss that I *have* a big dick, than I *am* a big dick." He grinned at her. "Go upstairs. Get naked. I'll be right up."

"Are you going to punish me?"

"Nope. I'm gonna reward you."

"For what?"

He lifted an eyebrow. "I need a reason? Fine. It's Tuesday."

"That works for me."

# Chapter Twenty-one

*"Y*ou sure you don't mind going along with me?"

Tobin took Jade's hand. "They just want to meet you in an informal setting." He kissed her knuckles. "It'll be fine."

"Will I have to buy a uniform?"

He frowned. "Uniform? We don't wear uniforms."

"But you do wear chaps and spurs, right? I never get to see you in those. I imagine the cutout in the back frames your tight little butt and the front accentuates that delicious meat club."

"Jesus, Jade."

"You're blushing. You're so cute when you blush. Pull the truck over and let's have a quickie."

His tiger was nervous. With him she'd babble from nerves, but the second she was in a group of strangers she'd clam up completely. "No quickie for us. But I appreciate the offer." He kissed the back of her hand. "You want to work here. It means we get to be together, remember?"

Jade reached over and stroked his cheek. "How could I forget?"

"You happy?"

"With you? Very."

At the main entrance to the Split Rock, Tobin downshifted and they bumped into the parking lot.

"How long will this take?"

"Not long. I assume most people brought their kids. They tend to get a little wild." Especially Janie and Abe's boys. Those two were hell on wheels.

Dust blew up around them as they crossed the parking lot. Tobin had gone with his usual boots and jeans, but opted for a short-sleeved shirt and his dress hat. He shot a look at Jade out of the corner of his eye. She'd worn a red and white floral sundress with white sandals.

"You're sneaking looks at me. Am I underdressed or overdressed for this job interview?"

"It's not an interview, tiger. You've got the job so stop worrying."

On the top stair, Tobin curled his fingers around the side of her neck and stroked the edge of her jaw with his thumb. "I'm so fucking proud of the fact you're my girlfriend."

"You are?"

"You're beautiful, smart, talented, a tiger in bed and you make me laugh. Every day I learn more about you and I like it. I like you. Hell, I love you."

She sucked in a quick breath. "What?"

"I'm not good at playing my cards close to the vest, am I? I want you to know before we walk in there . . . if you get overwhelmed, look at me. And imagine that's how I feel every time I look at you. I can't believe how lucky I am."

"That is so getting you laid later," she whispered. Then she placed her hand on his wrist and pulled him in for a kiss. An achingly sweet kiss.

The door banged open behind them. Tobin expected someone to yell, *Get a room!* but a small body smacked into their legs.

Looking down, he said, "Hey, Tyler, watch it, okay, little man?"

Tyler's hands were on his hips and he tilted his head back to peer at

Jade. "Do you know kung fu?" he demanded. "'Cause I do." With a loud *hi-yah!* he spun and karate chopped the boy behind him in the head.

But Bran's son didn't pull any punches. Tate never said a word; he never looked away. He just socked Tyler in the stomach with all his might.

Tyler doubled over.

Jade started to bend down to help, but Tobin tugged her away, inside the lodge.

"Trust me. You're better off just letting it go. Last time I got between them? I ended up with a damn black eye. From a fucking four-year-old."

She snickered. "Those kids are just allowed to run wild?"

"I could lie and say no, but the truth is . . . their parents own the business so they're around a lot. You want me to give you a tour?"

"I'm pretty sure I need a drink first."

Tobin ran his palm up the outside of her arm. "Still nervous?"

"Not as much as I was, now that I know you're in *lurrrve* with me." Jade snaked her arms around his neck. "I need a good-luck kiss."

He sensed her nerves leveling out at the touch of his lips to hers.

"I've gotten better at kissing you when you're wearing your cow-boy hat."

"It's like I told you. It just takes practice." Tobin gave her one last smooch and stepped back. He looked up to see they had an audience. Great.

Renner, cradling his sleeping son, Rhett.

Plus Abe with his youngest son, Dylan, slumped over his shoulder. And Fletch, who also held his sleeping son, Gus.

All three men were grinning at him.

"Hey, guys. What's up? Did your wives send you to the naughty corner already?"

"This is a far sight better than wranglin' the kids that ain't asleep," Renner said.

"Which is most of 'em," Abe said dryly.

"Yeah, we ran into Tyler out front. Or rather, he ran into us."

"Runnin' from Tate or chasin' him?" Abe asked.

"Couldn't tell as they were hitting one another," Tobin said.

Abe sighed. "His mama is supposed to be watching him."

When Tobin saw Abe staring at Jade expectantly he said, "This is my girlfriend, Jade Evans. She's Garnet's granddaughter. Jade, this is Abe Lawson. His wife, Janie, is the Split Rock GM—technically your new boss—and they're the parents of the karate chopper we met out front."

"Nice to meet you," Jade said. "I won't shake your hand as it appears yours are full." Then she looked at Renner and smiled. "Good to see you, Renner. What's your son's name?"

"Rhett. We're mighty glad you're comin' to work here."

Fletch was a big enough guy he could juggle a sleeping toddler and a horse. He offered Jade his hand and an enormous grin. "Well, well. Tobin's girlfriend. I'm very happy to meet you, Jade. I get a huge kick outta your grandma."

"I'm afraid I'm not nearly as entertaining as she is," Jade said.

"Sugar, no one is."

"I'm sorry. I didn't catch your name."

"Sorry. I'm August Fletcher—you can call me Fletch. The little guy is Gus. I'm a veterinarian so me'n Tobin work together a lot."

"Is Tanna here?" Tobin asked.

Fletch shook his head. "She's got a touch of morning sickness again. My dad fusses over her like a mother hen, so he's with her. But she sent me with very clear instructions, Tobin; you are to bring your *girlfriend* by sooner rather than later."

"Go ahead and tell her I saluted."

Everyone laughed.

"So am I good to take Jade inside? Or did you all wanna gawk at my beautiful girlfriend before she's officially on the Split Rock payroll?"

Jade groaned and turned her face into Tobin's arm.

"She's a damn sight prettier than you," Fletch said. "Tell you what. Leave her here with us. We'll take good care of her."

"Fuck that." Tobin steered Jade inside the entrance and across the main room to the bar and dining area.

"Do they always give you that much crap?"

"In the way only friends can do and not get punched." Tobin headed to the bar and stepped behind it. "It's serve yourself, so what're you drinking?"

"I'll just have a Coke."

Tobin loaded a glass with ice, filled it with soda and dropped two cherries in the top. "Here you go."

"Nice touch."

"I thought an umbrella might be over the top." He popped the top on a Budweiser. "Let's make the rounds."

The first person they ran into was Tierney. And she jumped right in. "Hi. Jade, right? I'm Tierney Jackson. I do the finances around here and some other stuff."

"Nice to meet you. I saw your darling son with Renner."

Tierney beamed. "He is a doll. Our daughter Isabelle is running around someplace. I wanted to say welcome and if you need anything, just swing by my office. Garnet is family. And you are too." She shot Tobin a soft look. "Doubly so now."

"Thanks."

A child's bloodcurdling scream echoed across the space and Jade jumped.

Tierney sighed. "I never thought I'd get used to that, but I am now."

Tobin watched as Isabelle raced in and tried to hide in front of her mother.

But Tierney neatly stepped aside.

A sweaty boy, covered in mud, stalked closer to them.

Harper, a chubby baby boy on her hip, shouted, "Jake Turner. You stop right there."

He spun around.

"Oh good lord, you were *not* raised in a barn! Why on earth would you think it's okay to track mud across the lodge carpeting? Get out on the patio. Sit there and wait."

He shuffled off.

Isa giggled. Too late she clapped her hand over her mouth when her mother heard it.

"And you can sit on the bench outside my office, Isabelle Jackson. I'll send your father to get you when it's time but you'd better not move."

Tobin looked at Jade, who watched the interplay like a tennis match.

Harper sauntered over. "Sorry. It's usually not like this."

"Yes it is," Tobin mock-whispered to Jade.

"I'm Harper. We met briefly at Bernice's a few weeks back."

"Oh. Yes. Nice to see you again."

Harper hoisted her baby higher on her hip. "This is Gage. The youngest of my three boys. The only one not covered in mud, or blood, but I sorta smell something worse."

Tobin stepped back.

She laughed. "Just you wait, buster. Bran was grossed out too, changing diapers with kid number one. Which boggles my mind because the man regularly sticks his entire arm up a cow's—"

"She gets it, Harper," Tierney said. "Don't forget Tobin often has his arm up there too."

"Great, ladies. Thanks."

Just then Janie Lawson came in from outside, her hand clamped around her son Tyler's upper arm. "You are grounded from watching TV. You do *not* karate chop people, do you hear me? Especially not your friends. You're lucky that Bran stepped in before Tate throttled you." Janie stopped. "Oh. Hey. Sorry. Just having a special little one-on-one time with my son."

"Janie, meet my girlfriend, Jade. Jade, Janie Lawson is the big boss here at the Split Rock."

"She's the boss at work but Daddy's the boss at home," Tyler announced.

Such a precocious little shit.

"Nice to meet you, Mrs. Lawson," Jade said.

"Trust me, the pleasure is mine. Welcome to the Split Rock family. Please, call me Janie. Do you have any questions?"

"About a million."

"The job is pretty straightforward. Dodie is in charge of the kitchen and she'll set the schedule. If there's a personal issue, come to me or Renner. If we have an employment issue, we'll come to you. That's rare, trust me."

"Does the kitchen staff wear uniforms?" Jade asked.

"Mama, watch this," Tyler said.

"Not now, honey, I'm talking." She looked at Jade. "Did you wear uniforms in New York?"

"Yes. Not that I brought them with me. But prep cooks wore white. Line cooks wore black."

"You can wear whatever you're comfortable in."

"All right. Then I'll have my parents send my prep uniforms."

"So you're both living in Garnet's house?" Janie asked. "And she just left the two of you alone for three weeks?"

Jade blinked at the abrupt change in topic.

"Mama, I said watch!" Just then Tyler Lawson attempted to do a karate kick, and the toe of his boot connected with Jade's shin as he uttered a loud, "Hi-yah!"

Startled, Jade dropped her glass and it shattered on the floor.

When she leaned down to pick up the broken glass, Tobin didn't hear Janie yelling or Tyler crying—all he saw was Jade draw her hand back really fast and then blood dripping onto the tile.

She said, "Shit."

She never swore.

He wrapped his fingers around her right wrist and brought her hand up so he could get a better look. He winced. "Baby. Your fingers are bleeding."

"It's okay, Tobin. It's my—"

"No, it's not goddamned okay. You sliced your fingers and you're supposed to audition in Casper this week. What if there are shards of glass embedded in the pads of your fingers? We've gotta get this cleaned up right now." He slipped his arm beneath her knees, lifted and carried her into the kitchen since it was closer than the restroom.

He set her on the counter by the sink and flipped on the cold water. "Tobin."

"Let me do this for you." He held her hand under the stream of water. A little pinkish water swirled down the drain but not much. "Does it hurt?

"No."

"Good." He cast his hat aside so he could press his forehead to hers. "Your first day you're attacked by 'Children of the Corn.'"

Jade laughed. "'Children of the Corn'?"

"I figured calling him 'Chucky' might be a little extreme."

"I don't think 'Chucky' did it maliciously. He's just excitable and like any boy wants to show off his mad skills. Besides, I'm the dumb one who reached for the glass." She nudged him. "You've sufficiently numbed the cut. Thank you."

Tobin shut off the water and grabbed paper towels from the dispenser. "Let me see it."

"Tobin, it's—"

"Don't say fine or I'll start to lose my fuckin' cool, sweetheart. Now let me see it."

Jade put her hand behind her back.

"Real mature, Jade."

She wrapped her fingers beneath his jaw and forced him to look at her. "For future reference? My right hand? Bow hand. My left hand? On the strings."

His eyes widened. "So you really are—"

"Fine. But I loved that you went all macho-cowboy he-man and carried me in here." She traced the side of his face. Then the shape of his lips. "I really love that I'm the first woman you've brought here and introduced to your friends. That makes me feel special."

"You are special. You know that."

"That's why I'm in love with you. Because not only do you make me feel special, you've shown me that this thing between us has been special since day one. I don't know what will happen when GG comes back, but I want to be with you."

His happiness meter? Off the charts right now. "Thank fuck for that."

"Come here, crazy man, and kiss me."

After the surprisingly sweet soul kiss, Tobin helped her down and they walked hand in hand out of the kitchen.

Someone had cleaned up the glass.

"Children of the Corn" were nowhere to be found.

Tierney, Janie and Harper quit gabbing the instant he and Jade strolled into view.

Janie spoke first. "Jade, are you okay? My sister-in-law Lainie is a nurse. I've already called her and she can be here in ten minutes."

"Fletch is still hanging around out front," Harper said. "I know he's a veterinarian, but if you need him to check out the cuts . . ."

"Thank you. Really. I'm sorry to be a nuisance. Tobin overreacted. I have two tiny cuts on the thumb of my bow hand. So it's all good. It won't keep me from coming to work here this week." She smiled.

Tierney smiled back. "Quick thinking on your part, Tobin."

"Yes. Totally romantic, swoon-worthy moment when you picked her up and carried her off to take care of her," Harper said with a sigh.

"You get props for that from me too," Janie added with a wink.

He wondered if his cheeks could actually burst into flame from embarrassment.

If he had to walk past the gauntlet of Abe, Fletch and Renner, that was a distinct possibility.

"I promised Jade I'd show her around a little before we leave, so we'll just head out the back."

## Chapter Twenty-two

⟋⟍⟋⟍⟋⟍

𝒯obin's head was in the clouds the next week after his interview with LME went well. Turned out, he'd gone to school with one of the owners' brother. They hadn't offered him the job on the spot, but the second half of the interview where they'd toured the facility indicated he pretty much had it in the bag. Since the position was part-time, they were more than willing to work around his schedule, which was just another bonus. With his mind elsewhere, he hadn't considered Renner's summons might be serious. But the instant he walked in and saw Renner staring out the back window, his hands in his back pockets, his shoulders scrunched up, he thought, *Oh shit.*

Still, Tobin attempted to keep the mood light. "You bellowed, boss?"

Renner turned around. "Yeah. Have a seat. A couple of things we need to talk about."

"It's late enough in the day, should I grab beer? Or is this a whiskey conversation?"

He rubbed the back of his neck. "I'm not sure. Let's get the first part outta the way."

A two parter. That was a little unsettling. Especially when Renner didn't sit down behind his desk.

"I have an applicant for your job. A qualified applicant."

The elation and sense of freedom Tobin expected to feel didn't come.

"Okay." He felt Renner studying him and he looked up. "What? Is there a catch or something?"

"Maybe. You tell me. I don't want to get in the middle of this. The truth is he came to me. He also said if you have a problem with him applying for the job, he'll withdraw the application."

Confused, Tobin said, "Who?"

"Your brother Streeter."

He must've looked like a train had hit him because Renner groaned. "A complete shock to you, I take it?"

"Uh, yeah." Tobin rested his forearms on his knees and tried to wrap his head around the fact his brother had applied for his job. Did that mean he'd quit working at the Hale ranch? "Can I ask when Streeter applied?"

"Last week."

Tobin's gaze connected with Renner's. "Did he interview here last week?"

"No. The application came in the mail. It had a Post-it requesting I clear the interview process with you first. Which was really fucking weird, to be honest."

"I'll bet."

"So I have to ask . . . has anything changed for you? Are you still looking to get out of the area altogether?"

"You're asking because I'm involved with Jade." He scrubbed his hands over his face. "Jade and I . . . we've been in this bubble, for lack of a better term. I can split our relationship right down the middle. The two and a half weeks before Jade and I became lovers that we were living with Miz G, and the past two and a half weeks we've been lovers and Miz G ain't been around at all."

"So Garnet doesn't know?"

"She's on a cruise ship. She'll be back next week and we've asked the

Mud Lilies to let Jade and me be the ones to tell her about our relation-ship. We have no idea how she'll take it."

Renner opened his mouth and then closed it.

"What? It's not like you to hold back, Ren."

"I'm not. But I want to focus on this first. What are Jade's plans?"

"She's working here. She'll be playing in the symphony in Casper. She has a line on teaching a class at the community college next semester. We planned on finding a place together halfway between Casper and Muddy Gap."

"So you're not leaving?"

"If I do, Jade will go with me. She's . . . everything, man. And yeah, I get the irony. After I made solid plans to get more outta my life than just bein' a lonely hired hand, Jade shows up."

"Yeah, that's some irony all right," Renner said.

Tobin's focus snapped to Renner because his tone sounded off.

"You know I don't want to lose you. I've told you the job is still yours if you opt to stick around."

"But?"

"But Streeter is the only applicant I've had for your job. And at the risk of pissing you off"—Renner flashed his teeth—"he has more ranch-ing experience than you do. I'll hazard a guess he has close to the same work ethic you do. So the work ain't gonna be a shock to him any more than the weather is. From an employer's perspective? If I can't have you? He's the next best thing. It was really fucking hard not just offering him the job over the goddamned phone, T."

"I can imagine. What held you back?"

"You. I wouldn't just cut you a check and hand you your hat. I know I'm your boss, but we're friends too. I've hated the thought of you leavin' since you told me you wanted to. And not just because that fucker Hugh bailed on me too."

Tobin laughed.

"And without bein' a total dick, your brother has been through some serious shit in the last year. Stuff I hope we never have to deal with. That may have affected his ability to work, so who am I supposed to ask . . . ?"

It clicked. "I wouldn't want to saddle you with him, just because he's my brother, if he won't be worth a damn, Ren. I know you won't ask me to talk to my family, so I'll just throw it out there that I'll do it anyway. Might give us both some peace of mind."

"I appreciate that. And I'll hold off on setting up an interview time until we both have more information."

He paused. "What else?"

Renner sighed. "It may be in order for you to have the life you want— stability and challenge—you'll have to wear a bunch of different hats. If you're workin' cattle as a ranch hand, that's not to say you can't be doin' stuff in the lab in Casper too. You've been an integral part of this opera- tion. I couldn't have built it into what it is now without you. This was supposed to be a temporary stop in your life while you waited for some- thing better to come along. I understand you wanting to use them fancy degrees you worked so hard to earn. But if you really hated ranching? You wouldn't have stayed here this long."

"Amen, brother," Tobin said softly. He'd been thinking along those lines too.

"Now that I've said my piece . . . damn my throat hurts." He smirked. "I'm goin' home. And bein' a husband and a father? That's who I am— who I've always wanted to be, and at the end of the day those are the only things that matter." He walked out.

Tobin didn't move for the longest time. He just closed his eyes, leaned back, and let it sink in.

❧

Jade wasn't waiting on the porch when he pulled up.

Disappointment dogged him. He'd gotten used to that. He climbed the porch steps. No scent of supper cooking wafting out the windows either.

But then he heard it.

Music.

He paused to take his boots off and heard her stop and start the same progression of notes. Her dedication amazed him. Moved him.

Although he'd been hot and dusty all day and needed a shower, he'd wait. He'd rather listen. After he whipped off his shirt and ditched his jeans, he sank into the easy chair and closed his eyes.

Something inside him shifted gears completely when he heard her play. It sounded sappy as hell but through her playing he had an entirely different connection to music. It seemed vibrant. Alive. Hauntingly heartbreaking. Playful. Majestic.

Tobin didn't mind when she played the same section over and over. He couldn't tell if the notes or the tone or the rhythm was improving; he wasn't sure if any of that had been her objective. He just waited for that moment when she played something that made the hair stand up on the back of his neck. That made it difficult to breathe. That suspended moment . . . almost exactly like right before he came.

Every piece had a climactic point. Some were slow buildups—just like sex. Some were fast and furious—just like sex. Some were there and gone so fleetingly you looked around wondering if you'd missed it somehow. He suspected Jade wouldn't enjoy the orgasm and musical climax comparison so he'd kept that observation to himself.

She'd drilled herself on the runs a dozen times before she moved on to chords.

Dissonant chords.

He loved these. He'd felt completely uneducated last week when he'd called these progressions chords. Jade, the wonder violinist, had gone into a long-winded explanation about partitas as techniques. The sassy woman had no idea how hard her musical instruction made him. So he'd had no choice but to show her. Twice.

The music stopped abruptly and he heard her make a strangled groan and smack her bow on the strings a few times.

Yeah. Her temper made him hard too.

Pretty much everything about her made him hard.

The door slammed open.

Bare feet slapped down the hallway. Words were muttered. The footsteps stopped, as did the feet. "Tobin?"

He opened his eyes and smiled at her. "Hey."

She squinted at the grandfather clock. "Omigod. It's after five thirty! Why didn't you knock on the door?"

"I knew you'd have to come out sooner or later."

Jade's gaze homed in on him—specifically that he wore a sleeveless T-shirt and boxer briefs. "How long have you been out there waiting for me?"

He shrugged. "I wasn't keeping track."

"But . . . you're probably starved."

"I'm good." Tobin held out his hand. "But I'd take a kiss or ten if you're offering."

She crawled onto his lap and popped the footrest on the recliner so his body was almost horizontal. Then she fused her mouth to his. Feeding him kiss after kiss. Then backing off. Nipping on his lips. Gifting him with soft smooches. Gliding her tongue across the upper and lower bow of his lips, teasing the seam until he smiled.

Jade smiled back. "Hey."

Tobin swept his hands down the middle of her back to cup her ass. Then he trailed his hand back up. "Did you have a good day?"

"Yes, if a little bizarre."

"Bizarre . . . how?"

"Vivien and Bernice came over. Which was fine. I mean they've both gone out of their way to be nice after the . . . misunderstanding."

"What did they want?"

"That's it. I don't know. Bernice asked if GG had planted any black-eyed Susans in her flower garden this year and I told her I wasn't sure. So she said she'd go take a look. I thought Vivien would tag along, but she plopped down and asked about the Casper Symphony audition. She said all the Mud Lilies had bought season tickets to this year's performances since I'll be concertmaster. She asked how it was with both of us working at the Split Rock. Then we talked about canning and I asked her to look at the okra because it still doesn't look right. When we were in the kitchen, I just happened to glance across the yard and I swear I saw Bernice carrying something out of the herb garden and putting it in the backseat of her car."

"Miz G is very particular about not mixing flowers and herbs."

"I know, right?"

"Did you get a chance to peek in her car?"

"No. They asked a bunch of questions like if I knew when GG would be back. They tsk-tsked and said they'd be in touch. So should I be worried?"

Tobin had his suspicions that the marijuana plants were gone. But that wasn't something his little rule follower needed to worry about. "Nah."

Jade traced his eyebrows. Then his hairline. And the stubble on his cheeks and chin. "Anything exciting happen to my handsome cowboy today?"

He snorted. Handsome. Right. He didn't feel that way, but he liked that's what *she* saw when she looked at him. "A weird thing happened at the end of the day. Renner called me into his office." He relayed the basics about Streeter applying for the job, purposely not giving commentary on how he'd feel being out of a job and where he'd go from here.

She blinked at him. "You didn't have any idea?"

"None."

"Dude."

"I know. I'm not sure if Streeter is even working there now or if he's unemployed."

"How long does it take to get to your family's ranch?"

"An hour and a half."

She wore a thoughtful look. "Would they split the difference with you? Meet you in Rawlins or whatever town is halfway between here and there?"

"Maybe if I offered to buy them a steak."

"Then call and ask if they'd meet you. That would answer your questions about Streeter sooner rather than later."

Tobin kept running his hand up and down her back. "Why are you pushing me on this?"

"I'm not." She kissed him quickly and then rubbed her cheek over his. "All right. Maybe I am. If Streeter always counted on his wife and she's not there? And he always counted on your dad and your older brother and now they're not in the picture either? I shudder to think how alone he must feel. Neither of us are strangers to that feeling of loneliness."

"You have that same big heart Miz G does, don't you?"

Those golden eyes got a little teary. "Thank you."

Tobin kissed her. "I'll call my dad and brother on one condition. You come with so I can introduce you as my woman."

Jade shook her head. "Not for the entire meal. I'll swing by for dessert and coffee. They won't talk freely if I'm there, and you need to get to the bottom of what's going on."

"You're so damn smart." He kissed her again. Longer. Slower. Against her lips, he murmured, "Can we be done talking now?"

"Got something else in mind we could be doing, cowboy?"

"I need a shower first."

"I'll come along and wash your back."

&bull;

Thirty minutes later he growled, "I love fucking you in the shower."

"I'd love it if you'd let me come."

"Let you come *again*," he said, nipping her earlobe.

"Tobin."

He had her bent at the waist with her palms flat on the wall. He stood behind her, his cock buried deep in that sweet, sweet pussy, slowly tunneling in and out. His hands were clamped on the backs of her thighs below the curve of her ass, keeping her spread wide so he could enjoy the show.

"This isn't fair," she panted.

Tobin chuckled and hoisted her slightly higher.

She automatically curled the tops of her feet around the side of his calves. "No, no!"

"Keep complaining, tiger, and your hands will be on the floor as I'm slamming into you."

"Oh god."

She'd tortured him earlier and he'd warned her what goes around comes around.

Had she *ever* tortured him.

He'd been standing in the shower, drying his hair with a towel after washing off the grime of the day when his naked woman had stepped into the enclosure with him.

Immediately Jade had pushed him against the wall, dropped to her knees and gone to town on his cock. Since she'd started when it was soft and relaxed, she'd stuffed the entire thing in her mouth. But as soon as his dick had gotten with the *holy fuck she's sucking on me* program, she switched it up. She'd sucked his balls until his damn legs shook. Until he was pretty sure the next swipe of her tongue would have him coming on her face.

The truth was, the wide width of his dick stretched a mouth to the point of discomfort, and his length . . . he'd never felt a woman's teeth at the base. Heck, he'd never felt a woman's mouth past the halfway point. So he'd become accustomed to slick hand jobs with a sucking mouth over the head of his cock, figuring that was as close as he'd ever get to a normal blow job.

But Jade was determined. She said, "Let's see how far I can take you." Then she angled her head differently and sucked him in halfway.

"Jesus."

She released his shaft slowly. "You like that."

"I fucking love that. But baby, don't make it uncomfortable for yourself. Please." He traced her stretched lips with his thumbs.

She nuzzled the hair between his legs. "I love the way you smell. I get the barest whiff of you and I'm instantly drenched." She peered up at him with a cocky smile. "Drenched because my body knows how much lube it needs to take you now."

"Let me fuck you."

Her superior smirk vanished. "Let me taste you first. No pulling out, Tobin. I want your come in my mouth. All of it."

He knew she'd change her mind once he hit that point, but he agreed.

Then she'd absolutely blown his fucking mind.

She used both of her hands on his shaft and his balls. Her mouth was an unstoppable force of suction and wet heat.

Normally he didn't allow himself to hold on to her head because in that moment when his body erupted, his brain shorted out and he couldn't guarantee he wouldn't pull her hair and shove his cock in deeper than expected.

This time when his balls drew up and her mouth was still halfway down his cock, he grabbed that black silk in his hand. He'd been so focused on that, that the finger sliding in his ass as he started to come had caught him off guard completely.

And he'd shouted.

*Shouted.*

Loud.

For like an hour. Because it seemed like he came for an hour amid her sucking mouth and stroking finger.

After he'd come that fucking hard, he'd had to goddamned *sit down* in the shower.

Sit down.

Jade had soothed him with loving touches and sweet nuzzles until he'd caught his breath.

Then she'd stood, her beautiful face a mix of pride and need as she straddled his mouth with her juicy cunt and said, "As long as you're down there . . ."

Smart-ass.

He'd made her come so hard *she* screamed.

Then again, she usually did since she was a screamer.

At that point Tobin was ready to fuck her.

Which was what he was currently doing as she begged him to let her come again.

"You close, sweetheart?" he managed.

"Yes!"

Grinning, Tobin dropped her feet to the floor for two seconds before he picked her up around the waist, spun her around and pinned her to the wall.

One hard shove and he was back in that tight hot cunt.

With her legs spread wide and the friction on her clit, his little screamer . . .

Screamed again.

Fuck. He loved that.

Her orgasm drove him to the edge.

Then Jade's teeth scraping down his neck with her fingernails digging into his scalp kicked him over.

They clung to each other. Bodies wet. Breathing labored. Minds scrambled. Tobin placed a soft kiss below her ear. "Every time I think it can't get better, you prove me wrong. I love bein' with you like this."

He didn't have to explain what he meant by "this" because Jade understood he meant more than just sex.

"Me too."

"Although . . . now that I know you can get my cock halfway in your mouth . . . we could try . . . ?"

Jade snickered against his neck. "You really think you'll be able to stop if you get this cock halfway up my ass?"

"We'll never know unless we try."

⤜⤛

The next night Tobin let Jade drive to Rawlins so she could drop him off at the restaurant and return for the dessert course. But he knew even when it was her car, he'd be driving it home. The woman hadn't lied; she was a shitty driver.

He found his dad and Driscoll at a table in the back of the restaurant. He'd arrived on time but it appeared they'd already knocked back a couple of Jack and Cokes. "Hey."

The cocktail waitress took his order and he stuck with beer.

"So we were mighty surprised to get the call from you," Driscoll said. "Kind of a shocker to find out you have a serious girlfriend."

Puzzled, he said, "Why?"

"Kinda always thought you were gay."

And how did he respond to that? Like a dickhead little brother. "Really? That's funny. I kinda always thought *you* were gay. You've had way more years to settle down than I have. I don't know that I ever remember seeing you with a woman neither. Not that it matters, Dris. I'd be fine with you havin' a boyfriend."

"Enough," their dad said. "Gives me the fuckin' creeps to talk about that stuff."

Tobin's beer arrived.

They ordered steaks. Since his dad and brother believed the meal was on Tobin's dime, they ordered crab legs too.

"Besides you finding a girlfriend, what else is goin' on up at the Split Rock?"

"I haven't worked at the lodge much since Renner expanded the cattle company. I heard from the GM there isn't an open room from mid-September until the first part of November during huntin' season."

"It still burns my ass that as soon as *you* went to work for them, they stopped askin' me to be a huntin' guide," his dad complained.

"I recall you only did it for a few weeks during the grand opening. Besides, Renner hired me because of my educational background to help him get a genetics lab up and running, but that hasn't panned out yet." He sipped his beer. "What's goin' on at the ranch?"

"Not much. Nothin' really changes."

"How's Streeter doin'?"

His dad and his brother both stiffened.

Jackpot.

"We have no idea how Streeter is doin' since he don't work for us no more."

"Whoa. What do you mean he doesn't work for you? I thought Dad owned forty percent and you and Streeter each owned thirty percent?"

"It's complicated."

"Luckily I've got a couple of college degrees so I can probably follow along just fine."

"Always were a smart-ass," his dad grumbled. "Bottom line? Streeter's been distracted, missing work a lot because he's babysitting."

"Babysitting," Tobin repeated. "He's Olivia's only parent so I don't see how that is babysitting. He's taking care of his child."

"Whatever. He ain't taking care of his responsibilities at the ranch. The calf weights are already low this year."

Tobin wanted to ask how that was Streeter's fault. "Did you buy him out? Or give him a year's pay on the buyout?"

Driscoll gaped at Tobin as if he'd sprouted alien tentacles. "No. Why would we?"

"How is he supposed to support himself and Olivia? He's been earning a ranch salary from you since he was what? Seventeen?"

"He got a life insurance settlement."

Was that why they'd cut him out? They saw Streeter's money as a windfall for him, which meant they'd no longer have to shell out wages and could split the profits two ways instead of three? "When did all of this happen?"

"Maybe three weeks ago."

"So the whole 'nothin' much really changes' was a lie? Because you guys kicking Streeter out of the cattle business is a whole lot of something."

Driscoll leaned back in his chair. He picked up his lowball glass and studied Tobin over the rim. "Dad's name is on the deed. No one else's. It's his decision who he wants to pass the land down to. Since you ain't on that list, I don't see how it's any of your concern."

"My concern is that you turned my brother and my niece out."

"If you're so worried, why don't you invite them to live with you?" Driscoll smirked. "Right. Not a lot of room in the trailer you rent up at the Split Rock, is there?"

Tobin's neck heated. His brother still knew how to push his buttons.

If the food hadn't arrived, no doubt Driscoll would've tossed off a smart comment about Tobin's degrees being worthless. There'd been a time when Tobin would've argued that his brother owed his entire way of life to being born first. He'd never had to leave the familiar and try to make his own way. And not for the first time, Tobin was thankful he'd been spared from spending his life in the small world his father and brother lived in.

He ate so fast he didn't taste anything. That antsy feeling dogged him—he kept waiting for his phone to buzz so he could grab Jade, ground himself and get the hell out of here.

Then his phone did buzz with a text message. He said, "Excuse me," and strode away from the table.

Jade waited by the hostess stand. Her eyes lit up at seeing him.

Everything in him settled. This woman was his future. She was joy and sweetness and kindness. Loving and smart and understanding. She got him. He pulled her into his arms and kissed her. "Hey. You ready for the trainwreck that is the Hale family?"

"What's going on?"

"I'll explain later." He set his hand in the small of her back and directed her to the back of the restaurant.

Neither his brother nor his dad stood when Tobin and Jade reached the table.

He comforted himself with the fact that his mother would've been appalled by their lack of manners.

"Jade, this is my father, Dan Hale, and my oldest brother, Driscoll. This is my girlfriend, Jade Evans."

"She ain't white," rolled out of his dad's mouth.

Jade patted her face and her hair. "Omigod, I'm not?" She gaped at Tobin. "Did you *know* this about me?"

"Yeah, darlin', I did."

"And you like me anyway?"

"Very much."

"Oh. Well then. We're good."

Tobin pulled out his wallet. "It was an enlightening conversation if nothin' else."

Driscoll's judgmental gaze winged between Tobin and Jade. "I thought you said your girlfriend was staying for dessert? Now you're takin' off?"

"We have more important things to do than sit here and listen to a pair of windbags pass judgment and gas." Tobin floated a fifty-dollar bill on the table. "That oughta cover my portion."

His dad dropped his elbows on the table. "Now wait just a damn minute. You invited *us.* You said *you* were payin'."

"You thought asking to meet you here meant I was paying for both of your dinners?" He snorted. "Hardly. When I said I'm paying, I meant for my own meal. I didn't expect you to buy mine."

"That's a shitty trick," Driscoll snapped. "Letting us order—"

"What you ordered went in your belly, not mine. And besides, Dris"—he hated that nickname—"I live in a rental trailer and I'm nothin' but a lowly hired hand, right? I've gotta budget my money a lot tighter than two fat-cat landowners."

He draped his arm over Jade's shoulder and didn't look back.

## Chapter Twenty-three

❧

*J*ade had to go upstairs because watching Tobin pace was driving her crazy.

His nerves didn't surprise her; he was a bit more high-strung than most people noticed.

But she noticed everything about him.

Everything.

She loved everything about him.

Now she had what she'd always wanted: A happy life doing the things she loved without living up to anyone's definition of success but her own. Even though she and Tobin had only been together a short time, in her heart and her soul, she believed this love would stand the test of time. They'd already become more to each other than they'd known they could be. And it made her a little giddy to think this love would continue to expand.

"Jade? Baby, they're here."

She reached the bottom step just as Streeter and Olivia came through the door.

The first thing she noticed was that Streeter resembled Tobin more than his dad or brother did. He looked a little gaunt—understandable given what he'd been through the last eight months.

Olivia clung to her father, her face buried in his neck so all Jade could see were two tiny brown pigtails sticking up.

Tobin rested his hand above Jade's behind as he steered her closer. "Streeter, this is my girlfriend, Jade Evans. Jade, Streeter."

"It's good to meet you," Streeter said.

"Same here."

Olivia lifted her head and stared at Jade.

Jade said, "Hi, Olivia."

"Can you say hi, honey?" Streeter urged Olivia.

She shook her head and burrowed back into him.

Streeter tried to set Olivia down and she shrieked. "This ain't gonna work. She's a little monkey today."

"Under normal circumstances I'd say we could deal with it another time, but sorry, bro, that ain't the case." He squeezed Jade's shoulder and pulled her a little closer. "Jade's my life now. We have to make decisions about our future. So you can trust that whatever you say won't leave this room."

After a bit, Streeter sighed. He said, "Understood." Then he perched on the edge of the recliner.

Olivia let her father maneuver her around—as long as there wasn't more than a foot's distance between their heads.

Tobin directed Jade to the couch and sat beside her. "So Renner offered you my job."

"A version of it anyway. I wouldn't be full-time. He doesn't want to hold you back from doin' what you need to do, but he doesn't feel comfortable just cutting you loose."

"Sounds like him. I'll be blunt, Street. How can you support yourself and a kid on part-time wages?"

"I always did my part on the ranch. Not bragging to say I worked harder than either Dad or Driscoll because it's the truth. They turned nasty after Danica . . ." He stopped and cleared his throat. "When I had other responsibilities and wasn't there all the time doin' their work. They started giving me reminders that I'd be expected to make up for the hours I missed. Which they never did if *they* missed time. It was getting to be unbearable. The week before Danica's life insurance policy cleared, my paycheck was a quarter of the amount it should have been. When I asked why, they said it was an actual accounting of the hours I'd worked and that's how I'd be paid from there on out."

Tobin's entire body went rigid. "Those bastards."

"I quit on the spot." A smile ghosted the corners of his mouth. "Of course, that was before I knew how hard jobs were to come by. It's worse when you're a single parent, sole provider and sole caretaker."

"I don't even know what the hell to say to you," Tobin said quietly.

"No one does." Streeter folded and refolded the hem on Olivia's dress. "My life ain't the same as it was a year ago. Most days I don't remember that guy I used to be. Dad and Driscoll—their way of dealing is to tell you to suck it up 'cause we've all got problems. They're gruff and self-centered. They don't understand I'm not 'babysitting' and I'm all Olivia has. Every bit of her care falls to me for the long term. Olivia acts out. Some of it is her age. Some of it isn't. I don't know which is which, but it's up to me to figure it out.

"And I sure as heck can't do that where everyone in town knows the ugliness my wife left us with. People I barely know whisper when we walk into a room. Olivia isn't Olivia Hale. Now she's referred to as 'that poor little girl.' Makes me freakin' nuts. People I've known my whole life act as if they have a right to ask whatever inappropriate question that pops into their fool head. I can't live like that." He briefly closed his eyes. "I need to get out of the area and start over where what happened isn't common knowledge and openly speculated about in the local diner. Isolating Olivia isn't the answer. There's a child therapist in Casper who we've met with several times and I have high hopes we're on the right track." He kissed the top of Olivia's head. "The insurance money is payin' for all of that. Which is ridiculous and sad and just plain pisses me off because the only reason Olivia has to go into therapy is because of what her mother done."

Jade ducked her head, to hide her tears. This poor family.

*This is your family now too.*

Streeter sighed. "I've always been a ranch hand; I don't know how to be anything else. It seemed like a sign when I found the therapist in Casper and then I heard you were leaving your job. Muddy Gap is a helluva lot closer to Casper than Saratoga is. Still . . . I debated before I applied. Renner said hirin' me was all dependent on you."

"No pressure," Tobin muttered.

"You heard the negative. Now here's the upside. Job sharing would let us both do what we love. I agree with Renner that you wouldn't have stuck around this long if you hated it. Splitting the workload would let you explore other options and let me get my sh—stuff together as far as Olivia. You could get to know your niece. Hell, Tobin, we could get to know each other again."

"I'd like that." He cleared his throat. "Where would you live? The foreman's cabin?"

Streeter shook his head. "A trailer would work better. Olivia needs her own room."

"Will that give you enough room for all your stuff?"

"I got rid of most of it in the move after the funeral. But if I get the job I'd insist on Dad and Driscoll handing over the livestock that belongs to me. So I'd need to lease a parcel or two for that."

Tobin studied him. "You wouldn't have an issue with taking orders from your younger brother? I recall that's been a problem in the past."

"I disagree. We ain't really ever worked together. Dad and Driscoll didn't want your input before or after you graduated college. I had no opinion one way or the other since I had my own shit to shovel. As far as the work and how things get done . . . I learned Dad's way, T. I never thought that was the *only* way."

Olivia had started to get restless. Streeter stood. "We'd better git before the total meltdown hits. Thanks for talkin' to me, Tobin. I hope this works out for us some way."

Jade wasn't surprised when Tobin acted noncommittal. "Renner will be in touch. Drive safe."

"Nice meeting you, Jade."

"Likewise. Take care. And if you need anything . . . I don't know how I can help you, I just know that I want to."

When Streeter said, "You're the first person who's said that to me that I actually believe means it," Jade's heart broke all over again.

&cs;

Jade left Tobin alone to think.

She walked out to the garden. Twilight was her favorite time of day, when the soil still held the heat of the sun's rays, perfuming the air with that loamy scent. When the plants were bouncing back from hours in the sun and soaking up water from the irrigation system. Although she hadn't started these plants from seedlings, she had a sense of accomplishment they were thriving under her care.

What would it be like to plan out a growing season? Would the connection to this chunk of earth get stronger with each passing year? Or would the rose-colored glasses come off and it'd become another chore?

Being born and raised a city girl, Jade wondered whether a life rooted so deeply in the country would lose the charm. If she'd miss the conveniences and choices of living in a metro area. She knew she'd miss her parents, but she also knew they wanted her to spread her wings.

Maybe they just hadn't expected her to fly so far away.

Jade heard Tobin's boots shuffling across the yard. She loved being so attuned to him. She turned to watch him walk toward her, and. immediately that overwhelming sense of elation filled her. This wonderful man was hers. She was his. There was no question they'd both do everything within their power to keep this level of connection to each other. And if she had to work three part-time jobs to build a life with him, she'd do it. She knew he'd do it too.

She took off at a dead run wanting to reach him as fast as possible.

Laughing, he caught her in those big strong arms of his and crushed her against his chest. "Hey. What a great welcome."

"I'll do that every night if you want."

"Oh, I want." Without setting her down, he angled his head to gaze into her eyes. "I don't even have to ask, Jade. I know how you feel about me. It's right there every time you look at me."

"Was there ever any question?"

"Only why you'd hitch your wagon to a guy who's maybe got one horse here, and one horse there," he joked.

"As long as you let me sit beside you in the wagon, I'm good with it."

He rested his forehead to hers.

"What did you decide to do about Streeter and the job-sharing situation?"

"I'll try it for a while and see how working part-time at both places works out. As much as Renner doesn't want to just cut me loose, I don't want to just walk away either. The position LME offered is a great opportunity, but the company and the work is a huge unknown. Maybe easing into it is the best way to see if it's what I even want."

Jade grinned and kissed him. "I'm so relieved to hear that."

"You are?"

"You were torn and it ripped me up. Now you can have both worlds, because there's no doubt in my mind you need both of them to make you happy."

"*You* make me happy."

"So finding a place to live in Muddy Gap would be ideal, but we'll likely need to check out the listings in Casper too." He set her down and smoothed his hand over her head. "This all seems surreal."

"It does. But it also feels right." She stepped back. "Tell you what, if you can catch me before we get back to the house? I'll remind you on my knees how real this is."

And when he caught her within the first twenty feet, she didn't mind losing.

## Chapter Twenty-four

❦

Tobin had spent the morning online looking for places to rent.

Jade said she'd be fine staying at his old trailer at the Split Rock since they both worked there, but he wanted them to start someplace new.

They were both a little on edge, not knowing when Miz G would return. Not knowing how she'd react to the news they were a couple in love, the head-over-heels-crazy-forever kind of love. Not knowing if she'd let them stay together in this house for one night, even if Tobin promised he'd ask Jade to be his wife.

He'd poured his third cup of coffee and was sorting through various screens on his laptop when he heard a rumble outside. Then he heard it again.

What the hell?

Jade came down the stairs at a good clip, muttering to herself.

She didn't even stop when he called her name; she just sailed out the door.

Tobin followed her and froze on the top porch step when he saw what had made that rumble.

A moving van.

He stomped down the steps.

Jade was already in the van driver's face. "—back this rig up now or I will call the sheriff and have you arrested for trespassing."

"Lady, I don't give a damn what you think you're gonna do. I'm gonna do my job, which is to instruct my guys to pack up the rooms on this list."

"By whose order?"

He spun the clipboard around. "Last name Evans. First name . . . starts with a G."

"No. This can't be right!"

Tobin said, "Excuse us." He took Jade's hand and towed her around the side of the house. "I thought you sent your dad an e-mail telling him that your grandma was fine to live on her own."

"I did! It was two pages long. It had bullet points. I e-mailed a copy to his personal address and to his office e-mail. I texted him and attached the PDF. I've been completely transparent about this situation with you, Tobin. Nothing has changed."

His eyes searched hers. "Then why is there a moving van in the goddamned driveway?"

"I don't know."

"Why does that guy have a detailed fucking *list* of where to start boxing up?"

He wanted to stop yelling at Jade but he couldn't for some reason.

*Take a moment and fucking breathe.*

Tobin attempted to stay calm. "Your dad must have signed that document."

She looked away and wiped her tears.

"When did you send the e-mails?"

"Over a week ago."

"Is there even a slight chance he didn't get them?"

"No. I have a digital receipt from his secretary."

"Well somebody fucked up."

"And how nice that you assume it's me." She whirled away from him and headed back to the front of the house.

Tobin closed his eyes and counted to ten. What had gone wrong here?

When he found Jade, she was pacing with her cell phone to her ear. Pacing but not talking. She dialed another number and started pacing again.

Then she stopped to watch the movers pull down the ramp at the back of the semi. Another couple of guys slid open the door on the side. Flat stacks of cardboard were unloaded and dragged into the house up another temporary ramp they'd assembled that stretched to the top of the porch steps.

Neither of them moved until the first loaded box marked *kitchen* rolled down the ramp and up in to the van.

"Who were you trying to call?" he asked her.

"My dad. My mom. My dad's office. GG."

Tobin took out his phone.

He called Miz Maybelle.

No answer.

He called Tilda.

No answer.

He called Vivien.

No answer.

He called Bernice.

No answer.

No answer for either Miz G or Pearl's phone.

Just for shits and giggles he called Jade's phone.

It buzzed in her hand.

She frowned at the caller ID and then at Tobin. "What?"

"Since neither of us is able to get through to anyone, I wanted to rule out that we've fallen in some weird dead zone out here."

"But my phone worked and disproved that theory," she said dully.

"Yeah."

"God. This sucks."

"Short of chaining ourselves across the front and back doors, there's nothing we can do."

"That first day I showed up here, you told me you'd do whatever it took to keep the movers out, including coming out swinging."

"I was a fuckin' blowhard." He exhaled. "I really don't need assault charges on my record either."

"So we just sit here and watch them dismantle her life?"

"Fuck if I know, Jade."

"I can't believe my dad would do this."

*I can't believe you thought he wouldn't.*

More time passed in a silent void.

Eventually they both sat down in the shade.

Tobin hated that it was so fucking peaceful.

Jade cleared her throat. "Are we supposed to pack up our own stuff and get out?"

"I don't think so. I didn't see our bedrooms on the master list."

She squinted at him. "You saw the master list?"

"Yeah."

"How do you remember . . ." She briefly closed her eyes. "Right. That photographic memory. Did you see anything else?"

"Nope."

She pulled her phone out and made another round of calls.

Nothing.

Tobin didn't bother.

Something fishy was going on here. Why couldn't they get a hold of anyone?

Needing to do something—anything—he stood.

"Where are you going?"

"To check on something. I'll be back." He walked over to the driver. "Hey. Can I see that authorization paper again?"

"Sure. But it's all legit."

"I believe you. It just sucks because this is not what we were expecting."

"I hear ya. Glad this ain't a foreclosure. Those are the freakin' worst." He passed Tobin the clipboard.

This time Tobin took his time flipping through the pages. Everything was laid out, exactly how it should be packed.

Nothing from the barn was on the list.

Nor the garage.

He reached the last page.

The signature and the date on the last page.

If he'd eaten anything he might be sick.

The moving van, the packing, everything had been set in motion . . . the day after Jade had arrived in Wyoming. The date? TBD. To be determined.

Miz G never had a chance.

But he knew Jade didn't have a damn thing to do with any of it.

Not only would she be upset for her grandmother, she'd have to deal with the fact her father had lied to her from the start. And in the end . . . he'd betrayed both his mother and his daughter.

*Jade will need you more than ever.*

Tobin's boots felt encased in cement as he crossed back over to her.

She scrambled to her feet. "What did you find?"

He wrapped his arms around her. "I love you. I am here for you today, tomorrow, next week, next month, next year and the next decade. Please tell me you believe in us. That we'll get through this and not only be together, but be stronger together."

"I promise. I love you. Now tell me."

And he did.

Her tears were so silent he feared she'd stopped breathing.

He just held her.

Later, when they were sitting on the ground, Jade curled against his chest and lost in thought, the side doors on the moving van clanged shut. The ramps were loaded up in the back.

The driver ambled over. "We're done."

Tobin and Jade got to their feet.

"You don't need to sign nothin'. We gotta git so we can unload before dark."

Tobin almost asked where the stuff was being stored, but did it really matter?

They held hands as they walked into the house. It was hard not to stop and stare in shock at the bareness of the rooms in front of them that had been so full of stuff. Full of life.

Living room: empty of furniture.

Dining room: no table, no china cabinet.

Tobin clutched Jade's hand as they entered the kitchen together.

She made a soft gasp.

Not a dish. Not a towel. Not a knickknack. Not a cookbook.

Just the appliances.

And one lone jar of strawberry champagne preserves on the counter.

"Is this some kind of sick joke?" she demanded hoarsely.

Tobin kissed her forehead. "Let's get out of here. Go grab something to eat and figure out what to do next, okay?"

She nodded.

As they were walking out of the kitchen, the screen door slammed.

Miz G stormed in.

The three of them stood in the empty living room, staring at one another.

Then Miz G noticed Tobin had his arm around Jade. Her eyes narrowed. "Who can explain what in tarnation is goin' on here?"

Jade had wondered all day what she'd say to GG.

But now, standing in front of her, Jade's mind blanked, her vocal cords shorted out and she couldn't move away from Tobin's side.

He didn't miss a beat. He kissed Jade's forehead, knowing full well that GG watched. "We're wondering the same thing. The day started like any other, then the next thing we knew, a moving van showed up. Me'n Jade both looked at the paperwork, but there wasn't a damn thing we could do but stand outside and watch as they loaded everything. We tried calling your son, since it was his goddamned signature—"

GG held up her hand, stopping Tobin's flow of words before she turned away, toward the front door.

Jade could see she'd put her hand over her mouth. Probably to keep herself from crying.

Then GG slowly walked the width of the room and the length, down along the wall to the staircase, keeping her back to them the entire time. The floor squeaked more loudly in the empty space. Her footfalls faded as she headed into the sitting room. And then down the hallway. The doors to the bedrooms and closets were opened and closed.

Through it all, Tobin kept Jade wrapped in his arms. His big hands in constant motion as he tried to soothe her.

The footsteps returned and Jade's heart jumped into her throat. The saloon doors clattered—angrily?—as GG entered the kitchen.

Tobin kissed the top of Jade's head. "Come on, tiger. Let's face it head-on. Together."

"Okay." Clasping Tobin's hand, Jade led him into the kitchen.

GG had her hands on her hips as she stood in the spot where the small table and chairs used to be.

"GG?"

"Dadgummit. They were supposed to leave the table and chairs here."

"Excuse me?"

"Shoot. It's probably too late for them to bring 'em back."

She was babbling. Probably from shock. "Grandma. Can we talk about this?"

"Yep, because the time is finally right." GG faced them. Her eyes were wet and her chin trembled.

Tobin's hands tightened on Jade's shoulders.

GG noticed. Then her enormous smile nearly swallowed her entire face. Tears still fell freely as she clapped her hands and cackled. "I knew it!" Then she bounced up and down as she repeated, "I knew it, I knew it, I knew it, I knew it!"

"Miz G, you need to calm down."

"I will not. I've been waiting for this moment for . . ." She tapped her chin. "Seems like it's been years, but it's prolly only been a couple of months. Anyway, it doesn't matter. What does matter is that I was *right*."

"About?"

"About you two being perfect for each other."

Jade hadn't moved but she still went completely motionless.

As did Tobin.

"You're in love, aren't you? The crazy, hot, 'I'm wild for you, I can't live without you' kinda love. You're both there, aren't you?"

He cleared his throat. "Speaking for myself? Yep. That's exactly where I'm at."

"And you, girlie-girl?" GG prompted.

"I'm right there too."

GG dusted off her hands. "Then my work here is done." She started to walk out of the kitchen.

"Whoa, whoa, whoa, there. We're *not* done here—bein's that me and Jade have no freakin' clue about what's goin' on and it sounds like there's a lot."

"And we want to hear every single detail of your planning and scheming, GG," Jade said firmly. "We can sit in here on the floor or there's still furniture on the porch. Choose."

But GG's focus was on Tobin's hand cupped on the ball of Jade's shoulder. She sent them both a soft smile. "He's sweet, isn't he? Always gotta be touchin' you I'll bet. Partially because he loves you and wants to show you, but also because he is thankful for you. That he's finally got a woman he can love on anytime he wants." Her chin wobbled again. "That's all I ever wanted for you two."

Neither Jade nor Tobin knew what to say after that, so GG jumped right in again.

"My old bones can't take sitting on the floor. I'll meet you on the porch." She patted Tobin's hand on Jade's shoulder as she shuffled past them and out the door.

Jade immediately started after her, but Tobin spun her around and said, "Hang on. Let's take a moment to talk this through."

"Talk what through? How she manipulated both of us . . . for our own good?"

Tobin groaned, but he wore a resigned smile. "She's gonna be cocky about this forever, you know that, right?"

"She's entitled. Nothing she tells us about her stealthy matchmaking skills will change the happy fact that it worked." She shot a quick look over her shoulder. "But we are entitled to know every tiny detail so we have to keep her on task."

"Agreed." Tobin gave her a smacking kiss on the mouth. "The suspense is killing me. We're both smart and we should've seen this coming a mile away."

She laughed. "I'm pretty sure she counted on us not looking at anything besides each other."

Outside on the porch, they settled side by side on the love seat. Tobin had nestled his arm behind Jade's shoulders. GG was right about one thing; Tobin always had to be touching her. It was still new and sweet and thrilling and she hoped the day never came where she took it for granted.

"All right, Miz G. Talk. Don't leave nothin' out."

Garnet folded her arms on the table and looked at Tobin. "Of all the guys around here, Tobin, you're my favorite. You always have been. Everyone knows it. I'm gonna get into all the embarrassing particulars about why so you'll just hush up and listen. I liked that you just showed up to check on me—winter and summer—or to watch one of my TV shows with me. You've fixed stuff around here. You've kept me from getting too out of hand a few times. You never told me to act my age. You never judged me. You're a hard worker. You're loyal to your friends. You have a kind heart and a great sense of humor. You're exactly the kind of man I wanted for my granddaughter."

Jade turned her head and kissed Tobin's knuckles.

"But I knew I couldn't force it. Heck, if I would've introduced you two to each other, you really would've rejected my attempt at match-making."

"Too true."

"And it wasn't like I thought 'these two are perfect for each other' from the start. It never crossed my mind, to be honest. But that changed when I watched you getting more and more discouraged, Tobin. Your life wasn't bad; it just wasn't the life you wanted."

GG looked at Jade. "Same with you, sweetheart. You never ventured far from your life in the city. I started to think it was just a habit, easier to stay than go. It's pained me knowing you were working yourself damn near to exhaustion as you struggled to find your own place in the world. You weren't to the miserable stage yet, but that's where you were heading."

"GG, how did you know all of that?" She squirmed under her grandmother's increased scrutiny. "I'm not trying to be contrary, but we see each other less than half a dozen times a year. We talk on the phone every couple of weeks. So that doesn't seem like enough contact or context to fill in the blanks about the level of happiness in someone's life."

She nodded. "You're right. But your dad and mom have always kept me in the loop when it comes to you. Sometimes they even asked for parenting advice."

Jade's jaw dropped. "They did?"

"Uh-huh, and I'll be gol-durned if they didn't even take it a couple of times! Anyway. Your daddy's been a lot more worried about you since you had that breakdown."

For once, she didn't even bother to correct her and claim it was the flu. "How often do you and my dad talk?"

GG tapped her fingers on her arm as if she was counting. "Oh, at least twice a week. Sometimes more."

"Then he knew you'd be fine living by yourself! So his 'I won't make a decision until I hear from you' promise was a lie. He signed those papers for the moving van the day *after* I arrived in Wyoming. So regardless of what he said, he——"

"Now, just a dadgum minute, girlie. Don't you be blaming nothin' on your daddy."

Tobin squeezed Jade's shoulder to keep her from lashing out.

"But he signed the papers. We saw it, Grandma."

"Nope. You saw *G. Evans'* signature and assumed it was his, when it was mine." She smirked. "Neat trick, huh?"

"You wouldn't say that if you saw how upset Jade got over this today," Tobin said sharply. "And I was plenty upset myself, Miz G."

"Oh pooh. Lemme finish and then you can throw rotten tomatoes at me." She shook her finger at them. "Some of those are past canning stage and I don't gotta ask what the two of you have been doin' instead of putting up my tomatoes."

When Jade felt Tobin's abdominals shaking she elbowed him.

"So where was I?" GG closed her eyes and mumbled to herself before she said, "Aha! Now I remember. So Jade is unhappy. Tobin is unhappy. I knew you'd be happy together, but I couldn't force it so I had to . . . resort to tomfoolery."

Tobin snorted.

"It started months back. I got a drunk and disorderly charge on purpose. Pearl made sure that happened."

Jade noticed the hard set to Tobin's jaw. He'd been there the next morning to take her home. He'd told Jade that in retrospect, he felt he'd failed Garnet by not keeping a better eye on her.

"You know, I wondered at the time why you weren't more embarrassed about that, Miz G."

"I don't know what I was so gol-durn afraid of. I had my own cell. And those jumpsuits are pretty comfy. I thought about getting some purple plaid material and having Tilda make me a couple of pairs to wear around the house."

"Getting offtrack again," Tobin said. "Back to it."

She sighed. "Anyway. Pearl called Garwood and told him about the arrest. She's been feeding him stuff, mostly baloney, ever since." GG looked at Tobin. "Then you gave notice at the Split Rock. We had to think fast. So the next part is kind of a blur for reals."

"Was my dad in on this?" Jade asked.

"Not really. After Pearl tattled to him about the pistol-firing incident, Gar did call me. I told him I had a friend staying with me. A male friend. A young male friend." She slapped the table. "That put the starch in his spine. I told him if he didn't like it maybe he oughta send Jade out here and *she* could make sure he wasn't fleecing me. Then everything just fell into place from there."

"Your son never threatened to lock you away in Cheyenne, did he?"

"No. I kinda feel . . . bad about him bein' the patsy on that."

"You didn't consider me the patsy?" Tobin said tightly. "Because I was more than a little nasty to Jade about it."

"And I didn't trust him and his charming ways from the start," Jade inserted.

"Because he wasn't using his charms on you, girlie. He was being himself—not the Boy Scout or the 'nice kid' everyone's made him out to be."

Jade sensed Tobin's surprise—and maybe his relief—that GG had picked up on that.

"So the whole . . . 'you two can't be in the same room together' rule?" Tobin asked.

"It worked, didn't it?" A smug expression settled on GG's face. "Lordy, was it ever entertaining watching you two try and get around that rule every gol-durn time I had my back turned! If I would've insisted you buck up and figure out a way to get along . . . you would've resisted. But insisting you keep away from each other at all times. Pretty smart idea, if I do say so myself."

Tobin laughed. "I will grant you that one, Miz G. It drove me crazy that every time I had this gorgeous woman to myself, you interrupted."

GG buffed her nails on her shirt.

"I will say the lie detector test went over the top, though."

GG blinked at Tobin. "What lie detector test?"

Jade elbowed him again. "Just some fun and games that backfired on me. Trust me; you don't want to know the details." Evidently not all of the Mud Lilies were part of this matchmaking operation. No wonder they grilled her about GG's plans. They believed everything she'd been telling them.

"This next part? Let's keep it PG, kiddos. You two hitting the sheets was inevitable. The last thing you lovebirds needed was an old woman around all the time cooling your ardor."

Jade grinned at the lovely phrasing—so different than Tobin's self-declared "sex-fest."

"Pretty amazing that you became this"—she gestured between

them—"in such a short amount of time. I'm plumb tickled. And maybe feelin' like a hotshot because I was right. You both love me, and I love both of you, so how can you not love each other?"

"You do have a point." Tobin looked at Jade. "I don't care how this came about. I only care that we're together from here on out."

"We are. We'll make this life work, no matter where we end up."

"Oh. That's so . . ." GG sniffled. Then she frowned. "What do you mean 'no matter where you end up'? You're where you belong. That's why I cleared out."

Their heads swiveled toward her.

"Run that by us again," Tobin said.

"This house and the land? Are yours. Well, as soon as you get married and both your names can be transferred to the deed. I'm old-fashioned that way."

"What? GG. That's so"—*crazy pants*—"insanely generous, but you don't have to move out and give us your house. We'd be happy if you lived with us. Heck, we'd just be happy to have a place to live because everything is so up in the air right now."

"What Jade said, Miz G. I wouldn't feel right booting you out of your house."

"I'm thankful you'd even offer, honey. Both of you. You're not booting me out. I'm bailing out. It is a lot of work for an old broad like me to take care of this place. It needs new memories. A family that make it more than just a house. It'll become a home. Your home. Your place to set down roots."

"But GG . . . it's so much . . ." She could hardly speak.

"Jade doll, you're my only grandchild. I can be generous to you if I want and you just have to suck it up and take it."

She laughed, even through her tears. "What about you?"

"Me'n Pearl and Tilda and Maybelle bought that piece of land across from Bernice's that's been for sale forever. We've all got these family

homes out in the country and it's time for us to have a swingin' bache-
lorette pad in the city."

"If one can even call Muddy Gap a city," Tobin said wryly.

"Oh hush, you. Anyway Holt is building us a fourplex, ranch-style
spread out all on one level. We'll each have our own space. In the middle
it'll have one of them shared courtyard thingies like in New Orleans.
There are two spots to add on for when Vivien is ready to make a change
and for Bernice if she ever divorces Bob. Holt has promised we'll be
roasting chestnuts and drinking eggnog on Christmas Eve in our new
digs."

"I'm excited for you. But are you sure?"

"Yep. That's why all my stuff is gone. I wanted this to be a new start
for both of you, from buying dishes and pots and pans together, to furniture." She waggled her eyebrows. "I'm assuming Tobin's king-sized
bed is all the furniture you have."

"Hell, in my opinion, it's the only furniture we need," Tobin said
with a grin.

GG snickered.

Jade whispered, "You are such a guy."

"Don't hear you complaining about that," he whispered back.

"That said, I am giving you the kitchen table and chairs," GG said.
"They were my mother's so they're gen-u-wine antiques."

"I'd—we'd—love that. Thank you."

GG stood. "I'm staying with Pearl until the Mud Lilies Pad is done."

"The sheriff is gonna lose his mind when he finds out you're all living in the same place."

"We're saving that announcement for Election Day, so don't spoil our
fun, sonny."

Jade stood and hugged GG for a long time. "This is better than winning the lottery. I've got the man of my dreams who loves me and wants
to build a life with me. I have a chance to do what I love and get paid for

it. Now we have this awesome house. And for the first time in my life I get to live close to you, GG. I'm excited about that."

"Me too, girlie. But I'll make a suggestion; that you always call first before you come over and I'll do the same."

"Deal."

Tobin picked GG up off the ground and spun her one time. "I'm happy to see the wacky outfits are back in rotation."

"I have no idea what you're talking about." GG adjusted her tunic that resembled a painter's drop cloth and slipped on a pink-and-gold-striped beret.

Tobin kissed her cheek. "Thank you for Jade, Miz G. Everything else is just icing."

"Love like that feels good, doesn't it?" She patted his chest. "And no more of this Miz G business. From now on you can call me Grandma."

**Keep reading for a preview of Lorelei James's**

# *Just What I Needed,*

**available now!**

———

Trinity Carlson might be having the worst day ever. And that was before she started drinking in a dive bar, right across from her ex and his new girlfriend. So when she finally decides enough is enough, she grabs hold of a hot, blond stranger and gives him the kiss of his life.

Walker Lund never expected that a chance at love would hit him right on the mouth. Since the moment his brother decided to settle down, Walker has been dodging his family's hopes that he'll do the same. He's never been interested in following in anyone's footsteps. But when he discovers his sexy assailant has given him a fake name and number he suddenly finds himself in the mood for a little hot pursuit . . .

*A*fter lunch, which I ate alone in my car, I started on the first set, a forest scene. It wasn't a happy bright blue sky, but an ominous gray. The pine trees were dark, angry slashes of green. I began to add layers, smaller trees, bushes and a rock-strewn path. These layers were softer, with feathery-looking pine needles, and a faint hint of light glowed beneath the lowest boughs.

I stepped back to gauge the image as a whole. It needed more distinct branches in the trees in the middle. Add a few dabs of yellow-green to balance the gray shadows and then this one was done. I snatched my bottle of water off the table and drained it.

"I hate to admit it, but you are one amazingly talented artist."

Startled by the deep voice, I dropped the bottle on the floor and whirled around. "God. Don't sneak up on me like that."

Walker had his hands in the pockets of his well-worn jeans. "Sneak up on you? I've been right here watching you for the last half hour." He paused. "You didn't know I was here?"

I shook my head. "People have said bombs could go off around me when I'm working and I wouldn't notice."

"I don't know if I've ever experienced that level of concentration—to say nothing of harnessing it repeatedly on cue to create something like that."

LORELEI JAMES     306

Usually I let compliments—and criticisms—roll off me. Yet his praise struck a chord since it wasn't about the finished product, but his appreciation of the process. "Thank you." Feeling self-conscious, I grabbed a smaller round brush and returned to painting.

I twisted the brush as I moved down the image. After the third pass, when I still felt him watching me, I said, "I'm sorry."

"For?" he said behind me, closer than he'd been a few minutes ago.

"For not correcting your assumption my name was Amelia."

During his silence, I fought the urge to fill the conversational void.

Finally he sighed. "I've spent the last four days pissed off, directing my anger outward because I knew exactly where the blame belonged."

*On you.*

"Evidently my ego couldn't handle the fact *I* might've screwed up, so it conveniently blocked that part out."

I snickered.

"What's funny?"

"That typical male response. You admit you have an ego but act like it's a separate appendage you have no control over. Kind of like when guys claim the little head is always at war with the big head for who's in control."

He laughed.

God. He had such an awesome laugh.

"Can you stop painting happy little trees for a moment and look at me?"

I whirled around. "Did you seriously just make a Bob Ross reference?"

"Why? Do you hate him or something?"

"No! I love him. In fact, he's a large part of why I became an artist. He was so positive and encouraging, which was so not the norm in my childhood. And it's not the norm in the art world either. He took such joy in creating. I loved how he made it look so effortless, even when I kind of resented him for that too, because it's *not* easy. Some of the happiest times in my childhood were spent in front of an easel, just me and Bob Ross on the TV in the background, painting happy little trees."

Walker was studying me.

"What? Do I have paint on my face or something?"

He shook his head. I swear his mouth twitched as if he was trying not to laugh.

Then I realized I'd gone off on a tangent again. Annoyed with my-self, I said, "Stop staring at me."

"But I really like your face. And I thought I wouldn't see it again, sweetheart, so I'm gonna look my fill."

I had no idea how to respond to that.

"Can I ask you something?" He paused in speaking but kept inching forward. "Did you consider getting in touch with me?"

"I considered it."

"And?"

"And I concluded chances were slim you'd lay a big wet kiss on me if you saw *me* again after you discovered you had the wrong name and number for me *from* me, so I let it go."

"You didn't think about me at all?"

I hedged, pointing the paintbrush at him to stop his advancement. "I have to finish this. So if you want to continue talking, you'll be talking to my back."

As soon as I turned around, I heard, "Then you can't complain if I'm staring at your ass."

Shivers danced down my spine from the sexy, growly way he'd said that.

I switched brushes and colors.

"You were wrong to assume that I wouldn't want contact with you," he continued. "My brother offered to track you down with the little in-formation I had. But I told him I just wanted to forget the whole thing." He laughed softly. "Of course, you're here—the last place I expected to run into you."

Using the wooden end of the paintbrush, I dragged lines through the paint, adding another facet to the branches. "So what now?"

"You tell me."

"Tell you what?"

"That Tuesday night was a fluke."

His denial surprised me. Or was he baiting me? "I should admit I'd had too many drinks and that was the only reason I kissed you?"

"Was it?"

"No. But I think you know that."

He exhaled loudly. "I do. I mean I did and then I didn't, and now I'm really freakin' glad I didn't imagine this."

My hand stopped midair. "But you said you wanted to forget the whole thing."

"That was then." Walker had moved in close enough that his breath drifted across the nape of my neck. "This is now. As far as I'm concerned, we haven't even started."

"You are confusing me."

"Welcome to the club, sweetheart."

"Do I get to choose a welcome gift for becoming a new member of this club?"

He laughed. "You have a bizarre sense of humor."

"So I've heard. Sorry."

"Don't be. I like it."

"Really? Most people don't get it. Most people don't get me."

"Their loss. Because I get you."

I almost demanded he prove it because I didn't want to get my hopes up about this guy.

The soft bristles of his beard grazed my cheek. "Trinity."

Gooseflesh rippled down my arm from his mouth being so close to my skin. "What?"

"Can you look at me?"

I turned around. This man was just so . . . manly. Big athletic body, toned muscles, and I couldn't help but wonder if the hair on his chest was as thick as his beard.

Warm, rough-skinned fingers rested beneath my chin when he angled my head up to peer into my face. And those eyes of his. *Sigh.* Cerulean blue on the outer ring, a smoky gray by his pupil. Beautifully expressive and laser focused with intensity on me right now.

"There are millions of people in the Twin Cities. There are hundreds of bars, theaters and volunteer organizations. The chances of us randomly running into each other twice in one week are miniscule. But we did." His thumb brushed over the divot in my chin. "I'm considering it a sign."

Chills danced down my spine. I was glad he'd said it first. Part of me wanted to point out this connection could be a bad sign just as easily as a good one, but the hope—and, yes, forgiveness—on his face had the rebuttal drying on my tongue.

"Let's start over."

"You want to pretend that kiss never happened?"

"No. I want to pretend you gave me your real phone number and real name so I can spend time with the real you."

"That was the real me in the bar, Walker."

He smiled. "Good. Because I liked you."

"Past tense?"

"So literal for an artist," he murmured. "The past is past. But I want the future tense to belong to me."

Okay. His confidence? Completely sexy.

"Come out with me tonight. You owe me that much since you did agree to a date."

His insistence didn't surprise me. But I'd had an exhausting week. All I wanted was to slip between my sheets, try to shut down for a solid eight hours. "Thank you for the offer. But I'll be worthless company tonight."

"I doubt that." He touched my cheek. "Just dinner, then. You have to eat."

"Do I look like I miss many meals?"

Walker's eyes turned stormy. "Don't."

"Don't what?"

"Say shit like that about yourself. I like what I see when I look at you, Trinity."

"Oh." That was really sweet. "I like what I see when I look at you too."

"But that's not a point in my favor right now, is it? You're still turning me down for dinner."

I set my hand on his chest. As hard and muscular as I remembered. "Yes. Just for tonight, though."

"How about lunch tomorrow? A long lunch."

He smiled—*oh, hello, sexy dimples.* I wanted to press my lips to the deep divots and feel his beard tickling my lips. Next time I kissed him, I'd take it slow and explore.

"So is that a yes?" he pressed.

My focus snapped back to his eyes. "It depends on where you're taking me. I'm not a fan of bar food—chicken wings, nachos, all that fried crap."

"Got it. Any other things to avoid?"

"I spend so much time inside that I'd like to enjoy the fresh air—as long as it's not a hundred degrees in the shade." I could see the ideas churning in his head and then one clicked.

"You're all right with it just being us tomorrow? Not in a restaurant or a bar or surrounded by people?"

I appreciated that he'd asked and hadn't assumed. "Sounds good. Where are we meeting?" I knew he probably expected to pick me up, but I needed the option of being able to leave whenever I wanted.

"I'll text you around ten and let you know. I have to check on a couple of things before I decide exactly where we're going." His eyes roamed my face. "Bring a hat and sunscreen."

"Anything else I should bring?"

"Just your beautiful self."

"You are smooth." I slid my hand up and curled it around his neck, intending to pull his mouth down to mine. But something stopped me.

"I have no problem with you taking the lead," he murmured. "Kiss me anytime you get the overwhelming urge again. But this time, it's my turn."

I groaned when our lips met and he swallowed the sound in a hot and hungry kiss. I hadn't embellished this passion between us. And he seemed determined to remind me of that with every teasing flick of his tongue, with every soft growl, with every angle he moved my head so he could delve deeper into the kiss.

When he broke the seal of our mouths, my lips tingled and my head buzzed. I'd melted against him and was having a hard time remembering why I couldn't stay right there forever.

Oh yeah. I'd opted to give up more of this to go home alone to my quiet house and my neurotic, cranky cat who hated me.

Sometimes I'm a complete idiot.

Stepping back, he said, "Got that new number memorized yet?" and pulled out his phone.

I'd given the number out enough times in the past few days I could rattle it off without writing the digits on my wrist every morning.

Ten seconds later my phone buzzed in my purse.

He smirked at me. "Just checking."

"I'm glad you see the humor in it."

"I do now. But at the start of my day . . . let's just say being pissed off isn't always hell on productivity. I finished twice as many set cutouts as I'd planned."

"I'm taking credit for that."

"See you tomorrow, Trinity."

**Lorelei James** is the *New York Times* and *USA Today* bestselling author of contemporary erotic romances set in the modern-day Wild West. Lorelei lives in western South Dakota with her family . . . and a whole closetful of cowgirl boots.